# SHELTER FOR DANNI (SPECIAL FORCES: OPERATION ALPHA)

## BROKEN HEROES MENDED SOULS
### BOOK ONE

### JEN TALTY

Dear Readers,

*Welcome to the Special Forces: Operation Alpha Fan-Fiction world!*

If you are new to this amazing world, in a nutshell the author wrote a story using one or more of my characters in it. Sometimes that character has a major role in the story, and other times they are only mentioned briefly. This is perfectly legal and allowable because they are going through Aces Press to publish the story.

This book is entirely the work of the author who wrote it. While I might have assisted with brainstorming and other ideas about which of my characters to use, I didn't have any part in the process or writing or editing the story.

I'm proud and excited that so many authors loved my characters enough that they wanted to write them into their own story. Thank you for supporting them, and me!

READ ON!
  Xoxo
  Susan Stoker

# PRAISE FOR JEN TALTY

*"Deadly Secrets* is the best of romance and suspense in one hot read!" *NYT Bestselling Author Jennifer Probst*

"A charming setting and a steamy couple heat up the pages in a suspenseful story I couldn't put down!" *NY Times and USA today Bestselling Author Donna Grant*

"Jen Talty's books will grab your attention and pull you into a world of relatable characters, strong personalities, humor, and believable story-lines. You'll laugh, you'll cry, and you'll rush to get the next book she releases!" Natalie Ann USA Today Bestselling Author

"I positively loved *In Two Weeks*, and highly recommend it. The writing is wonderful, the story is fantastic, and the characters will keep you coming back for more. I can't wait to get my hands on future installments of the NYS Troopers series." *Long and Short Reviews*

"*In Two Weeks* hooks the reader from page one. This is a fast paced story where the development of the romance grabs you emotionally and the suspense keeps you sitting on the edge of your chair. Great characters, great writing, and a believable plot that can be a warning to all of us." *Desiree Holt, USA Today Bestseller*

"*Dark Water* delivers an engaging portrait of wounded hearts as the memorable characters take you on a healing journey of love. A mysterious death brings danger and intrigue into the drama, while sultry passions brew into a believable plot that melts the reader's heart. Jen Talty pens an entertaining romance that grips the heart as the colorful and dangerous story unfolds into a chilling ending." *Night Owl Reviews*

"This is not the typical love story, nor is it the typical mystery. The characters are well rounded and interesting." *You Gotta Read Reviews*

"*Murder in Paradise Bay* is a fast-paced romantic thriller with plenty of twists and turns to keep you guessing until the end. You won't want to miss this one..." *USA Today bestselling author Janice Maynard*

*For Kris Norris. Thanks for answering the phone and solving my plot problem. You rock sister!*

TEN YEARS AGO

*D*anni Hagar bolted up the stairs with her heart in her chest. If only she'd known. If only her parents had told her that *he* had returned. That *he* was coming to her party.

Not that she would have expected him to blow it off if he were in town. They were next-door neighbors. Their parents were best friends.

And he was… her friend.

He returned her letters. He'd always been nice. Always kind. Always treated her with respect. He'd never teased or picked on her—not even when his friends had.

Thor Armstrong had been her friend, even though he didn't have to be, considering he was four years older.

But none of that should matter now. She was eighteen—an adult—a high school graduate. Sure, he was twenty-two and about to enter Navy SEAL training, something that was more important to him than anything.

Once in the comforts of her bedroom, she kicked off her pumps, shed her graduating gown, and yanked open her closet. The basic dress she'd picked for the party wouldn't cut it. Not when she had a man to impress—and not any man—the man she would marry.

She laughed. She'd once told him that when she'd been twelve and he'd been sixteen. Thor patted her on the head, smiled, and told her she was too young to think about stuff like that. He also mentioned that he had a girlfriend at the time.

Danni knew all about *her*. She'd babysat her a few times and she didn't like that girl much. All she did was pump her for information on Thor. But that relationship hadn't lasted.

They never did. Thor was the kind of man who had goals. He didn't need distractions, and so far, he'd achieved everything he set out to do. Danni couldn't be prouder.

She riffled through her closet until she found *the dress*. The one she'd bought without her parents' knowledge. The one she knew would get *his* attention. It was a little black-and-white number that came down to the center of her thighs. It had a slit up the right leg. It wasn't a big opening, but it showed just enough skin. Just enough of her toned muscles from playing ice hockey—a sport he enjoyed, and he'd come to a few games and cheered her on.

He wouldn't have done that if he didn't care.

Now all she had to do was show him she wasn't the cute kid next door.

She tore off the modest dress her mother had helped

pick out. It was a nice dress. She liked it. It fit her body, but it didn't scream 'notice me.' Ripping off her bra, she pulled the more sophisticated one over her head. The spaghetti straps hung on her shoulders, showing off the tan she'd been working on for the last couple of weeks, thanks to warmer weather that had rolled through Delaware during her final exams.

The dress plunged between her small breasts. She sighed as she cupped them. Unless she went to a surgeon, they were never getting any bigger. It didn't bother her that she barely filled out a B cup, except that the women she saw draped on Thor's arm had at least a C or D.

Why were most men into big boobs?

She twisted her body, glancing at her ass in the mirror. Now, she could fill out anything with her backside. She'd been graced with what her mom referred to as a bubble butt. Danni sucked in a deep breath, fluffing her long dark hair that she'd curled and put one side back in a clip. She was glad she hadn't pulled it back in a ponytail like usual. No, this was more grown-up.

Racing into her bathroom, she fumbled in her makeup kit, found her lip gloss, and dotted it across her lips. Taking a step back, she gave herself the once-over. "This is going to have to do." She nodded.

*Knock. Knock.*

She jumped.

"Come in," she called, figuring it was one of her parents wondering where she'd run off to. Might as well face the music about the change in attire. Her mom would understand. Her dad? He'd have a freaking heart

JEN TALTY

attack. He struggled with the idea that his little girl was, indeed, one, a girl. And two, leaving for college soon.

The party had been planned. Her parents had invited all her cousins, half the neighborhood, and a bunch of family friends. She was happy to celebrate her accomplishments with this crowd versus dashing off and going to one party after the other that her friends were having. Of course, Danni didn't have many friends. Not because she was strange or considered unpopular.

But Danni had been focused on hockey and because she was a girl and there wasn't a team for her to play on at her school, it meant a travel team. It meant most of her close girlfriends ended up going to other schools. Her team was the best of the best and almost every girl had either gone to a prep school their senior year in hopes of playing D1 or did what Danni had—and wound up going to a D3 school.

She couldn't wait for that to begin.

"Danni? Where are you? Are you trying to sneak in a documentary on religious cults before your party?" Thor's voice bounced off the walls, landing on her body like a warm bath. It was sexy and smooth, and if she knew what whiskey tasted like, she suspected it would be that.

With her heart hammering in her throat, she stepped from the bathroom and did her best to smile— seductively. Not that she had a clue as to how to seduce a man. She'd never been with one before. Sure, she'd had a couple of boyfriends. She'd kissed and done things with a boy.

But sex?

4

She was too busy getting good grades, training year-round, and ensuring a path to one of New England's best women's hockey programs.

She stared at him. All of him. Every single inch of his sexy swagger. Part of her was a little disappointed he wasn't in his Navy uniform. He was so handsome when he wore that. But his jeans hugged his hips nicely and she loved the untucked purple button-down shirt he'd chosen. It was her favorite color on him.

"Of course not." She inched closer. Ever since she'd turned sixteen and her feelings for him exploded, she'd always been a little nervous, but this was next level. She reached for the side of her dress in search of pockets. But the darn thing had none. There was no place to put her shaky hands to hide the tremble rattling her body from the inside out. "I can't believe you're here."

"Surprise." He smiled. "I told both our parents not to tell you in part because I wasn't sure if I'd be able to make it in time, and I didn't want to disappoint you, like I did for your sweet sixteen."

"I wasn't disappointed. I totally understood and you came home for a visit a few weeks later."

"You're always so understanding." He winked. He actually winked at her. Her stomach flipped and flopped.

"My folks sent me the article that was picked up by the local paper. It was really good. I'm impressed. My dad said you spent most of this past year working on that piece—interviewing people who used to be cult members. I was especially touched by how delicately you handled the family who lost a child to that crazy religion."

"I knew that girl. She was a grade ahead of me." Danni swallowed the thick emotion that always bubbled from her gut when she thought about what happened to that young lady. "It was a real tragedy what happened. I was grateful her parents were willing to speak with me and let me tell their story."

"You have a wonderful way with words, Danni. You really did a fantastic job. Are you still considering going into journalism?"

"Probably," she admitted. "But I don't have to declare a major right away."

"Are you going to stay over there, or do I get a hug?" He stretched out his arms.

Thank God she hadn't had a chance to put on her big heels, because she would have fallen on her face if she had to walk across the room in those things with the way her muscles vibrated. "It's good to see you, Thor."

"You too." He tugged her close to his chest, wrapping his strong arms around her body and holding her... tight. He smelled like a combination of salty air and earth. It was intoxicating. He pressed his warm lips against her temple. He'd kissed her like that every time he'd come home and every time he left. But this... felt different. His lips lingered. His embrace seemed more... intimate. More compelling. More real. "Let me get a good look at the high school graduate." He held her by the biceps and took a step back. His gaze dipped from her face and slowly devoured her body. "Wow," he whispered. "That's some dress." He cocked a brow.

"Why, thank you." She did a little curtsy. "I got it special for this occasion."

"Very grown-up." He nodded.

She rolled her eyes. "Because I am."

"I guess you are." He chuckled. "I got you something." He dug his hand into his jean pocket and pulled out a small box. "I saw it when I returned Stateside a couple of months ago and I thought of you."

"You've held on to it this long?" She glanced at the box, then up at him. Her stomach pitched like a sailboat tilting sideways catching the wind.

"You always said you were going to play college hockey, and you made that dream come true. I thought this would be a fitting graduation gift." He lifted the lid and pulled out a silver necklace with a single hockey charm. He held it up.

"Oh my. It's beautiful." She fingered the female figure. "Will you help me put it on?"

"Sure. Turn around."

She did as instructed, lifting her hair and holding her breath.

Men didn't buy women gifts for no reason and they sure as heck didn't randomly think of them at odd times. Not unless there was something there.

Her mother always told her never to make the first move. That guys didn't like an aggressive woman, and her father would burst out laughing, telling her aggressive and going for what you want were two totally different things.

Well, she wanted Thor.

7

His fingers danced across her neck. He brushed a few stray strands of hair off her skin.

This was it. This was her moment.

"Let me see how it looks," he said softly. He pressed his hands on her shoulders and stepped around to face her. He traced a path down the chain to the hockey figure dangling dangerously in her nonexistent cleavage.

She stared at his hand. Her pulse pounding in her ears drowned out any noise. Her chest heaved up and down.

"You grew up real nice." He dropped his hand to his side.

With a shaky hand, she reached up and palmed his cheek.

He took a quick intake of breath.

Raising up on tiptoe, she leaned into his body, curling her fingers around his neck, drawing his face closer. His mouth closer.

His lips parted. He gripped her hips with both hands, squeezing.

She pressed her mouth against his and closed her eyes. It didn't start off as a kiss to end all kisses. It was slightly awkward as they stood there, holding each other, lips locked, doing nothing. But then, without warning, his tongue darted into her mouth, swirling around hers and commanding she participate—and she did. It was electrifying, passionate, wet, even a little sloppy. But more importantly, he was full-on kissing her like a man was supposed to.

His arms wrapped around her body, and he practically lifted her right off the floor. A deep guttural groan vibrated from his throat to hers as they stumbled into the wall. Her back slammed into the hard structure. His knee wedged between her legs. She dug her fingernails into his back and hung on for the ride of her life.

And then he took a step back, breaking off the kiss... breaking off all contact in a split second. He stared at her with wide, confused eyes. "Danni," he said in more of a breathless pant. "What are you doing?" He stuffed both hands in his pockets. "We're friends... we shouldn't be... doing that."

"Kissing?" She blinked.

"Yeah. You shouldn't have done that."

"Seriously? You're the one who shoved me up against the wall." Now was not the time to be defensive, but she couldn't help herself.

"I got caught up in the..." He ran a hand over his face. "You're just a kid."

"I'm not a child. I'm eighteen. I'm an adult. I could join the military and die for this country, just like you."

He let out a long breath and rubbed the back of his neck. "Not what I meant."

"But it's what you said and come on, you're going to stand there and tell me you haven't thought about that? Because that kiss tells me otherwise."

"No, Danni. I haven't." He shook his head.

"Seriously? You bought me a necklace. You came up to my bedroom to give it to me—alone. And you took part in that kiss, and it wasn't a kiss that someone accidentally gets caught up in." She planted her hands on her hips. All her nerves flew out the window and were replaced with frustration and a twinge of anger.

9

Not because he was rejecting her, but because he refused to see what was standing right in front of him.

"I've been in this room before, and I buy you presents for your birthday. It's what friends do." He narrowed his stare, and his lips drew in a tight line. "But friends don't kiss and while you've grown into a beautiful young woman—you're still incredibly young. You've got the entire world to experience. Your life has barely begun." He cocked a brow. "I'm twenty-two."

"And? Your point?"

"That's too old for you."

She laughed. "My dad is five years older than my mom." She poked his chest. "Your dad is four years older than your mom. The same exact age difference between us. That argument doesn't fly."

"It does, for us." He snagged her wrist. "I don't want to hurt your feelings, and I certainly don't want to lose you as a friend, but I don't see you that way."

"Tell that to your tongue." She waved her hand. "And the rest of your body." She made a beeline for her closet and bent over, not caring that she was in a dress and it wasn't ladylike to show her ass. She snagged her heels and marched right past him. "I'll see you downstairs." She glanced over her shoulder. "Thanks for the necklace. I do love it."

"You're welcome," he mumbled.

Her parents had told her Thor was only there for the weekend. She had two days to show him that he was making a mistake.

But she wasn't giving up. Not yet.

Thor leaned against the fence that separated Danni's home from his parents'. He brought his beer to his lips and sipped while he tried not to stare at... *her*.

But for the last hour, she always seemed to be in his line of sight. No matter where he went, she and that damn dress graced his vision. He'd always liked Danni. That was a no-brainer. She was a kind, sweet girl who, over the last few years, had become more than the pesky little girl that lived next door.

She'd become his friend... his best friend.

He could admit that he valued that friendship. He was proud of the young woman she was becoming and all he wanted for her was to go out in the world and live her dreams.

Danni was the kind of person who rarely took no for an answer. He remembered when she'd first gone out for the all-girls elite travel hockey team. She'd been cut and named as an alternate. Instead of getting mad or upset, she looked that coach square in the eye and asked him what she needed to do to get better and get called up.

Two months later, she was on the team full-time. The following year, she was an assistant captain. She always knew how to make lemonade from lemons. Nothing stood in her way. Every challenge that came her way, she lifted her chin, gritted her teeth, and did whatever it took.

He admired that in part because he wasn't any different.

She stood at a table by the pool with one of her

cousins and another neighbor. She glanced in his direction, waved, and smiled, though it was more sarcastic in nature than anything else.

He sighed, gulping his beer, which soured his belly, and eyed his old man who strolled across the lawn.

"Hey, son. Why are you over here all by yourself?" His dad handed him a fresh, cold brew.

"Just tired. Between my last deployment, packing up my stuff to move across the country, and nearly missing my flight this morning, I'm not firing on a full tank."

"How are your ribs?"

"Sore," he admitted.

"And the rest of you?" His dad tapped his temple. "I know you can't talk about it, but you did mention that things went a little sideways on that last deployment."

Mindlessly, Thor rubbed his side. All deployments were grueling, even if nothing happened. Sometimes it was the hurry up and wait part that he struggled with most. Sitting around and waiting for something to happen could be just as hard as when the shit hit the fan. "I'm good." He nodded. "But two members of the other team we went in with aren't doing well." He sucked in a deep breath and let it out slowly. "This ex-military guy named Brick just opened a ranch called The Refuge. It's for anyone who is suffering from PTSD or needs some space to get their head on straight. They're going to head there for a few days."

His dad held his gaze with pain and concern etched in his eyes. "Are you sure you're okay?"

"My team got there after it was mostly over."

"Your mother and I worry about you."

"I know." Thor nodded. "You can let Mom know I spoke with a therapist. I'm taking care of myself both physically and mentally."

"Good. Good." His dad nodded. "Now, when do you leave for Coronado?"

"Five days." Thor wiggled five fingers. "Then it's nearly two years of crazy intense training, but it's all I've ever wanted."

"You've worked hard for this chance and while I don't pretend to have any idea what's ahead of you, I know you'll approach it like everything else. With raw, gut-wrenching determination." His dad slapped him on the back. "Though, I suspect the real reason you're standing over here with a sourpuss look on your face is you noticed Danni isn't the cute little girl next door anymore." His dad lowered his chin. "She's a woman—"

"Oh my God. Seriously, Dad? You're going to use the word woman to describe Danni?"

"Absolutely." His dad nodded. "Just like I had to learn to see you as a man." He waggled his finger. "You graduated from high school and two weeks later left for bootcamp. That was a tough pill to swallow." He held up his hand. "I've been watching ever since you came down from giving her the present you bought her, and it's been painful."

"I have no idea what you're talking about."

His dad pushed his sunglasses up on the top of his head. "Look, you and Danni have always had a special bond. We never thought anything of it. We raised you to be kind and the Hagars are more than our best friends. They're family. Danni's always had a bit of a crush on you." His dad chuckled. "She always had two strange fetishes. One was for old, creepy cemeteries and you always humored her by walking around them with her. The other one, which she still has, is for religious cults. I guess that started when that girl from her high school got involved with that cult and died. It really affected her, and it showed with that piece she wrote. Her mom told us she drew from that for her college essay."

"I'm not surprised. She's never understood how a rational person could be lured into something like that, but the more she watches those documentaries, the more she gets how predators like that hit people in their weak spots and Misty was a troubled teenager who was looking for a place to fit in." Thor wiped his mouth, but he couldn't rid the sensation of her lips from his skin. "Many of her letters to me have been about the research she did for that piece. I'm always in awe of the way she uses language."

"Danni's a damn good writer and her investigative skills on that piece were that of a pro. But she scared the crap out of her parents with that one. Did you know she attended some of that crazy cult's meetings? Alone. Her dad damn near followed her once with his shotgun."

"I would have done the same thing." Thor shook his head. "But when Danni sets her mind to something, there's no stopping her." He brought his fingers to his lips again. The memory of that kiss might forever be etched in his brain, and he wasn't sure where to file that.

"No, I suppose that's true. While it's a good quality

to have, it could get her into trouble." His dad chuckled. "But that determination seems to have landed on you."

"Dad, you're talking in circles. What's your point?"

"Until now, it really wouldn't have been appropriate for you to notice Danni. Although, your mother and I have been wondering for the last year or two when it was going to happen."

"Jesus. Now you're just making this really freaking awkward."

His father laughed harder, then cleared his throat. "Kind of hard to make something work when she'll be in Rhode Island for the next four years and you'll be in Southern California for the next two."

"There's nothing to get going," Thor mumbled. "Besides, even if I was interested, which I'm not, I don't have time for a relationship. SEAL training is insanely intense and I'm not going to screw this up."

"I get it. I do." His dad squeezed his shoulder. "But whatever is keeping you standing over here, looking like you swallowed a lemon, I'd deal with it before you leave because it's affecting her too."

"Why do you say that?"

"For starters, that wasn't the dress she wore to graduation." His dad shook his head. "And she's been glaring at you with some mighty big daggers, son. Your mom— and hers—are wondering what happened in that bedroom to make the two of you act like you suddenly hate each other."

"Nothing happened," Thor said quickly. Too quickly.

"I know I said I understood, and mostly, I do. But if

you like her, long distance can be done. Your mother and I did it for three years."

"Oh my God. I can't believe you even suggested that." Thor chugged his beer. "I need to dump these two empties and grab some food." He pushed from the fence, telling himself he wasn't going to glance in Danni's direction. But his gaze defied him, only she wasn't where he last spotted her and that made his heart sink.

He sighed. How could one kiss with a girl he'd known his entire life turn his world upside down?

*Thor*

The following morning, Thor sat on his parents' back deck and stared at his cell. He felt like a real asshole for ignoring Danni yesterday, especially since it had been her big day.

But that kiss. His lips still burned with the sensation.

She was right. He had participated. No doubt about that—and he'd liked it—a lot. It had come out of left field, and at first, he had every intention of pushing her away, not slamming her against the wall.

"Come on, Danni. Text me back." He set his phone aside, reached for his coffee mug, and sighed. He knew she was home because her car was still in the driveway.

Unless one of her friends had come and picked her up, which was possible. Or she could have gone for a run. Or to the gym. The girl was a machine. The way she looked at it, she had four more years to play the sport she loved more than anything else. After that, she had some tough decisions to make with her life, though she had a pretty good idea what she wanted to do.

She loved writing, and investigative journalism intrigued her, so she planned on studying it in college.

Good on her.

*Tap. Tap.*

He jerked, glancing over his shoulder.

"Hey," Danni said softly, standing on the other side of the sliders.

"Hey, yourself." He jumped to his feet. "Care to join me outside?"

"Sure."

He pulled open the door, stepping aside. "Do you want some coffee? Juice? Are you hungry?"

She waved her travel mug. "I've got a smoothie." She eased into one of the lounge chairs and stretched out her legs. She wore a pair of white shorts and a dark T-shirt. She'd pulled her long hair up into one of those messy buns on top of her head, and she wore little to no makeup.

If he were honest with himself, he'd noticed her the last time he'd visited. Noticed how pretty she'd become. How grown-up she looked. But he hadn't really spent much time looking.

This morning—he looked.

But it wasn't just her beauty he noticed.

He pulled the other lounge chair close and sat down. "Thanks for coming over."

"You said you wanted to talk before you left tomorrow morning and I've got practice for summer league in two hours along with dry land training." She glanced at her watch. "That will take me well into the dinner hour and I'm sure you want to see your friends."

"No one's around anymore." He laughed. "But I have to leave here at three in the morning for a five a.m. flight."

"That sucks for you."

"I'm used to it these days." He took a big sip of his bitter brew, rolling his thoughts around his brain. "Look, I'm sorry about how I behaved yesterday. You caught me off guard."

"I'm sorry too." She crossed her ankles. "But not for kissing you."

He groaned.

"You regret it?"

"I don't know," he admitted. "But what I do know is that I'm moving to California next week and I'll be spending the next two years in SEAL training." He reached out and covered her mouth when she opened it. "You're headed to Rhode Island. You've got your own thing going, and even if that kiss had been planned and something that I'd been thinking about or wanted more of, I don't have time for anyone in my life." He dropped his hand. "Except for a friend." He arched a brow. "I do care about you. We've been friends forever and I don't want that to change."

"I can't say that's the conversation I was hoping to have this morning." She held his gaze with an unwavering stare. This wasn't the teenaged girl he'd spent time with even a year ago.

She'd changed. This was a mature young woman, and he had no idea how to deal with her anymore.

But it didn't matter. Their lives were going in different directions, and he needed to focus.

"But I understand." She shifted, pulling something from her back pocket. She placed a small piece of paper and a picture on his leg.

"What's this?"

"My address at college and my senior picture." She swung her legs to the side. "I hope you'll write. If you do, I'll return the letters. I know guys keep pictures when they're deployed." She shrugged. "I don't expect you to keep mine, but I wanted you to have it." She leaned over and kissed his cheek. "Take care of yourself." Jumping to her feet, she strolled through the sliders and disappeared into the house, leaving him there, alone.

"Damn," he whispered. He lifted the image and swallowed. She was so beautiful. Snagging his wallet from his pocket, he tucked the picture, and her address, into his billfold. He would write, like he had been for the last year, because it was nice to have someone to send his thoughts to.

The school picture? He wasn't sure what he was going to do with that, but for now, it felt right to have it.

2

TWO YEARS LATER...

*D*anni leaned back on the sofa. She lifted the remote and hit pause on the documentary. She picked up her notebook and jotted down a few jumbled thoughts. The assignment was simple enough. Write an investigative piece from the opposing point of view.

But that was impossible to do when writing about cults. They sucked. How could Danni argue that they weren't pure evil? How could she write a piece defending them when she believed they were one of the most dangerous organized organizations created by man?

But it was too late to change it now. The stupid paper was due in three days.

"You've got mail." Jessie, one of Danni's roommates, tossed a letter at her as she slammed the side door closed. "Oh my God. You're watching another documentary on cults. How do you find them?" She stood in the center of the room with her hands on her hips.

"This one is actually for class." Danni held up her hand. "Can I have my mail, please?"

"Who writes conventional letters anymore? Haven't you heard of email?" Jessie asked, snagging a loaf of bread and a jar of Nutella. The girl lived on those two things, and it was amazing that she had never gained a single pound in their little over two years in college.

Not that Danni had either, but she didn't eat garbage. If she had extra calories, she preferred to drink them. Not that she drank all that much. Technically, playing a sport, she signed a contract not to partake, and she wasn't twenty-one yet.

"Thor likes to write longhand." Danni had never accepted that she and Thor would remain only friends forever. But it was hard. It didn't matter that he was stationed back in Virginia. He was deployed more than he was in the States.

"That's weird, and he's not even your boyfriend."

"He's my best friend." She took the letter and raced into her room, closing the door.

She shared this house with three of her teammates. They had moved in at the start of their junior year. It was a nice house right on the main drag. She plopped herself on her bed and tore open the letter.

Thor wrote almost every week, sometimes more, and she always wrote back, though often his letters didn't get to her right away. Especially when he was deployed in a foreign country and couldn't tell her which one—or he'd been injured, like this time, except she only knew that because her parents had called to tell her what happened.

21

But she lived for their letters. She told him everything. Well, almost everything. There were a few things she chose to keep to herself, like the few dates she went on. She couldn't live under a rock.

And she suspected he dated.

Or maybe he didn't. Sometimes, he sounded so exhausted. Beaten down, even.

It had been nearly four weeks since she'd heard from him, and it had been pure hell. In his last letter, he'd warned her, again, that he was being deployed. He always informed her when that happened. He was good that way. Sometimes, he even called. She loved it when he did that.

She flattened the two-page letter and sighed. This time, the distance had been harder because he'd been injured.

*My dearest Danni,*

*I hope this letter finds you well. It took a while for your last two letters to reach me. Things here have been—crazy. We'll get to that in a few seconds.*

*You and cults. While I get your fascination with them, and I understand your drive to expose them for what they are, you're playing with fire. There are other stories to write about. Other stories to investigate. I'd like to see you try one for a change. I know. I know. You want to eventually write a book about the subject. I support that. I do. It's just that you're such an amazing writer and you're passionate about so many things. Maybe try your hand at something else?*

She rolled her eyes. She'd heard it all before. But when she picked investigative journalism as a career, she also made the decision that the mark she'd leave on society would be exposing cults and she'd start with the Origins of God. It wasn't a well-known cult. It flew under the radar, but something about them gave her the creeps.

*Enough about that and please keep sending me the articles and papers you write. I love reading them. I really do.*

*On to something else...*

*Wow. A hat trick. That's amazing. I wish I could have been there to see that. I told you that you'd find your footing on the team. That all you needed to do was settle in and get your bearings. You always do. It took you a full year when you made the all-girls travel team, but you did and see, you're shining in college too.*

*I'm sorry that Stella is being a bitch about your success on the team. It sounds like she's jealous. I know you find that to be a worthless emotion, but just because you generally don't feel it, doesn't mean others aren't inflicted. I'm glad she found another house to live in. That would have been disastrous for you, but I'm glad you and she are getting along better, both on and off the ice.*

*You always find a way to get along.*

*I have to laugh. Even though the team relentlessly picks on me for the photographs you send me, feel free to send more. It's nice to have stuff from home, even if Rhode Island and your college house aren't home. LOL.*

*Mouse keeps asking me what I'm going to do if I actually get a girlfriend and you keep sending me letters and pictures, how that's all going to play out.*

Danni frowned as she rolled to her side.

*Of course, Jupiter thinks you are my girl and if you're not, then I'm the biggest fool on the planet. Kawan and Sloan totally agree. Lief, is as always, Switzerland on the subject, but he did recently make the observation that for the last two years, all I ever talk about is you. That it's Danni did this, Danni accomplished that, Danni authored another fantastic article. I'm always complaining that the few times I made it back to Delaware, you were either out of the country with family or friends or couldn't get away from college.*

*I get more shit about my love life, or lack thereof, than any other guy on the team. But I don't care. I don't know how to say this. I'm afraid it will upset you before it lands on your ears right. If that makes any sense.*

*I have no regrets. Not when it comes to us. I wasn't ready for that kiss. I'm probably still not. I don't know. It's been over two years since it happened. We haven't seen each other since. We haven't talked about it. Not even in these letters.*

*But I haven't stopped thinking about it.*

*Or you.*

"Holy crap." She bolted upright. Her stomach rolled. Her heart fluttered. She reread the last few words. Not once. Not twice. But three times before continuing with the letter.

*I wish I could see your face right now. You're probably sitting on your bed—I'm so glad we had the chance to FaceTime when you first moved in so I could see it—with your mouth gaping open, wondering if I'm teasing you.*

*Well, I'm not.*

*But I'll be honest. It's taken a lot to get me to this point—to understand what I've been feeling and why I've been fighting it so damn hard.*

"What the hell does that mean?"

*You know, when I left for SEAL training, I was quite confused about that kiss. About you. I saw you as a kid. My dorky little friend who lived next door. The little girl who had always been around since I could remember. The girl who would come over and play video games with me. Or that my parents would make me take trick-or-treating. I never minded. You were always fun and energetic. Wise beyond your years. We always had fun together. If I'm being honest, I probably started noticing you when you were sixteen. But I was twenty, and it would have been wrong for me to act on it.*

*When I came home for your graduation and I saw you in that dress, you stole my breath. But it wasn't just because you were so damn beautiful. So damn grown-up. It was because I saw you. All of you. Because I was heading to Coronado for SEAL training, I had to compartmentalize. I had to walk away. I know that's selfish and I'm sorry.*

*I also had to let you chase your dream.*

*I'm so proud of you and so grateful that you continued to write and share your life with me.*

*And you have so much left to do. I want you to know I support you.*

*Now, we get to the heart of this letter.*

*I know your parents told you I took a bullet to the shoulder on this last mission and I'm sorry I haven't called or written until now. It's been a difficult road. Your cookies were the best by the way. I had to hide them from all the guys because if I didn't, I wouldn't have been able to enjoy them.*

Tears welled in her eyes.

*I want you to know that I'm fine. I really am. Me and the guys are healing. Jupiter is being a big baby, as usual. Mouse is bouncing back faster than we could have imagined, which is great. After Germany, because of some of the things we went through, it was decided that we would spend a long weekend at The Refuge. It's this awesome ranch out in New Mexico. It was started by seven ex-military guys who all suffered some kind of PTSD and decided to start a place where anyone could go and deal with their demons.*

*That mission went sideways so fast. We're so lucky that we all walked away with barely a scratch.*

"Are you kidding me? You were shot."

*I want you to know that the letters, the pictures, and that sweet kiss helped me survive sitting in a hospital and then back at The Refuge and rehabbing this shoulder. Doctor says I'll be as good as new. Don't worry. I'm actually exceptionally good at my job. And I love it. I wouldn't want to do anything else.*

*But since I've got some time off, I'd like to come see you… see if a kiss might be as explosive as the last time. Would that be okay with you? Let me know your schedule. You can message me… or email me. That would be quicker.*

*Of course, if I made this weird, well, you can let me know that too.*

*Your… not sure what now… Thor*

"Oh my God." She fingered her necklace. She hadn't taken the thing off since Thor had given it to her. She bolted from the bed, pulled back her chair, and fired up her laptop. Should she message or email?

Screw it. She'd do both. Quickly, she sent him an email, letting him know she got his letter. She told him that she was sorry about his injuries and that she was glad that he and his friends were healing nicely. That she would love to see him and sent her schedule.

After that, she opened the messaging app they occasionally chatted on. He wasn't live, but that was okay. She copied what she sent in email and sent it. But she left it open. She sat there and stared it. Willing him to come on. She opened another tab, checking what time it was in New Mexico.

He should be around, but he could be off doing something.

She lifted her cell, making sure the push notifications were turned on for the app. She would have to be patient. He would reach out when he could. In the meantime, she'd write a letter. No matter where he was in the world, as long as she sent it to the base, it would find him.

---

Thor made sure he strolled into the rink five minutes late. He didn't want Danni to know he'd come. He didn't want to distract her from the big game. He'd been following the last two and a half years as best he could between her letters, their phone calls, and conversations with his parents. He knew this was an important game. The team she was playing was her biggest rival. It had been five years since her college team had beaten them, so if they did it today, it would be huge.

He couldn't believe she'd messaged him when he'd been an hour away from Rhode Island. It had been a calculated risk to get in his car and drive, but he had to see her. He had to know if something was there or if he was holding on to a memory.

He strolled into the rink and immediately cringed. A group of men—students—stood by the plexiglass. They were shirtless. They painted the starting lineup numbers on their bodies.

Danni was the starting right wing—number nine.

Some dude had number nine on his back and chest.

Some man who was closer to her age than Thor. Some human who had a different connection. Someone who saw her day in and day out.

Suddenly, at twenty-four, Thor felt old.

Jesus, what the heck was he doing? All over a kiss that had happened two years ago? He'd lost his ever-lovin' mind. He'd been warned that being shot would change him fundamentally, and it had. Not that he ever believed for one second that he was invincible. He understood that what he did was dangerous. That he could die. It wasn't that he didn't fear it, because he did. However, he and the team used that fear to stay alive. It had become their compass.

But he hadn't expected it to draw her into the fold with such fierce intensity.

Of course, that had been building. He'd been thinking about her every day, pulling out that damn picture and looking at it every night. Using it to bring him a piece of home. It gave him a reason to go on when he thought he was done. When he thought he couldn't continue. She gave him strength. She reminded him that he had that extra ten or twenty percent needed to forge on to the next step.

He wasn't sure he would have made it through the training if it hadn't been for her.

She had wormed her way under his skin, and he treated it like she belonged to him—as if she were his girl—his Danni.

He cracked his neck and found a spot against the

glass in the far corner. When he'd gone to her games in the past, he'd always watched from behind the net, on the side where she would score. Next period, he'd move.

He rubbed his hands together before shoving them into his pockets. He'd forgotten how cold ice rinks could be.

She flew across the ice, handling the puck with grace and precision. He understood the sport. He'd played it all through high school, but even he could admit she was much better than he ever was. He smiled. His chest puffed out with pride. He was here. He was her friend. That would never change, and he missed her. He thought when he'd been assigned to SEAL team four, which was technically stationed out of Little Creek in Virginia, he'd get the chance to see her a few months ago. But his unit was quickly deployed, and he barely had a chance to drop his shit off in some run-down old house he and a couple of the guys rented.

Danni passed the puck to her center, who muscled through two players while Danni skated across the blue line and into the zone, circling the net. Her team seemed to have a good feel for each other, passing and shooting, but that goalie was good and stopped every attempt. After forty-five seconds, Danni skated off the ice with her line.

By the time the third period came around, the score was tied at two and Danni's team was beginning to fall apart. They were tired. They were being outplayed, outskated, outshot, and the worst part was, they were defeated.

The guys who were half-naked, sporting the starting

line's numbers, were banging on the glass, doing their best to not only rile up the team, but rattle the opposing one.

Danni's line skated onto the ice. She set her stick down with sheer determination. She eyed the other winger before quickly glancing at the ref as he dropped the puck. Her center picked it up and hustled forward. Danni slammed her stick on the ice. She was wide open, and the center flicked her wrist, sending the puck in Danni's direction.

A collective gasp filled the air as Danni gathered the puck with perfect perfection and crossed the blue line with only one defenseman staring her down, the other one chasing from behind. But damn, was that girl fast.

"Don't slow down, Danni," Thor whispered.

Danni skated to the right and the defenseman she faced moved up, making a play for the puck, but missed.

The crowd went wild.

Thor pounded on the glass. "Take the shot, Danni. Take the shot."

Danni wound up just as the other defenseman caught up with her. Danni flicked her wrist, and the opposing player tried to muscle her arm in front of Danni, but instead, she tripped her, and Danni face-planted, nearly hitting her head on the goal post.

"That was a cheap shot. She could have been hurt." Thor pounded on the glass. "Come on, ref, call the tripping."

The shirtless men glanced in his direction.

He ignored them and focused on Danni, who

jumped to her feet and shook it off. She always shook it off, even when she shouldn't have.

The ref called a two and a ten. Perhaps that was a little much considering there was only forty-eight seconds left in the game, but Thor would take it, and Danni's coach left her out on the ice for the power play. The misconduct penalty would carry over to the next game.

Interestingly enough, Danni was on point. That surprised him, even though she'd mentioned that a few times in her letters. She had great stick skills and speed. He suspected she could hold the blue line, but she was only five-five. Not very big for someone playing a defensive role. If one of those girls got past her, he wondered if her size would be a detriment.

He rubbed his tender shoulder and held his breath.

Her team spent the next thirty-five seconds passing the puck and dominating. Thor couldn't understand why they hadn't taken a single shot, until the front line shifted. It was a slight change, but he understood that shift. He watched the center skate to the right side of the net. The left wing shot the puck back to Danni, who wound up with a... slap shot?

Holy cow. She nailed it and the puck went flying. She hit it so hard, her back knee smacked the ice shortly after the puck sailed through the air.

The center muscled the defenseman out of the way. The goalie got a piece of the puck, and the right wing came over and pushed the puck right through the goalie's legs.

The crowd went wild.

Thor pounded on the plexiglass and yelled Danni's name. She didn't hear him because everyone in the stands was screaming.

The ref blew the whistle. There was four seconds left in the game.

But it was over. Puck dropped and that was that.

The girls dropped their sticks and gloves and jumped on each other.

Thor laughed. His hockey days ended when he'd been eighteen. Even if he'd gone to college versus the Navy, he wasn't good enough to play anything other than club or beer league.

This was amazing. He couldn't be happier for Danni. He sighed. Did he belong here? Belong in her life?

He glanced at his watch. Newport was a Navy and college town. It was also damn impossible to get a hotel room close to campus, so he'd reached out to a few buddies who'd been stationed here to see if he could couch surf. Thankfully, a dude he knew from bootcamp was here and said it would be no problem, just to reach out when he rolled into town. Now, Thor wondered if he should just drive back to Virginia—though he would have to leave at three in the morning since he had a meeting at four in the afternoon tomorrow and he and Danni certainly weren't ready for anything other than a conversation... and maybe a few kisses.

At least he wasn't.

He considered himself a confident man. At least when it came to his chosen profession. He was good at it and thrived in the environment. Everyone told him so.

32

He wasn't arrogant or cocky. Humility went a long way in the military.

But when it came to women, somewhere along the way, he'd lost his touch—if he ever had it. He hadn't really dated anyone since he'd been twenty and even then, they weren't real relationships, and he hadn't been the one to make the connection. He didn't pursue anyone.

Once again, he let his brain flop back to the friend thing, because no matter anything else—that was real.

He watched the girls file off the ice. Their friends and community cheered, fist-pumped, and patted their shoulders as they made their way to the locker room. Thor could wait until she'd had the chance to shower and do whatever kind of team celebration they did. He meandered into the food shack and got himself a cup of coffee before perching himself against the wall by the door.

Ten minutes ticked by.

Twenty.

Thirty.

Finally, forty minutes later, the door opened. His nose twitched. He was assaulted with a combination of skunk scent and vanilla. Strange mix.

Five more girls shuffled out before his eyes were graced with one of the prettiest women he'd ever seen. His pulse increased. His palms got sweaty. Air got stuck in his throat.

"I don't know," Danni said.

"All you do is study." One of the other girls shook her head. "Just come out for a little while."

"I want to go home first and—"

"Check your computer and see if Navy man responded." One of the girls laughed, waving her hand, interrupting Danni.

It was hard for Thor not to smile. He inched a little closer, dumping his empty coffee cup into the trash, then stepping in front of the entrance to the lobby. He didn't want her to pass right on by.

"I guess I can hitch a ride with someone else." The other hockey player waggled her finger. "But you have to promise to meet us out after you—"

"Thor?" Danni paused dead in her tracks. Her lips parted. Her eyes went wide.

"We all know his name. You've told us a million times," the other girl said. "You've shown us his picture and mentioned how freaking awesome he is."

"Oh my God. What are you doing here?" She blinked.

"I can leave if you don't want to—"

"Hell no." She flung herself at him, wrapping her arms and legs around his body.

He stumbled backward, hitting the wall. He gripped her thighs and groaned. His shoulder, while mostly healed, wasn't quite ready for impact. But holy hell, her lips. Her damn fucking lips molding against his mouth, while unexpected, were a welcome treat. Her tongue snagged his, twisting and rolling. It was hot, passionate, and part of him didn't care that he thought he heard some dude cheering on number nine.

He dug his fingers into her solid muscles as he turned his body, pushing her against the wall, taking control of the kiss, which absolutely didn't belong in an ice rink. A few of Danni's teammates made some comments as they strode past, but he ignored them... ignored everything... but his Danni. He'd thought about this moment for a long time, and he hadn't ever expected it to go quite like this.

Not that he was complaining.

Gently, he untangled her legs from his waist, setting her feet on the floor. He smoothed his hands over her round ass, up her back, and cupped her neck. "Hi," he whispered, staring into her deep blue eyes.

Her face turned bright red.

He chuckled, running his thumb across her cheek.

"That was so aggressive. I don't know why I did that," she mumbled. "I just got your letter today. I sent you an email and a message." She shifted her gaze to his shoulder. "Oh no. Did I hurt you?"

"It's still sore, but no. I'm fine." He dipped his head and kissed her softly. He needed more. Just a taste. "I got your message, which is how I knew to come here." He chuckled. "The base wasn't forwarding our mail to The Refuge, so I didn't get most of your letters until I returned, and I needed to see my folks before I drove up here."

She narrowed her stare. "That means my parents knew you were back and didn't tell me."

"I stopped there for a night, so I wasn't really back." He palmed her cheek. "I was an hour away when I got your message."

She exhaled and furrowed her brow. "You're not freaking out."

"Not even a little a bit." He heaved her tighter to his chest and ran his hand up and down her back. "But people are staring and I'm starving. I saw a pub down the road. Can we get something to eat?"

She nodded.

He laced his fingers through hers, and it didn't feel strange. He thought it might, but it didn't. Their age difference still worried him, as did the distance. His career as a SEAL wouldn't change and she still had three semesters of college left.

But whatever this was, he was willing to make a go of it. She was worth it.

## 3

A YEAR LATER... DURING THE HOLIDAYS...

*D*anni sat in the living room of her parents' home. A headlight from a vehicle shone through the windows, but it was the neighbors and not Thor. Her heart lurched to her throat. It had been months since she'd seen Thor. He warned her that being in a relationship with him wouldn't be easy.

That was an understatement.

They had been technically dating for a little over a year, but during that time, she'd only had a few weekends with him. These weekends were always shared with family, her hockey teammates, or his SEAL team, and they had very few moments alone.

Actually, they were rarely alone, and that meant—they hadn't had sex—she hadn't had sex, and that was super embarrassing, mainly because he didn't know. Or at least, she didn't think he knew. They had all sorts of sexy talk, and she even sent him a couple of partially nude photos. He appreciated them but told her not to do it again. He worried his buddies would see them or someone would magically snag them from the airwaves.

That made her laugh. However, she appreciated his protectiveness.

But this last deployment had been especially harsh. He'd left six months ago. While they had letters, emails, and video chats, it wasn't the same. However, he'd landed Stateside five days ago. He'd missed Christmas with the family, which couldn't be helped, and everyone understood. It's just that she was heading back to school in three days, and while she knew he'd come with her to Rhode Island if she asked, that wouldn't be fair to his parents.

He had only five days of leave. He needed to spend this time with his family. They missed him too. He wasn't scheduled to be deployed for the next month or so—that she knew of—so she'd get a long weekend soon. She hoped. They'd make something work.

She sipped her wine and stared at the computer screen. For so many years, her world had been hockey. It was all that mattered. However, that was about to come to a screeching halt, and it was time to find a job. She knew what she wanted to do, and she had prospects. She just didn't know which one would make the most sense.

Lights flashed and a vehicle pulled into the driveway next door.

Finally.

She set her laptop on the sofa, chugged the rest of her beverage, and bolted for the front door. Wearing her slippers, she raced through the dotting of snow on the lawn. "Thor!"

"Hey, babe." He slammed the driver's side door of his pickup closed and held his arms out, scooping her up and twirling her around. "I missed you."

"Not as much as I missed you."

"I doubt that." He pressed her against the truck, wedged his body between her legs, and kissed her, hard. His mouth bruised her lips. His tongue devoured hers as if it were on a search and destroy mission. His hands roamed up and down her back, her ass, her hips, and climbed back up under her arms. He cupped her breast, fanning his thumb over her tight nipple.

She moaned.

"I can't believe at twenty-five this is coming out of my mouth, but where are our parents?" he asked breathlessly.

"Still out to dinner. I don't expect them back for at least two hours." She took his hand and shimmied it under her shirt. Every erotic nerve ending in her body ignited. Quickly, she unhooked the front clasp of her bra and pressed his warm palm against her bare skin.

"That's playing with fire, sweetheart."

"I've waited too long for this. I'd do it right here if that's the only choice I was given."

He growled low and deep. His index finger and thumb twisted and plucked at her nipple. "Don't tempt me."

Gripping his shoulders, she jumped, wrapping her legs around his waist. She wiggled her hips.

"Sweet, Jesus, woman. You're going to be the death of me." He nibbled on her ear. "I no longer have a room since last year. My dad turned it into an office for my mom, and now I get to sleep on a futon, so perhaps we should—"

"Just shut up and start walking toward my house," she said.

"I don't need to be told twice."

She'd waited a lifetime for this. She'd saved herself for this moment—for him. God, she needed to tell him. There should be no secrets between two people who cared for one another. It didn't matter they hadn't uttered those three little words yet, though she did love him with all her soul.

However, he needed to know she'd never been with a man before.

"You don't have to carry me the whole way." She buried her face in his neck and closed her eyes. She should've had sex her freshman year when she had the chance. At least she would have had the experience.

"I want to." He opened the front door, kicked off his shoes, and took the stairs with ease. Once inside her bedroom, he laid her down on her bed and eased in next to her, running his fingers across her midsection. "What's wrong?" He kissed her nose. "And don't tell me it's nothing because whenever you scrunch up your nose like that and your lower lip twitches, something's bothering you."

She tossed her arm over her eyes and groaned. "I should have told you this a long time ago."

"If it's about birth control, I bought a box of condoms in case you weren't on the pill since we never discussed this."

"Oh my God. That's so sweet, but no. It's not that."

"Phew. I hate those things, but I'd have used them if we needed to." He tugged at her arm. "Will you look at me, please?"

"I don't want to." She sighed, catching his gaze. "I am on the pill, and I wouldn't know anything about what a condom feels like because I've never used one."

He narrowed his stare. "My first thought is well, of course not, you're a girl. But my second thought is even though you're on the pill, because of disease, you should always consider them. Only reason I'm not is because I haven't had sex since we started dating and I would hope you haven't—"

"Of course not." She covered his mouth. "The reason I wouldn't know anything about condoms is because I've never had sex. Like ever. I'm a freaking twenty-one-year-old virgin. Go figure."

He blinked. And blinked. And blinked some more. He stared at her with his lips slightly parted but said nothing. However, to his credit, he continued to hold her, to run his hand across her bare skin.

"Cat got your tongue?" she asked.

"Little bit." He nodded.

"Are you going to start freaking out and run for the hills?"

"No," he said. "Just rethinking my strategy."

"Excuse me." She swallowed her breath. "What does that mean?"

"It means, hard, wild, and bent over the dresser probably isn't the way to go for our first time." He rolled on top of her, stretching her arms over her head, gripping her wrists. He kissed her temple, her cheek, her

41

neck, and the space between her breasts. "Slow and tortuous and the old-fashioned way might be a better option. Except fast might be the only speed since it's been forever, and men are only built one way."

She gasped.

He chuckled, lifted her shirt over her head, and tossed it and her bra aside. "You're so beautiful," he murmured right before his mouth took her nipple.

"Oh God." She clutched his head, threading her fingers through his short flattop hair.

He gave both breasts attention while he fumbled with her jeans, tugging them to her ankles.

In a swift, fluid motion, he pulled away from her just long enough to remove his shirt—flinging it carelessly to the side. His chest was a mass of hard muscle, dusted with a trail of dark hair that led tantalizingly toward his waist. She fingered the anchor and compass tattoo on his biceps before bringing her hand to the scar on his shoulder. She pressed her lips on the damaged skin.

He repositioned himself on top of her, igniting sparks of desire that shot through her entire body. He dipped his head down and captured one of her nipples in his mouth again. The sensation had her eyes rolling back in pleasure. His teeth grazed against her skin—not enough to hurt, but just enough to make her gasp.

Shifting to the side, his hand slid across her belly and cupped her between her legs. His thumb found her hard, throbbing clit. With the lightness of a feather, he drew circles around it before slipping his index finger inside.

She arched her back, moaning, gripping his shoulders. Instinctively, she rolled her hips with the movement of his hands. She might not have had sex before, but she was a sexual being. She did have some experience. She understood her body. She knew what she liked and God, she loved the way he touched her.

He kissed his way down her stomach. He lifted his head, catching her gaze while he licked his finger.

She swallowed, unable to suck in a deep breath.

"You taste so good." He dipped his head, flicking out his tongue, swirling it across her folds.

"Oh, Thor." She dug her heels into the mattress and curled her fingers into his scalp. A slow buildup started in her belly. It worked its way lower, spreading like a wildfire until she exploded. Her body shook like a volcano. Heat poured out of her. It covered her like a blanket.

He lifted his head, licked his lips, and smiled as he pawed at the button of his jeans. "Mind if I get rid of these?"

"I wish you would," she managed, her body still convulsing with the aftershocks of her orgasm. She watched as he unwound himself from her. The overhead light cast an illuminating glow over his sculptured physique as he rose off the bed. He stood there for a moment, letting her take in the view, before working on freeing himself from the confines of his own jeans.

Her heart pounded like a drum in her chest as he kicked off his last piece of clothing and climbed back onto the bed with predatory grace. This time when their bodies met, there were no barriers between them.

He brushed a string of unruly hair from her face.

"Remember," he said with husky intensity, "you're in control." His words were punctuated with hot kisses tracing down her neck and onto her chest.

"God," she managed, "I want you."

"And I want you," he responded, pressing himself firmly against her. "But only when you're ready."

Shyly, she reached out to touch him. At her first contact, he let out a hiss of pleasure. Emboldened, she stroked him lightly, exploring. He shuddered beneath her touch and groaned, leaning into her hand. It was all the encouragement she needed. She brought her mouth to him, taking the tip, and only the tip. She would start slow.

"You don't have to do... oh God," he muttered as she took more and squeezed the base. His chest heaved up and down. He pooled her hair on top of her head. "Two minutes. That's all I'll be able to handle."

She continued to lick, suck, touch, and savor him. She enjoyed this as much as she loved what he'd done to her. Being with him was freeing. It was what love and relationships were supposed to be like.

"As much as I really like what you are doing, babe, I need you to stop." He tugged at her hair and gently pushed her back on the bed.

With a subtle shift of his body, he met her gaze, those electric blue eyes of his now darkened with lust. His skin radiated an ethereal glow, the light casting dancing shadows on the valleys and peaks of his strong, chiseled form.

He lowered himself onto her, careful and gentle as he parted her. She gasped at the sensation. It was overwhelming, the feel of him against her—raw and intoxicating.

"Are you okay?" he asked tenderly as concern darkened his eyes, contrasting with the carnal desire that still lingered.

She smiled, appreciating his concern. "I'm wonderful." She ran her fingers down his back, cupping his ass, and encouraged him to go deeper. Harder. She needed him, wanted him, and she wasn't going to let him treat her with kid gloves.

His movements were slow at first—allowing her to adjust to him, but soon urgency took over. Each thrust sending shivers down her spine as she wrapped her legs around him for better leverage. His eyes never left hers. It was intense, like he was laying not just his body but his soul bare to her as well.

As their rhythm quickened, their breaths grew ragged and hushed moans were shared between stolen kisses. He buried his face in the crook of her neck, where he had previously been nibbling and whispered three words she wasn't expecting. "I love you."

She gasped audibly this time and held on to him tighter. The sudden confession added a layer of depth to their intimacy that she hadn't expected yet welcomed all the same.

"Yes," she whimpered against his ear, "I love you, too."

And with that shared proclamation of love between them, they rode out the wave of pleasure together until they both succumbed to the intense euphoria that washed over them.

Exhausted yet sated, they lay entangled within each other's arms, basking in the sweet afterglow of their shared passion. With languid strokes, he drew lazy circles on her arm and stared into her eyes.

"I meant what I said," he murmured, his voice husky from their recent exertion. He kissed her forehead softly, pulling her even closer to him. "I love you."

But before she could even enjoy the purest of moments, she heard the garage door hum to life.

"Is that what I think it is?" Thor pulled her closer.

She nodded. "Unless my folks walk over to your parents' house, there is no way they won't know we've been up here."

Thor cupped her chin. "I really don't want to get out of this bed. I'd rather lie here, hold you, and enjoy the moment, and while we're adults, this is your parents' home. I don't need the death stare from your dad." He shifted, moving toward the other side.

She laughed, shaking her head, grabbing his arm. "Death stare?"

"I saw him give it to that dude you dated your sophomore year in high school. That boy was a creeper. I didn't approve." Thor kissed her cheek. "We better get dressed."

"Our parents will stand in the driveway for a half hour before they part. They always do." She patted his chest. "I was only trying to make you jealous."

"I was too old for that." He laughed. "But maybe I was." He held up his index finger and thumb. "Just a little." He palmed her cheek. "There won't be any hanging out. They will come looking for me."

46

"I hadn't thought about that." She sighed.

"Are you okay? Did I hurt you? I can go downstairs and tell them you're not feeling well."

"Oh my God. I'm fine." She kissed him. Hard. "Did I act like it hurt? Or am I crying like some crazy woman?"

"Well, no." He pursed his lips.

"Open up that drawer and pull out the pink box." She waved toward her nightstand. Heat rose to her cheeks, but what the hell.

He rolled and did as she asked. "What's this?"

"Just look inside."

He lifted the lid and both brows shot up. "A vibrator?"

"Just so you understand that while no man has ever been inside me until you, that has."

"I'm oddly impressed, thrilled, and a little scared." He placed it back in the box and closed the drawer. "Can we use that? Together?"

She shrugged. "I don't see why not."

"Damn. My girlfriend's a little vixen." He patted her ass.

"Danni? Pumpkin, are you up here?" her dad called.

"Shit. Did you lock the door?" She pulled the covers up to her neck.

"No." He stared at her with wide eyes.

"Um, yeah, Dad. I'll be out in a couple of minutes, okay?"

"Sure thing," her father said. "Oh, and Thor, we appreciate you taking your shoes off. Always the *gentleman*." Her dad emphasized the word. "Your parents

47

are looking for you too. I'll let them know you're here. We'll have dessert together." Her dad laughed. "We have a fresh apple pie and brought home some ice cream. I'll open a bottle of wine."

Thor groaned, dropping his head, and covering it with the sheets. "Your father has always had a weird sense of humor."

"His way of letting us know he approves."

Thor swung his legs to the side of the bed. "I already knew he was on board with us dating. My parents are over the moon. But you know how they get when they've been drinking."

"Honey, they don't need booze to make either one of us blush." She padded across her room, naked, and it didn't feel strange at all. Not one bit. She found a fresh outfit and dressed. "When they left, your mom told me I was too young to make her a grandmother."

"She did not say that."

"Hand to God, she did." She turned and smiled. "Well, we might as well go face the weird music that is our family."

---

"My opinion doesn't matter." Thor raised his beer and stared at Danni from across the table in her parents' kitchen. The evening had been normal, considering everything.

It's not like he and Danni hadn't talked about being together. It had consumed his thoughts this last deployment. It felt unnatural not to be with the woman he loved and God, he had known he loved her for months now. It hit him like a ton of bricks when the enemy had come down on them, bullets flying, barely missing him and his buddies.

When he lay under the stars that night, grateful he and his team had completed their mission—successfully and without injury—all he wanted was to see her face, not just in a picture. He wanted to hear her voice, hold her body against his, and feel her breath tickle his skin.

She'd become his rock—his gravity—his center. She balanced him, and he wanted to be that for her. He wanted her to have everything she desired. He didn't want to be the reason she didn't chase her goals—he wanted to be the person who supported them.

However, the one thing he hadn't considered was that his sweet, adorable Danni had never been with anyone else. It humbled him. He remembered his first time and it wasn't anything to write home about. He'd been nineteen, and it had ended about the same time it started, and the girl he'd been with had been highly disappointed.

He wasn't a horndog. He didn't date much, and it's not like he had a ton of sex. He didn't. He had one relationship that lasted eight months. That was something, and he cared about her, but that was about the extent of his love life until Danni. Because of his career, they resorted to sexy talk and a few interesting video chats.

It amazed him how comfortable she'd been with her own body. How well she knew it and now he was sitting around the table with their parents. It shouldn't be weird at all, and mostly it wasn't. But they were talking about their future—something he knew he wanted—with Danni.

"Why would you say that?" Danni scrunched her nose.

"Because this is your career. It's the beginning of something amazing, and where I'm stationed shouldn't factor into it."

"I disagree with that." Danni pursed her lips. "One of the jobs is much closer to the base. I could get an apartment right there. The other one is about forty minutes away. I could commute, but I hear the traffic is a nightmare, especially over that bridge."

"Babe, I don't want you making this decision based on how close the job is to the base, especially when both are in the area. What you need to consider is, which one excites you more?" He tapped the screen. "You've been working on this piece about the Origins of God for this magazine for a while now. Heck, you've been writing about this cult since high school."

"I agree," her father said. "You've put your heart and soul into that project. Your entire college thesis is based on that."

"It doesn't mean I have to take the job they offer." Danni folded her arms, leaned back, and sighed. "Besides, everyone here is constantly getting their panties in a wad about my obsession with cults or how I'm always interviewing people in the cults. You're always worried about me doing that."

Thor did worry—a lot. But he didn't want to stifle the woman either. "Come on, babe. You wanted to follow up on that story, and the one in Newport News isn't all that far away. It's just on the other side of the river. There are lots of wonderful places where traffic wouldn't be as bad." He let out a long breath. "And the cult story won't be the only story they will have you working on."

"Maybe not, and it's possible the one in Norfolk will let me run with the story on the Origins of God. I haven't asked. Besides, it's less about the first potential assignment and more about where the job can take me. I want something where I'll have the flexibility to move around with the possibility to work from home, and I still want to write a book and take down something like the Origins of God—now that's major."

Thor admired her ambition. "Babe, I think you just made your decision." Thor pushed the paperwork in front of her. "I don't want to put a damper on any of this, but I could be transferred to a different base at any time, and I'm deployed so much that this will be hard." He rubbed his temples. Any SEAL who was in a relationship got a lecture from some other career SEAL about how impossible it was for relationships to last. The divorce rate was through the roof. But they weren't just anyone. They had already defied the odds. "I'm only home for a month, and then I don't know how long I'll be gone. Hopefully, it won't be six months again, but we must keep in mind that—"

"Thor. I get that," Danni said. "I'm not looking at it only from the perspective of how close to the base I will be. If you get transferred, I have to consider if I can pick up quickly and move too, so I need to ask that question regarding both offers." She arched a brow. "But you're right, the one in Newport News does seem like a better fit." She cocked a brow. "But that story, it could take years. It could consume me and my career, which means if I'm in the middle of it and you get transferred, I might not want to leave right away."

"The likelihood I will be shifted out of SEAL team four isn't very high. It was just something I needed to put out there." Thor took her hand and squeezed. "I want you to take the job that is going to make you happy. We'll work out the logistics of where you live when that happens. No matter what, I love and support you." He swallowed. Admitting that to himself—to her —that was one thing. But saying it in front of all their parents, well, by the smirks and chuckles, it must have landed… maybe, right?

"I'm glad to hear you say that." His mom stood, stretched, and yawned. "Come on, honey, it's late. Time to call it a night."

His father rose, looping his arm around his mom. "Thanks for a wonderful evening." He nodded. "It's exciting to watch our kids tackle their next phase of life."

Thor wanted to roll his eyes, but instead, he just smiled. "I'll be over in a bit."

His dad laughed, glancing over his shoulder as he paused at the back door. "I will never forget when we moved into this neighborhood. Thor was eight and Danni was four. Danni came running over, wanting to know who the new neighbors were. She stood in our kitchen and told us all about her family and then asked Thor if he wanted to go swimming in her pool. I figured that boy would produce any excuse not to have to hang out with a kid half his age, but he begged his mom to find his swim trunks."

"I actually remember that day too." Thor nodded. "Swimming beat helping you two unpack."

His mom smiled. "Perhaps, but the two of you always had a bond. She'd come flying over after school and if you weren't doing anything, you'd gladly sit on the sofa and play video games with her or build a snowman. Even when you got to high school, you always made room for Danni."

"She was always my friend." Thor shrugged. "And as families, we went on vacations together. I don't see why you're making a big deal about this all of a sudden."

Danni's father leaned closer. "The moms are hearing wedding bells—for real—and that's something they have spent countless hours making jokes about since we all met." He tapped his knuckles on the table. "They spent all of dinner discussing how wonderful it was that you were together and even brought up grandbabies."

Thor pounded his chest and swallowed the thick lump that magically appeared in his throat. His life had taken a major turn—but not much had changed. He still had his best friend. She just turned into the woman he loved.

Those words had tumbled from his mouth in the throes of passion. He meant them. He just hadn't anticipated saying them at precisely that moment. Though he was glad he had, and he loved Danni with all his heart and soul.

"You're embarrassing the children." Gracefully, his mom rose, gathering the dessert dishes.

"Yeah, well, the kids can play at this game too." Danni rested her free hand on Thor's thigh, a little too high. Her fingers danced. "I only have two more nights before I have to drive back to school and since Thor won't be coming with me, he's going to be sleeping here, in my room, with me."

"Tell us something we don't know." His father opened the back door. "Your mother didn't even bother to open the futon and put sheets on it."

"Besides, when she graduates from college and gets that apartment, we all know this one"—her father slapped him on the back—"will be moving off base and in with her." He stood, helping his wife with the dishes. "I suppose we need to get used to the idea of them sleeping in the same bed."

Thor dropped his forehead to the table and groaned.

Danni wrapped her arm around his shoulders, her delicate fingers digging into his muscles. She pressed her lips against his temple. "You doing okay, big fella?"

He turned and sighed. "Ask me that in the morning when I try to decide if I'm crawling out your bedroom window to hightail it to my folks' for coffee, or if I sheepishly tiptoe past your father's shotgun."

"Good night, all." His father waved his hand over his head. "Let's all have dinner at our place tomorrow."

"Sounds like a plan." Thor sat up taller, tugging Danni closer. As weird as it all felt, this was where he belonged. "I'll grill because you burn everything."

"I do not," his father balked. "But I won't say no to standing on the sidelines and having my son do it."

Thor laughed.

Danni rested her head on his biceps. She was his heart and his soul. He knew without a doubt that someday they would get married and have a family of their own.

TWO YEARS LATER...

*D*anni stared at the diner's door with her heart in her chest. Her career had completely taken off. She'd become a trusted expert in religious cults. She'd authored more articles than she could count. However, Origins of God continued to be the bane of her existence. Finding members of the cult—both current and past—to interview had proved impossible.

She'd drive over to West Virginia and try to interview the people who went to the farmer's market and sold the produce they grew on the compound. Or the candles, jewelry, and clothing they made.

They all sang the praises of the religion they so vehemently followed.

However, none of them had ever met Christopher Bently, the leader of Origins of God—at least, that's their story. When she asked about him or where he was, they told her he was busy ensuring their place here on earth and in heaven. There was so much about the hierarchy of the Origins of God that Danni didn't understand, but she believed without a shadow of a doubt that there were members there who didn't want to be there or that were being held against their will.

At least that was the picture of some family members who lost loved ones to the religion.

But what was it that kept them there? Why were they afraid to leave? What did Christopher and his eight disciples have on their followers?

She was about to find out.

A young woman entered the diner clutching an over-sized bag hanging over her shoulder. She glanced to her right and then to her left, locking gazes with Danni, who gave the woman a slight nod.

Krista was about the same age as Danni, but as she lowered her head and shuffled her feet across the floor, Danni noticed how haggard the poor woman appeared. While she didn't have wrinkles, she wore years of being beaten down in her yellow-brown eyes. A sense of dread lifted from her skin and landed thickly in the air.

"Hi, Krista," Danni said softly. "Thank you so much for meeting with me."

Krista glanced over her shoulder. Her gaze nervously darted around the room. "Does anyone know you're interviewing me?"

"No one knows your name," Danni said softly. "However, my boss does know I'm interviewing some-one." She left out the fact she'd shared her location with Thor. That he knew everything. For starters, her boss at the magazine wouldn't have liked that she shared so much of her work with Thor. But he was her partner, the love of her life, and he was a fantastic sounding board.

He was also insanely overprotective and sometimes, he pounded his chest and acted like a baboon. But she had to admit, it was nice to have a badass Navy SEAL as a boyfriend.

"No one can know I'm speaking with you." Krista held her bag on her lap and hugged it like a security blanket.

"What if my editor decides your story needs to be told?" Danni rested her hand on the notebook she had on the table and leaned closer. "Because what little you've told me so far, I believe we're going to want to run with this story." She tapped her fingers on the pad of paper. "I've been researching Origins of God for years. I get the feeling they don't let people go and the fact that you managed to walk away—"

"I didn't walk away." Krista swiped at her cheeks. "I ran away, as fast as I could. I did it in the middle of the night and I did it with help."

"What do you mean?" Danni cocked her head. "Who helped you?"

"I can't tell you that. It would compromise them and what they do," Krista said. "All I can say about that is when Disciple Matt was left with no choice but to take me to the hospital, I met someone who lived something similar as me. I don't know why I believed and trusted them when I was suffering so badly, but I did." She spoke fast and with a slight tremble, but there was a sense of strength in her voice. "I went with them and never looked back... until now."

"Would you be willing to reach out to them and ask them if they would be willing to let me interview them?"

Krista shook her head. "The way it works is they help people like me get out. They help set us up with a new name, give us a little money, a couple of job prospects in a new town, and send us on our way."

"Why did you reach out to me?"

"I read the article you wrote about a different cult last year." Krista opened her bag and riffled through the contents. She pulled out a picture. "This is one of my little brothers. He's about to be eighteen. That means he will go through what Origins of God call the Enlightenment Ceremony. It's for men who have come of age. It tells high council of each branch what that young man's role will be."

"I've never heard that term before." Danni picked up her pen and opened the notebook. "What is it and what does it mean for your brother?"

"It will decide his fate inside the organization." Krista fingered the image. "We were born and raised in Origins of God. So were my parents. My father is a Spiritual Teacher, or what is also known as a Keeper of the Truth. That's a big deal. My mother was plucked during her ceremony to be a Divine Mother. For a woman, that is considered the ultimate calling. You are the purest of the pure. You are considered to be the closest to God. The community reveres you and everyone wants their daughters to be chosen."

"Is that what you were chosen to be?" Danni wrote as fast as she could. She'd already promised Krista there would be no audio devices. Right now, she wished she

59

hadn't agreed to that. This was good stuff. She'd gotten more out of Krista than she'd learned in all her years trying to pluck information about this religion from what little literature there had been on them.

Krista laughed. "I was an utter disappointment to my family. I questioned the teachings of our spiritual leaders. I didn't like being treated differently than the boys. And I certainly didn't want to be a Divine Mother. They are one of many wives and their only purpose is to have children and be quiet. People might have bowed their heads at my mother when she was allowed to roam the compound, but she wasn't treated like a Divine Mother. She was treated like an incubator and a human cow. Once children reach the age of three, they spend most of their time with the Sanctified, which are women who either can't bear children and are tossed aside by their husbands or they weren't considered worthy by God during their Enlightenment Ceremony."

Danni's heart pounded in her chest. "I'm sorry, but this doesn't sound like a religious cult anymore. It sounds like a prison."

Krista leaned forward. "For me, it was." She nodded. "Girls have their Enlightenment Ceremony at sixteen. At least at my compound they do."

"Would a parent's role have any bearing on what happens or where the child is placed?"

"It's not supposed to. The idea is that God speaks directly to the disciple and tells him what everyone's purpose is. It's all based on how the individual has lived and how they are perceived by the community and, more importantly, God. There's a lot of speaking in tongues. It's very ritualistic. When I had my ceremony, I expected God would have told Disciple Matt that my role would be as a Sanctified Woman. A woman who will not be married and not worthy of having a husband or children, but who will take care of the Divine Mothers and other women who are chosen to give birth. A woman who will cook and clean and serve. Basically, the lowest of women who might not even be godly."

Danni found herself sitting on the edge of her seat. "What happened?"

"Nothing. God found no purpose for me." Krista clutched the picture to her chest. "Disciple Matt rolled his eyes and said he had a vision. He said I was to be an Unseen."

"What is that?"

"The believers think it's a person who is cast out, released, or given the opportunity to relearn what Origins of God is all about. This is a person who is to beg God for a second chance. But no one inside the compound knows what that person chooses until they reappear some months later." Krista shook her head. "And everyone I've ever known who becomes an Unseen always comes back, but they aren't the same person. They are broken. They are void. They are a cog, and I didn't want to be that."

Danni swallowed. "What happened to you?"

"I was locked in a room. At first, I was given food and water. I was visited by a man I never saw before. He'd read to me from our bible. He'd give me lessons on our doctrine. I was expected to do the exercises left for me. I was expected to pray ten times a day. If I didn't meet those expectations, I was beaten—by this man. He would also rape me." Krista wiped the tears that fell from her eyes. "He would whisper in my ear that God commanded him to take me. That this was God driving himself into me."

"That's disgusting."

Krista nodded. "That man would stand over me and tell me I better do as I was told or God would punish me in the worst of ways. I figured nothing could get worse than what was happening. I almost never did what they asked. That man broke one of my ribs and punctured a lung. A few days later, Disciple Matt was forced to take me to the hospital. He told them that I had run away, and some boy had done that to me. He even gave them a name."

"Oh my God. That's crazy." Danni waved her hand. "I must ask. What happened to that young man?"

"He was picked up by the police, but I never gave a statement because the people who helped did so two days after I was brought in. That boy was released, I was gone, and the cops dropped it."

"You were sixteen, right?"

Krista nodded.

"You were a child. Didn't your parents—or anyone —file a missing persons?"

"That would have brought the police into the compound and while I had no idea anyone in the compound was doing anything illegal—and I still don't have proof—just an outline of how they do things—I suspect that not one of the higher-ups wants anyone poking around, so they actually told people that I had run away again. They gave the cops a note that I had written to my parents a different time I tried to run away and that was that, but I think the people who helped me might have mentioned something to one of the police officers. I can't be sure."

"I'm going to have to look into that," Danni said. "This was the group in Kentucky?"

"Correct," Krista said. "There are nine compounds altogether, but no one knows where Messiah Christopher lives. There are rumors about where that compound is, but nothing concrete."

"The eight disciples must know. I was told by Disciple Oliver in West Virginia that they have meetings every few months."

"I wouldn't know anything about that," Krista said. "I'm surprised he met with you."

"He didn't. I showed up at the compound after spending hours at the farmer's market. I think he believed it would make me go away. Obviously, that's not working."

"You don't want to upset these people." Krista sighed.

"What else can you tell me about the leader?"

"I know that Messiah Christopher does try to visit each compound a couple of times a year, but he's very sneaky about it. It's like he crawls in through a tunnel. He doesn't like attention from the outside world, except to have new worthy recruits, and he hates it when outsiders show up, but I've never met him."

Danni tapped her pencil on the table. "How is that possible?"

"I wasn't worthy to be in his presence," Krista said, swiping at her cheeks. "I would be locked away when he came to our compound."

"I've noticed he's camera shy." So far, Danni hadn't been able to find any images of Christopher Bently anywhere, except for a few from when he'd been younger.

"He won't allow any pictures taken of him or on the premises."

"I've spoken with a bunch of believers. I've seen parts of what everyone refers to as the farm at the West Virginia compound."

"That's sounds like what we used to call the playground in Kentucky. It's where the Anointed, the Keepers of the Faith, or anyone who is a true believer can roam free. It's also where new recruits come and hang out. It looks normal. When I was a little girl, my mom was allowed to go there once a day. She would take me and my siblings with the help of a few hand-picked Sanctified women. It was different there. People didn't bow to my mother. They didn't quite yet under-stand that she was seen as so pure that only a man of God could speak to her or touch her. That even her chil-dren were beneath her."

"Sounds like such a lonely way to live."

"It is." Krista nodded. "If you think the real world still doesn't give women a sense of equity and equality—well, you haven't seen anything like what happens in the Origins of God." Krista visibly shuddered. "I think because I could see and feel how different the play-ground was than the compound, that's why I acted out so strongly over the way women were treated. Actually, about the entire doctrine that we were taught."

"Do you know of anyone else who has ever left the Origins of God?"

"I don't." Krista shook her head. "I know people who have escaped other fundamentalist groups and cults. But I try to stay away from anyone who could have a connection to Origins of God."

"Are you afraid they might kidnap you? Or worse?"

"I'm absolutely terrified what they might do to me," Krista whispered. "The man who beat me. He would whisper in my ear that he would break me. That he would do this for as long as it took. That he never failed knocking the devil out of anyone." Krista swallowed. "He would hold me down while he was inside me and tell me that I would succumb, that I would be submissive, and that I would never again question God's commands. The way he said it, the timbre of his voice, and the way his hands crawled across my body, it made me start to question why I was fighting or what I was fighting. It was as if what I knew as right and wrong no longer mattered. I knew in that moment that he was right. That given enough time, he would and could make me into a shell of nothing. If they find me, because I betrayed them at the highest level, they will finish what they started, and I don't think I have it in me to fight them again."

Danni reached across the table and took Krista's hand. "If I get the go-ahead to write this piece, I will make sure you are protected."

"I don't see how you can do that." Krista hiccupped.

"Even if you leave my name out, you print what I just told you, they will know it was me."

"What do you want me to do?"

Krista took the napkin and dabbed her wet cheeks. "I'm moving north. I know someone who escaped something similar. She's married to a retired military guy. They've offered me refuge if I decide to let you tell my story."

"My boyfriend is a Navy SEAL. He's got connections all over the globe." Danni squeezed her hand. "We have to put an end to organizations like this."

"Can I ask you a question?"

Danni nodded.

"Why is this story important to you?"

That was always a tough question for Danni to answer. "There was a church not far from where I grew up that was considered a cult. I also went to school with someone from that religion who was murdered by one of their members. It affected me deeply."

"I'm sorry." Krista lowered her gaze.

Danni tapped her pen to her temple. "What do you know about their recruiting methods?"

"Very little, to be honest," Krista said. "Those who come in from the outside are screened heavily. In the sixteen years I grew up there, I only knew a couple of converts and they never talked of their past or how they came to the compound. Only how they were chosen to serve the Messiah, his disciples, and God."

"So, most people are born into the cult."

Krista nodded. "My mother had nine children, that I know of. I wouldn't be surprised if she had more after

I left. Even women who aren't Divine Mothers have many children. It's really the only purpose women have outside of cooking, cleaning, and serving."

"What if a woman was chosen to be a Divine Mother but couldn't have children?"

"She would be seen as a sinner. As someone who must be doing something wrong or having evil and impure thoughts. She would either be Forsaken, Unseen, Veiled, or a combination of those, depending on if she prayed hard enough and somehow became pregnant. I never knew a Divine whom that happened to, but I did know a Devoted woman who was Forsaken because she couldn't have children. She was reduced to cooking for the high counsel. She was also a Veiled, which is like wearing a scarlet letter in public and she had very little chance at redemption."

"So, no chance of going to heaven?"

"Not according to the Origins of God," Krista said.

"Why would they stay?"

"Because there was always that little sliver of hope that God would somehow whisper in the Disciple's ear that a Forsaken would be forgiven. That they could move back into a godlier role." Krista raised her hand. "Let me tell you, if you were born into this, you believed it with everything that you are because you don't know any better. We were not taught to think for ourselves. We didn't have outside influences. If we showed any inclination of being influenced, we weren't allowed off the compound." She arched a brow. "But the real scary part is how people who aren't born into this end up believing it just as passionately. That's something that I don't understand. I get being beaten into submission. That was the only way they could make me do anything. But I will never understand the person who willingly seeks this crap out."

Danni did understand why some people sought comfort in the arms of religion. Oftentimes, spirituality gave people answers to things there were no answers for.

But this wasn't that at all. People like Disciple Matt and Oliver were predators. They got off on having power—on controlling others—and Danni planned on exposing them and their leader, Christopher Bently, for what they really were.

## 5

TWO YEARS LATER...

*P*op! Pop! Pop!

"*Take cover,*" Moose said.

"*I'm shot.*" Jupiter groaned. "*Sloan, Kawan, and Lief, all down. Calling for evac.*"

*Thor tried to open his mouth and use his vocal cords, but nothing happened. The taste of metal filled it. He tried to suck in a deep breath, but his lungs burned. He reached for the radio, but his vision blurred. He blinked. Something wet and tacky dribbled down his face. He raised his arm to wipe it away, but his arm didn't move.*

Beep. Beep. Beep.

He jolted. His eyes flew open. His body screamed in pain. "Danni," he whispered. Turning his head, he glanced around.

Fucking hospital room… same damn nightmare… mission gone sideways…

A woman wearing scrubs stood over him. She took his wrist in her cool hands and smiled. "Are you dreaming about Danni again?" she asked in a calm voice.

"Always," he managed, even though that nightmare had nothing to do with the woman he loved.

"I've got some good news," the woman said. "Moose has been discharged and he's sitting in the hallway." She jerked her thumb over her shoulder. "Jupiter, Kawan, Sloan, and Lief all will be discharged in a few days and returned to the States."

"That's good to know," he said. "And what about me?"

"Unfortunately, your injuries were a little more extensive. We will keep you here for at least five to seven days."

"Of course you will." He chuckled, then coughed. "Can you send Moose in?"

The woman nodded, turned around, and left.

He adjusted himself in the bed and did his best to purge the demons. Only they didn't disappear so easily this time.

The door swung open, and Moose casually strolled through it, his arm in a colorful cast and sling. "How are you feeling today?" he said.

"Like I got shot in the gut." His throat was dry, and it hurt to talk.

Moose handed him a cup of water.

He slurped it down, though he wished he hadn't because with each swallow, he wanted to ask for the nurse to give him something for the pain and he hated taking that crap.

"We all got our phones back and have been given

permission to communicate with the outside world." Moose set a phone on the side of the bed. "Danni, your parents, and hers, are going bonkers. I know I should've waited for you to give the thumbs-up, but since we made the news and your injuries weren't life-threatening, I made an executive decision to text everyone when I was discharged."

Thor arched a brow. "How on earth did we make the news and that fast? It's only been a few days."

"We're all getting medals." Moose smacked his forehead with his good hand. "The mission might have been a shit show, but we did achieve our goal."

"I wish I could remember getting the hostages on that helicopter with us." Thor twisted his body, lifting the phone. "But I'm surprised it landed so quickly back in the States."

"We did rescue journalists." Moose waved his hand over the cell. "You better call that girl of yours before she sends me another nasty text."

"Danni would never." Thor chuckled. However, he knew how impatient she could be.

"You can read them if you want," Moose said. "When you're done, text Brick from The Refuge."

"Why would I do that?" Thor frowned.

"Because he and Pipe are here."

"What on earth are they doing in Germany?"

"A favor for an old friend and when they heard what happened, they wanted to check on us. Now, they're offering all of us a repeater discount." Moose ran his good hand across his unshaven face. "We've cheated death before and we're not even thirty yet. I don't know about you, but I for one could use a little peace and quiet. I already told them yes and thank you." He lowered his chin. "For all of us."

Thor sighed. He'd been to The Refuge twice now. He valued what Brick and all the men and women there did for people who suffered from PTSD. He wasn't about to say no, but he didn't feel like dealing with it right now. All he wanted was to see and hear his beloved Danni's voice.

"You don't look overly thrilled about the prospect." Moose arched a brow.

"It's not that and I know I'll need it. We all will if we're going to be able to be at our best when we're cleared to get back in the saddle again. I just want to go home and wrap my arms around Danni. I'd have her fly out here, but by the time she gets here, I'll be heading home."

"This is a military hospital. I doubt they'd let her in," Moose said. "When are you going to put a ring on that girl's finger?"

Thor had heard it all before. He'd been razzed a million times by every single one of his teammates. Funny coming from them since they were all single. But Danni was only twenty-five. Heck, he wasn't even thirty yet. "I'm not even going to answer that."

Moose tapped the phone. "Call her and don't wait too long to ask that woman to marry you. She's the best thing that ever happened to you."

"You don't have to tell me that," Thor said. "It's not like we don't talk about it. We have a plan. Now, get out of here and let me call my girl."

Moose waved his good hand over his head and strolled out the door.

Thor lifted the phone, tapped the screen, and held his breath. He chose to video chat because he wanted to see her face. He needed to see the love in her eyes.

He was the luckiest bastard in the world.

"Oh my God. Thor. It's you." Danni tucked her hair behind her ears. She stared into the phone, leaning a little closer. "Are you okay?"

"Babe, I'm fine."

"I've been pacing a hole in the floor ever since Moose texted, but I'm so glad he did. Once the story hit and they plastered your image and name on the news, it would have been worse not to have the details. Freaking reporters are everywhere."

He chuckled, which cost him a shot of pain in the center of his gut. He coughed and then cleared his throat. "Babe, aren't you a reporter?"

"I'm an investigative journalist and while some of the reporters are top-notch, others are slime. Moose told me not to say anything to anyone and your parents were visited by the Navy. They instructed them not to discuss you with the press at this time. Your dad said the Navy will be contacting me since they know I'm your girl-friend and we're living together."

"Moose just told me that we made the news."

"The story broke five hours ago." She smiled wide. Tears dribbled down her beautiful cheeks. "I have so many emotions colliding inside me. When I saw a text from Moose's phone, my heart sank. I didn't even want to open it. I think I knew something had happened because I hadn't heard from you for an entire week. Sometimes it's hard to be strong—"

"I know, sweetheart. But I'm fine."

"Fine?" Her eyes grew wide with a combination of shock and anger. "You were shot—twice. I know this is the life I signed up for. I'm super proud of you and I love you—but because I love you, this is hard, Thor. It sucks not knowing sometimes and sucks more knowing you're lying in a hospital bed in Germany and I was oblivious to it, and I can't do anything about it." She swiped at her cheeks.

God, he hated how this hurt her and all he wanted to do was wrap his arms around her and hold her tight. "I'm sorry, babe."

"It's not your fault," she whispered. "I shouldn't have even said anything." She sighed. "I'm sorry. I'm just so grateful you're okay. Moose told me that the rest of the team will be going home soon and that he's staying behind with you."

That was news to Thor.

"He also said that after you get a clean bill of health, he wants the team to spend some time at The Refuge."

"He does." Thor rubbed his temple. He wasn't ready to talk about this, not even with Danni. No one died on this mission, and it had proven to be successful. According to the United States government, it was worthy of a medal.

"Nightmares?" Danni asked softly. Her voice was sweet and calm—not a single word was laced with judgment. It wasn't the first time a mission had gone sideways, causing him to jerk awake in the middle of the night. Or make him break out in a cold sweat when something triggered him. He always pushed through—always managed to sneak past the demons that lurked in his mind.

He did so because of Danni—and because he was the kind of man who knew he couldn't go it alone. He needed places like The Refuge. He needed to talk out the emotions that were created by the chaos of his career.

He shifted his gaze.

"It's okay if you don't want to talk to me about it," Danni said. "But I know just because no one died, doesn't mean—"

"I love you." He stared into the tiny screen, catching her gaze. "You mean everything to me, you know that, right?"

"Yes." She nodded.

He smiled. "We'll talk about this when I get home and can hold you in my arms. When I can feel your skin against mine." He lowered his chin. "I'll be home before I go to The Refuge."

She nodded.

"Now, tell me. What's been happening at home? How's things with work? I want to hear everything." He lifted his free hand and waggled his finger. "Do not leave anything out. I'm bored as heck sitting in this hospital and I'd rather talk to you, then listen to Moose babble about his chickens back home."

"For a badass SEAL, he's an odd man."

"You can say that again." Thor chuckled. "Now start talking." He shifted, doing his best not to grimace.

The last thing he wanted to do was bring the attention back to himself.

"My final piece on polygamist groups has been published and well received... except for by fundamental polygamist groups." She shook her head and laughed. "The main religion I went after has demanded a retraction, stating that my facts on men marrying girls under the age of seventeen is absolutely wrong and that they don't take on more than one wife."

Thor pinched the bridge of his nose, wishing he hadn't asked for an update. Now, all he'd do was worry about Danni and these crazy groups she wrote about in her articles.

At least it wasn't Origins of God. That group freaked him out, but only because the world knew so little about them. They weren't an organized religion. They hadn't asked for tax exemption. They called themselves a community, not a religion, but they had their own doctrine.

However, what really concerned Thor was Danni's obsession with them.

"Honey, you have nothing to worry about." Danni cocked her head. "I have proof of their practices. Half a dozen women have come forward in these past few weeks. Because of my hard work and all my articles and reporting, the police might actually be able to make some arrests soon."

"That's wonderful and don't get me wrong, I'm so proud of you. It's just that I worry about your safety, especially if the cops aren't ready to make those arrests right now. I don't like you being alone when this stuff goes down."

*Knock. Knock.*

Thor glanced over the cell and waved Brick and Pipe into the room.

"I don't have any control over that, and this is the first time one of my collections put a dent in any of this." She tilted her head. "I do understand your concerns. They're no different than mine."

He couldn't argue that point. "Promise me you'll contact Kawan's cop friend, Tim if—"

"I already have." She blew him a kiss. "Looks like you've got company." She squinted. "Only, I don't recognize those faces."

"Meet Brick and Pipe of The Refuge." He panned the phone and both men awkwardly waved. "They were here on other business and popped in to say hello. Call me when you climb into bed to say good night, okay?"

"I will," she said. "I love you, Thor."

"Love you, too, babe." Thor set the phone on the table by the bed.

Brick and Pipe leaned up against the far wall.

"It's been a couple of years," Brick said. "I'd say you look good, except you look like shit."

"And you're still ugly." Thor shifted, sitting taller. "All joking aside, I appreciate you stopping by—it wasn't necessary, even if you were in-country."

"You would've done the same thing if the table were turned," Pipe said in his wonderful British accent. "Do you need anything?"

"I'm good. I'm just ready to go home."

"You know how to reach us." Brick nodded. "We'll see you at the ranch in a few weeks. Feel free to call us if you need anything." He tapped his knuckles on the side of the bed. "Or if Danni needs anything. We're happy to help."

"I'll keep that in mind." Thor watched as Brick and Pipe stepped from the room. He suspected they either had already visited his buddies or were making their rounds. Everyone at The Refuge were good people and Thor was grateful to have such a great support system. Many people—including servicemen and women— didn't have the resources or the willingness to do the work. Thor would put in his time. He wasn't ready to give up his career. He had many years left.

He and Danni were both still young. He took what Moose said to heart. He had a plan and while marriage was definitely on the table, he'd made her father a promise when they moved in together that he'd give Danni the time and space to achieve some of her goals before they settled into marital bliss.

Thor had no regrets. He had his dream job and his dream girl. Funny how Danni had been right about that all those years ago.

## 6

A YEAR LATER...

*T*hor poked at the steaks on the grill. He loved a lazy Sunday afternoon with his buddies— and his girl.

"That was quite the series of articles Danni wrote." Mouse leaned against the fence in the backyard and sipped a beer. "Very informative, and her source, holy shit. That's terrifying what that poor girl had to live through."

Thor nodded. While he was incredibly proud of all the things Danni had accomplished, the attention to the articles about Origins of God and the young girl who had escaped the chains that tied her to the cult left a bad taste in Thor's mouth.

"You don't look as if you're pleased," Mouse said.

"She's gotten some weird emails this past week," Thor admitted. "They weren't threatening in nature, but they were alarming. She and her boss called the police. However, it wasn't enough for them to do anything about it. But Danni poked a big bear with this cult, and

I don't believe for one second they are going to take it sitting down."

"I heard the cult put out a rare statement denying everything," Kawan said. "That the girl's parents have come forward stating she ran away with some boy years ago and that they outed her true identity."

"Danni's magazine has unequivocally denied the connection between Danni's story and the identity the cult gave, but the damage was done." This was the part that truly terrified him. "I'm going to tell this to you guys because this does freak me out. The victim's real name is indeed Marybeth Quinn. I've spoken to the family that has given her refuge. A guy by the name of Phoenix Snow. He's ex-Delta Force. His wife was in a polygamous cult. She escaped years ago and exposed that cult with his help. He and his brothers— also ex-Delta—will protect her, but my Danni is hell-bent on taking this cult down. She doesn't feel as though these few articles she's written are enough and she's pushing for more, along with a book deal. Marybeth—or Krista as she prefers—has told Danni she couldn't identify her attacker and while she's given Danni a ton of information, it's nothing that the cops can use."

"What is Danni planning on doing next?" Lief asked.

"She wants to interview Disciple Oliver again and tour the compound." Thor shut the grill and guzzled his beer. "I know her and she's not going to stop until she proves they are keeping people against their will. That they are abusing women and children."

Mouse squeezed his shoulder. "She doesn't go it alone, does she?"

"She's an investigative reporter, of course she does." Thor sighed. "If I'm home, she lets me either follow her or track her movements. If I'm deployed, someone always knows where she is, or she'll sometimes bring a colleague with her." He shook his head. "Her argument with me is always the same, that the Origins of God need her to paint them in a good light. That they wouldn't do anything to harm her. She's too much in the spotlight, especially now."

"She's only partially right about that one," Kawan said. "Thing is that crazy people don't think logically and therefore—"

"You don't need to spell that out. Trust me, I know we're not dealing with rational people. But tell that one to my Danni." Thor stared at the back of the house they'd moved into a few weeks ago.

Danni appeared at the sliders. She carried a tray of snacks as she stepped out on the back patio. She never minded when the guys came over and none of them currently had girlfriends.

Well, Lief had a girl he occasionally hung out with, but it wasn't serious, and he chose not to bring her today.

"You boys should be careful what you say when the kitchen window is open." She set the tray on the table. "I heard every flipping word." She cocked her head and glared. "I appreciate your concern for my safety, but really, if you have something to say about what I'm doing, you can say it to my face."

Thor did not want to have this fight… again. He strolled across the patio, tugged her to his chest, and kissed her sweet lips. "I love you," he whispered. "I only want you to be safe."

"I know." She squeezed his biceps. "But I'm not giving up this story and I've been doing a dance with that book agent from New York. This could be a big deal for me."

"I never said I wanted you to give up." He rubbed his gut where a year ago a bullet had torn through it. The injury hadn't been life-threatening, but it had changed him fundamentally. Occasionally, he still had nightmares, and they weren't just about him. Somehow, Danni managed to sneak into those terrifying dreams. He'd gone back to The Refuge three months ago in hopes to reset those dreams. It worked—until recently. "But with me and the guys going away shortly, I worry, especially since you're trying to get a meeting with that wackadoo. Has that happened yet?"

She sighed. "No, but he will after my next article goes to print."

Thor cocked a brow. "What did you do?"

"I just got off the phone with a woman who lived at the compound in Ohio for eight years. She was a convert. She joined after her mother died by suicide. She was nineteen and feeling lost and alone in the world. She was on the fringe for the first seven years, staying in one of the cabins on the outer part of the compound. She didn't see any of what Krista—Mary-beth—witnessed, until they brought her in for her

Enlightenment Ceremony. She told me that was the beginning of the end for her."

"What happened?" Thor asked.

A tear escaped Danni's eye and rolled down her cheek. He wiped it away with his thumb. These stories always touched her soul so deeply. She was such a caring and empathic human, and he loved her even more because of it.

But he worried about her and how her emotions drove her deeper into this story. She couldn't save everyone.

He knew this firsthand.

"According to Heather—the woman I spoke with— she was told God called her to be a Pilgrams Guide, which is someone meant to recruit others. At first, she took this as a great honor. She was excited to share God's word with others. But for the next few months, she wasn't allowed to leave the compound. She felt like a prisoner and the doctrine changed. She saw things that horrified her but went along because she feared what might happen if she didn't. When she was sent out to sell candles, she took off. She's been in hiding ever since."

"How did you find her?" Kawan asked.

"She found me." Danni sucked in a deep breath. "My articles are doing good. I can't stop and a book deal would reach far more people. You must understand that what I'm doing is helping people."

Thor cupped her face. "I never said it wasn't and I'm not asking you give it up. I only want you to be safe." He kissed her softly. "These people are dangerous and you're putting yourself in harm's way. I'm being deployed again, and I don't know what I'd do if anything were to ever happen to you. I don't want you to go to this compound alone."

"My boss feels the same way." She nodded. "I don't know if they will agree to meet with me if someone comes along, but I will promise to have backup."

"What does that mean, exactly?" Thor arched a brow.

"If you're not at home to follow along, I'll have Charlie close by. I promise."

Thor liked Charlie. He was a good man. A good photographer. He'd worked in war zones. He would and could protect Danni if he had to. Thor would have to accept this because he knew Danni wouldn't give up this story and he wasn't the kind of man to tell the woman he loved with his entire soul she should give up her life's work.

"Okay," he agreed.

"What about Tim?" Kawan interjected. "He's a good cop and he's been following along with the story. Not to mention, he's the one who worked on those emails Danni got. He wouldn't mind. You'd just have to get him on his day off since that group is in West Virginia."

"That's a good idea." Thor held Danni's gaze. "You should put Tim on speed dial. It can't hurt to have a cop in your back pocket."

"While I think you're all being insanely overprotective, because of those emails, I will do it." She patted his chest. "And also because I know you won't let me say no."

"You're right. I won't. Now let's eat. I'm starving." Thor smiled. Loving Danni was easy. She was the light at the end of his dark tunnel. But sometimes, loving her meant he had to learn how to stuff his protective chest-pounding attitude, because right now, he wanted to lock her in the house and never let her leave.

But that wouldn't make him any better than the cult she was trying to take down.

---

Danni leaned against the doorjamb and sighed as she stared at Thor standing at the edge of the bed, stuffing the last few items into his rucksack. He wore Navy cammie pants with a white T-shirt. He looked so sexy, and she had to pinch herself often that he was all hers.

They had been living together for a little over four years, and they were happy. Their mothers had always been on the bandwagon of them getting married, while their dads had been more in the camp of, they had plenty of time. But now, even her dad was dropping hints that maybe it was time.

They discussed it—like they conversed about every-thing. She was lucky to have a partner in life. A man who viewed her as his equal and, at the same time, treated her like a princess.

Thor loved being a SEAL and Danni was proud to be on his arm. Their relationship—for the most part— was easy. They fought like any other couple. Mostly about stupid stuff—like Thor had this horrible habit of leaving dishes in the sink. It drove her batshit crazy.

But she didn't always make the bed, making him want to pull his hair out.

He glanced up, smiled, and sauntered across the room, taking her into his arms, and kissing her softly. "I'm only going to be gone five days." He tucked a few stray strands of hair from her ponytail that had fallen out behind her ear. "And then I've got a whole week of leave."

"I know." She rested her head on his chest. "I'm looking forward to our vacation. Lord knows we both need one."

He tilted her chin with his thumb. "Then why did you sigh so heavily?"

"It's this follow-up piece with the Origins of God. Heather doesn't want to make the trip here and she's not sure about telling me where she is, and I get that, but in-person interviews are always so much better. I'm trying to get her to at least agree to a Zoom call. However, she's not even sure she wants me to see her face—the whole thing has me on edge. The agent I signed with loves the direction I'm taking the book, but she doesn't think I have enough for a publisher to take the bait."

"How much of her story have you vetted?"

"That's the hard part," she said. "I've fact-checked as much as I could, but it's not like the Origins of God are going to give me a list of people who came and went. Plus, she's admitted Heather isn't the name she went by and like most of my sources, she won't give me her real name."

"So, it's possible she's not who she says she is." He arched a brow. "Could she be a plant from the cult? Could she be trying to find out what you know? Or give you false information? Or worse?"

Danni shook her head. "I don't think it's that. I've never learned my sources' real names until after I've interviewed them the first time. Besides, what she has told me is pretty damning."

"I know I've said this before, but any of these people who come forward now could be playing you."

"Trust me, I understand that. I've made the people at Origins of God nervous. But I can't ignore what Heather is telling me."

"Okay." He kissed her temple. "That organization is a cult. You know that. Unfortunately, they use religion and brainwashing techniques to keep their followers loyal. But if you can't verify facts, like you did with Krista, then this might not be the part of the story you need to chase."

She cocked her head and glared. "Thor... you can't talk me out of this." She sucked in a deep breath and puffed it out, taking a step back. "I spoke to Krista this morning and she told me that what Heather said about the doctrine matches. So I do have that vetted." She lowered her chin. "It's just that this is a different compound. A different disciple. Things at this one are run a little different than how Krista explained. I feel like I need to see Heather's expressions as I ask the questions. I get a lot from a person's body language. It's why visiting the compound is so important."

"Babe." He palmed her cheek. "I know you're passionate about this. I get that. I'm not saying you should stop your efforts in exposing the things that could be going on behind closed doors with the Origins of God." He reached out and palmed her cheek. "But Tim doesn't like how those emails keep coming—and you've gotten two more. While they aren't threatening in nature, there is an underlying tone that clearly states they don't want you meddling and find your articles to be defamatory."

"I'm writing the truth." She frowned.

"I didn't say you weren't. I'm just saying that I believe, and Tim agrees, these people are dangerous. I'd like for you to leave this alone while I'm gone."

"I don't want to argue with you minutes before Moose gets here to pick you up."

He kissed her gently. "We're not fighting."

"We're close." She chuckled. "I have half a mind to climb that fence in the middle of the night."

Thor growled. "Promise me you won't do that."

She didn't say a single word.

He narrowed his stare. "Danni?"

"Of course I'm not going to do that, but I'm not letting this go."

"I'm not asking you to. Just don't do anything crazy while I'm gone."

"My boss needs me to finish the Pearlman piece. What a scum-sucking asshole and I'll enjoy helping expose that man's exploits."

"Yeah, he's a piece of work, but why do you always have to pick things that are either controversial or dangerous?"

"Do you really have to ask that question?"

"I suppose not, and it is one of the reasons I love you so much." Thor pulled his cell from his pocket. "Moose just texted. He just pulled into the neighborhood." He cupped her face. "You are the air I breathe. I love you with everything I am. Take good care of yourself. I'll see you in five days."

"I love you, too." She raised up on tiptoe. "Be safe."

"I always am."

She kissed him passionately. Then she watched him fling his rucksack over his shoulder and stroll through the bedroom, into the family room, and out the front door of their house. She raced to the picture window and waved as he stomped across the driveway, heaving his bag into the back of Moose's pickup.

Both men waved before climbing into the cab.

She turned, wiping the single tear that dribbled down her cheek. She never let Thor see her cry when he left, but she suspected he knew it happened.

Time to dive into work. It's what kept her sane.

## 7

*T*hor stepped into the bungalow and smiled while Danni shook her cute little ass, dancing in front of the stove as she attempted to cook.

She wasn't the best. As a matter of fact, she kind of sucked at it. But he wasn't about to complain. He was the luckiest man in the world. Even luckier was that Danni had been patient enough to wait for him when she'd first kissed him, but he hadn't been ready.

So, was she ready for what he planned on proposing? If he ever got up the flipping nerve to do it. Last night should have been his big moment. A nice romantic dinner at a beautiful seaside restaurant, only he'd left the ring in his kit—and right now, well, he had other things on his mind—again. He couldn't get enough of her and doubted that would ever change.

"Hey, babe," he said.

"Shit." She jumped. "You scared me."

"Sorry." He sauntered across the small beachfront hideaway in South Florida. He reached around her, turned off the burner, and wrapped his arms around her body.

"Turning that off will only ruin dinner."

"We'll order pizza." He kissed her neck and nibbled on her ear while his hand slid under her shirt and unhooked the back of her bra. He found her nipple, then pinched and twisted it. He loved her body. "You're fucking gorgeous."

She squirmed under his hands, her skin blazing hot beneath the thin fabric of her shirt. Throwing her head back against his shoulder, she laughed. "You're a real romantic, Thor."

"Only for you, darling," he murmured in response, nipping gently at the tender skin along her throat. His hands roved lower, teasing the hem of her jean skirt. He slipped a hand inside, finding her already slick and warm.

She lifted her leg, placing her foot against the counter, giving him all the access he desired.

"Dinner can wait," she agreed breathlessly, reaching behind to stroke him through his jeans.

His breath caught in his throat. He turned her around swiftly, pressing her against the counter. His eyes drank in the sight of her—from the disheveled curls that framed her face to the flushed chest exposed by the shirt now hanging loose around her waist.

"Let's not keep me waiting," he growled. "I'm starving." He hoisted her ass onto the counter, yanking her tiny thong off and tossing it over his shoulder. Her fingers threaded through his hair as her heels dug into his shoulder blades. He licked her, circling her clit with his tongue, diving his finger deep inside.

"Oh God," she gasped out, the hand in his hair tightening into a death grip. "You…"

The rest of her sentence transformed into a moan, her head falling back to hit the cabinets behind her. She writhed under his touch, her hips moving against his mouth in a rhythm as ancient and undeniable as the tide rolling in from the ocean just outside their door.

"You taste so good," he purred, lifting his head just enough to shoot her a heated look.

She bit down on her lower lip. One hand gently pushing his head. The other cupping her perfect breast with her thumb fanning her tight nipple. Danni was perfection and she was his. All his.

He undid the button on his jeans with one hand, sliding them down just enough to free himself. Then he was back at her core, lapping at her like a man lost in the desert who'd just found an oasis.

It didn't take long. Her pleasure echoed against the tiled kitchen walls as the orgasm hit her hard. He took all she gave him, greedily lapping it up.

She waited a moment to get her breath back before tugging at him again. "My turn," she whispered huskily, "before I die of anticipation." She ran her fingers across his chest, digging her nails into his skin as she smiled at him, lowering herself.

He swallowed. She curled her fingers around his length, stroking him softly. Gently—like a feather. It was torture and he loved every second of it. He watched himself disappear into her hot mouth.

As she took him in, he groaned, the sound echoing richly in the quiet kitchen. His fingers twisted further into her hair, guiding her rhythm, holding her to him. He watched as her eyes shimmered with lust, her lips closed around him, taking him deeper.

Her mouth was a furnace, her tongue a lively serpent exploring him inch by inch. He gripped the edge of the counter, his knuckles white from the pressure. His gaze never left her face. Her dark lashes fluttered shut, her cheeks hollowing out like she was suckling on the sweetest candy. The sight alone made his head spin with an exquisite pleasure that was both maddening and intoxicating.

"Jesus," he gasped, his voice rough and broken. He could feel her smile around him, adding to the pleasurable torture he was experiencing.

She pressed soft kisses to his length before taking him in again. He could feel the buildup inside him, a slow climb that threatened to explode any moment. It was too much and not enough at the same time.

His universe narrowed to her. The taste of her still on his tongue. The feel of her mouth on him. The way her body had moved against his. The way she'd come apart under him.

"Oh fuck," he moaned. His hips pushed against her involuntarily, following the rhythm that she had set for them.

One of his hands slid from her hair down to grip her shoulder, pulling her up to meet his gaze. He kissed her fiercely.

"Sweet Jesus," he muttered against her lips. "I want

you," he growled, his words punctuated by hot kisses along the hollow of her neck. His hands descended lower, fingers teasing around the curve of her breast before squeezing it in a firm grasp.

He took in the sight of Danni against the white tiles and swallowed hard. He wanted to remember forever how she looked at this moment: wild-eyed and breathless with pleasure.

He stole one last glance into her eyes before she let out a quiet gasp again as he thrust himself inside her, hard and raw.

Every part of him was singing with intense pleasure as he finally let himself drown in Danni, losing himself in their shared dance until they both lost all control…

With rough hands, he cupped her ass, pushing himself deeper inside. Her back arched off the counter, her body matching his rhythm.

"Thor," she panted. He loved hearing his name on her lips. It was a sweet symphony. He kissed her deeply as if he could drink in the taste of her forever.

Pulling away from her mouth, he moved his kisses down her throat. Marking her as only he could. His thrusts became faster, deeper, spurred on by the sounds of her pleasure.

Her fingers tightened in his hair, keeping him close even as she fell apart beneath him. Her legs tightened around his waist, and she held him close as waves of pleasure crashed over them both.

Catching his breath, he rested his forehead against hers. His heart pounded in his chest as he watched the woman beneath him slowly regain control.

Her soft laughter echoed throughout the room as he helped lower her from the counter. With a smile that made his heart race all over again, she reached out to entwine their fingers together.

"I'm going to take a shower. You can clean up and order pizza," she said with a wink and litheness that suggested their night was far from over.

He swallowed. He really needed to grow a pair and ask the woman he loved the most important question of their lives. "Yes, dear." He gathered their clothing, hiked up his jeans, and watched her shamelessly pad across the room into the bathroom, naked.

He sighed. Both sets of parents expected them to return an engaged couple. He'd gone through the trouble of asking her dad for his blessing. He needed to get his head out of his ass. It wasn't like she would say no. They had discussed it. Figured in a year or two, but it took time to plan a wedding—though he'd elope just to save himself the hassle of dealing with their mothers. They already had ideas.

"Um, Thor? Can you come in here for a second?" Danni stood in the doorway of the bathroom in a towel.

"Is something wrong?"

"I need help with something." She waved her hand around wildly.

Danni wasn't generally a dramatic girl, but some-times, if bugs were concerned, especially cockroaches, she could be.

"What's going on?"

"Oh. Just come here." She took her hand and wiggled her fingers under his nose.

He laughed, pushing it away. "What's gotten into you? Did you start drinking while I was out?"

"Nope." She stuck her hand in his face before bringing it to her cheek. She smiled. "But a bottle of champagne would be nice."

"With pizza? That's odd, even for you." He laughed. "Now what's the problem that you took me from the dishes?"

"Hmmmm." She covered her mouth with her hand, tapping her fingers along the side of her face. "I was looking for nail clippers in your kit and I came—"

"You went through my kit?" He took her by the biceps, lifted her feet right off the floor, and moved her out of the doorway. His pulse raced out of control. Normally, he wouldn't have cared, but it was the only place he could think of to put the box with the ring in it.

He blinked. The little box sat wide open and empty on the edge of the sink. He turned. "You found it, opened it, and are wearing it?" He took her hand and stared at the six prong, round, full carat gracing her ring finger. "Wow. You couldn't leave it there and pretend you didn't see it and wait for me to pop the question?"

She giggled.

"It's not funny," he mumbled.

"Okay." She cleared her throat. "Answer me this, honestly. How long have you had the ring?"

"Three weeks." He raked his fingers through his hair. "I was just waiting for the right time."

"Did you have it in your pocket last night at dinner?" She arched a brow.

He blew out a puff of air. "No," he said quickly. "I forgot it."

"Probably on purpose." She laughed. "I kissed you at my high school graduation and I waited two years for you to figure out that you had feelings for me. I'm not waiting for you to muster up the nerve to ask me." She wiggled her finger. "The answer is yes." She leaned in and kissed him. "Why were you so scared to ask me anyway?"

"I wasn't scared." He took her hand and pressed his lips against the ring. It looked good on her finger. Real good. "At least not like you're thinking. It's just that you're so special and you mean the world to me. I know that you don't care about the grand gestures, but I had wanted this one to be done right. I'd even asked your dad."

"Oh, good grief. You did not." She covered her mouth.

"I did." He laughed. "It was more awkward than that first morning I spent the night."

"I imagine it was. While he thinks you're perfect for me, I will always be his little girl."

"When we have kids, I'm kind of hoping they are all boys. I can't imagine having to deal with a mini you as a kid."

She chuckled, patting his chest. "I'm sorry if I ruined your proposal, but I know you. It's possible we could have been almost home before you even brought it up and when I found it, there was no way I was going to be able to keep my big trap shut."

"Babe, it's okay." He kissed her nose. "I love you and

I want to spend the rest of my life showing you just how much."

"I love you, too." She groaned, dropping her head to his chest. "Our mothers are going to take over this wedding and make our lives miserable."

"We can always elope."

She jerked her head. "I have dreamed of this day since I was twelve. I'm wearing a white dress and you're going to be in your Navy blues."

"Yes, ma'am." He'd do whatever this woman asked. She was his anchor. The line that tethered him to shore. He'd die without her.

## 8

A YEAR LATER...

"Can we not fight about this now?" She glared at Thor.

"Are you going to change your mind about going to that compound while I'm gone?" He cocked his head.

"It's my job, Thor. I have to go, especially when it was my story that led to another girl coming forward about the abuse she allegedly suffered by the high council of the Origins of God and I'm this close to getting a book deal." She held up her thumb and fore-finger. "I've got two publishers interested and my agent said they are solid—like big-time solid."

"I get it. I just wish you could wait until I was in town because I know you and you'll push to go behind the communal area and you're quite persuasive when you want to be. If anyone can get one of those weirdo disciples to let them into their inner sanctuary, it's you." He ran his hand across his mouth. "Are you going to at least call Tim and let him know your plans?"

"Of course and Charlie will be my backup, just like I promised."

"That does make me feel better, but I don't like this. Origins of God has made it clear through those emails that they don't like you poking around. They have publicly called you a liar and even threatened legal action."

"They can threaten all they want, but they haven't done anything because I haven't done anything illegal. I have credible sources, and they are running scared."

"That's what frightens me."

"Origins of God needs me to paint them in a positive light. That's what this is all about. They want to show me how great they are. But by giving me the grand tour, I might be able to see something they don't want me to or plant a seed with someone who wants to leave. Or maybe someone will slip me a note or talk to me. But the bottom line is, Origins of God wants me to write a 'nice article' about them and that's what got me this interview. My willingness to see their side."

"But that's not what you're doing. Essentially, you're manipulating them."

"I don't want to argue about this—again." She pulled out all the things she needed from the cupboard and sighed. "In one month, we'll be married. Can you believe it?" Danni spread peanut butter across the bread. She snagged the jelly and squeezed it. She pressed the bread together and stuffed both sandwiches into a plastic bag. Her big strapping Navy SEAL still preferred a PB&J. He was a big kid, and she loved him. All of him.

She swallowed. Their lives were changing in so many ways. Some they were more than ready for.

One, well, she wasn't so sure of. They had talked about it, but it's kind of always landed on when she was closer to twenty-eight and he was in his thirties.

She was only twenty-seven and he thirty-one.

"My darling Danni, so good at changing the subject." Thor nodded like a bobblehead. "I honestly didn't want a year-long engagement, but our mothers insisted."

Danni pursed her lips. "Not true. We had to make sure you could get leave and that the country club would be available."

"I would have married you the day I asked."

"You didn't ask." She cocked her head.

"Not my fault you're the most impatient woman I've ever met." He leaned against the counter, brought a water bottle to his lips, and winked. "You wouldn't even let me remove all your clothes this morning and you know how much I love your boobs."

She tossed her head back and laughed. Hard. "Um, sailor. I'm not the one who bent me over the sink and forgot about foreplay."

He shrugged. "I can't help myself around you. Especially when I know I'm going to be gone—for three weeks, which sucks right before our wedding, but at least it's not a mission and just a training exercise."

"I am happy about that." Mindlessly, she bit down on her index finger.

"Babe, what's going on? Are you more worried

about this interview? Is there something you're not telling me that I need to know about?"

"Yes and no." She rested her hands on his strong shoulders.

"I don't like the sound of that."

"It has nothing to do with the investigative piece for the magazine and the book. I'm good with that. All my ducks are in a row, and I'll make sure people know where I am at all times. I promise."

"I know. I'm sorry I'm often overprotective, but I worry about you when I'm gone." He kissed her nose. "But you're crinkling your forehead and when you do that, something is weighing heavy on your mind."

"I have no idea how to tell you this."

"Just say it." He cocked a brow.

"I'm pregnant."

He opened his mouth, but no noise came out. He slammed it shut and opened it again. Still, silence.

He blinked and blinked and blinked some more.

His fingers dug into her hips.

"You okay?" she asked softly.

He nodded, still saying nothing.

"How do you feel about this?"

"Shocked… stunned… terrified… freaked out… happy… thrilled… ecstatic. You name it, I'm feeling it." He ran his fingers across his freshly cut flattop. "How did… I mean… you take your pills… I guess you forgot those two days we went home to visit our folks."

"I did." She nodded. "And I guess that's what happens."

"How do you feel about having a baby?" A slow smile spread across his face.

It was hard not to smile in response. "I'm surprisingly okay with the idea. A few years earlier than planned, but our parents will be over the moon."

"Especially our mothers. I think they have been secretly knitting booties together."

"Probably." She leaned into him, holding him close. "I love you, Thor."

"I love you more," he whispered, tilting her chin. "I don't want to beat a dead horse, cause an argument, or act like a jerk, but please, I beg of you, be safe when dealing with that story."

"I will." She ran her finger across his shoulder, pressing against his scar. "I worry about you too."

"Fair enough." He pressed his lips against her temple. "I'm going to be a father," he whispered. "That's a little scary."

"No more frightening than the fact I'm going to be a mom." She gazed up into his eyes. "I'm going to get all fat and ugly."

"You're going to be beautiful and isn't it true that pregnant women's boobs get bigger?"

She slapped his shoulder. "What's wrong with the size of my breasts now?"

"Nothing." He laughed. "But I've been told that it's like being with—"

"I wouldn't finish that statement if I were you." She cocked her head. "I hear Moose's truck in the driveway. You better get going. Your work wife hates waiting."

"Am I allowed to tell the guys?"

"If I say I'd rather wait until after the wedding, will you be able to keep your big trap shut?"

He shook his head. "That's like asking me not to have sex with you the morning before I leave on a mission."

"Fine," she mumbled. "But that means we have to tell our parents."

His brows shot up. "Yeah. You have fun with that one. Especially our mothers." He patted her bottom. "See you in three weeks." He leaned over and kissed her belly. "Bye, little baby."

"Oh my God. You're so weird."

"I'm the weird you chose to marry... when you were twelve." He snagged his lunch bag. "I love you."

"I love you, too." She watched him practically skip out of the kitchen and disappear into the family room.

Once she heard the front door close, she shed her first tear.

Every single time he left, she let loose a few drops. Not many and some of these were happy. Her life was everything she dreamed it would be. She had a wonderful job and the perfect man.

Nothing could ever take that away.

*A week later...*

Danni blinked open her eyes. A wave of nausea hit her like a ton of bricks. She swung her feet to the side of the bed and raced to the bathroom. She knelt in front of the toilet, gagging.

Morning sickness.

Of course it hit shortly after Thor had left.

She wiped her mouth, stood, and snagged her toothbrush. The room swayed. Normally, all she wanted in the morning was coffee and food.

Right now, neither appealed to her.

Maybe some crackers and soda would ease her unsettled stomach.

She padded back into the bedroom and stared at the mattress. God, she missed Thor. It had only been a week. She grabbed her cell. No messages from him and that didn't surprise her. Even though this was a training exercise, he was still busy.

Quickly, she sent a text to Charlie, confirming the time of their meeting in West Virginia later today. It was about a four-hour drive. He would follow her and wait outside the compound. They rented two hotel rooms where they would go over everything she learned, or didn't learn.

She then sent a text to Tim, letting him know the plan. He had the day off. She wondered if he'd taken the time off just because of her or if it had always been that way, but it didn't matter. This would ease her future husband's mind and if Tim wanted to spend his free time sitting in a car in West Virginia, that was his prerogative.

Both men responded back quickly. Charlie planned on meeting her at a gas station about five miles from her house. Tim would meet her at the hotel, but he planned on being at the compound and wanted to make sure he got a visual of her before she left the parking lot.

Fine. She could live with all that.

Needing to put something in her stomach before she gagged again, she made her way down the hallway.

As soon as she stepped into the kitchen, something sharp lodged into her foot.

"Ouch." She hobbled. "Crap." She glanced at her foot. A small piece of glass found its way into her skin. "What the hell?" Her gaze went to the tile floor. More glass. She glanced up. The sliders out the back had been shattered.

Her pulse raced.

She lifted her phone, but before she could hit Tim's number, something hard came down on the back of her head.

Her legs wobbled. Her vision blurred. She dropped her phone. Her knees hit the hard, cold floor. She glanced over her shoulder just as a silhouette holding something… metal… a gun… swung, landing on the side of her head… and the world went black.

---

"What do you mean she's missing?" Thor stared at his phone. He squeezed it. Sweat dripped from his brow. His body trembled. "You were supposed to be following her."

"She never made it. Your house was broken into," Tim said. "Her car is missing. But her purse and phone are still here."

"What are you saying?" Thor's legs could no longer hold his weight. He leaned against the desk in the CO's office.

"We believe she was taken," Tim said softly.

"Taken? By whom?" Thor ran his fingers across the top of his head.

"We don't know," Tim said. "It's an active crime scene. We're dusting for prints. It looks as though whoever it was broke the glass on the kitchen sliders. There's some blood on the floor—"

"Blood?" All the oxygen in Thor's lungs flew out.

"It's not a lot. Not enough to indicate she's—"

"I'm at the base. I'll be there in forty minutes." He waved to Moose who stood at the doorway with a solemn look. "I need your truck."

"I'll drive. Our CO will understand." Moose waved his keys.

"We should be able to let you in the house by then," Tim said.

"It's my fucking house, and that's my fiancée. I'm not sitting on the damn sidelines." Thor slammed his fist on the desk. "What the hell happened, Tim? You were supposed to keep an eye on her, not let some crazy-ass cult break into my house and kidnap her."

"We don't know that's what happened," Tim said calmly.

"Who else would do that?"

"I don't know, but I can't have you jumping to conclusions. Not at the beginning of an investigation and especially when that's not the only piece Danni was working on. That cult isn't the only group she's pissed off. Let's not forget she helped expose Pearlman, who is awaiting trial as we speak. He's been outspoken about what he believes was a witch hunt and he swears he's innocent."

"That man raped three young girls whom he coached on an elite soccer team. He's scum." Thor couldn't deny what Tim said made sense. But it didn't make him feel better. If anything, it made matters worse.

"Exactly," Tim said. "Listen, I have to go. I'll talk to you when you get here."

Thor tapped his cell, stuffed it in his pocket, and lifted his gaze. Tears burned his eyes.

"Come on, man. Let's get to your place. I'll text the team. We'll figure this out and we'll get Danni back."

"She's pregnant," Thor whispered. "I swear to God, whoever took her, if they hurt one hair on her head or our baby, I'll kill them."

## 9

## THE NEXT DAY...

*D*anni wiggled her arms and legs, grateful they were no longer bound together by rope. But the fact her engagement ring was gone tore her heart in two.

Add in the fact she had no idea who had taken her or where they had taken her—and worse, she had no idea how long she'd been knocked unconscious.

When she came to, she'd been in the back of a van and her captors had put something over her head. She rattled around in the back of that vehicle for what seemed like hours.

When it finally stopped, two men—she knew they were men by their voices—took her inside a hotel room. They let her use the bathroom and then tied her to the bed, where she spent the night alone—crying.

But not until after she tried to use the phone, which they had disconnected.

After that, she tried screaming—a lot. However, no one came to her rescue. She finally gave up and succumbed to tears and fitful sleep because every noise, every footstep, every creak of the hotel made her wonder if her next breath would be her last.

Before the sun rose, the two men came into the room wearing ski masks. They covered her face and tossed her back in the van, and they drove again… for hours. The longer they drove, the more she realized she was farther away from anyone finding her.

Farther away from Thor.

She blinked, glancing around the small room she'd been tossed into. The men had once again tied her to a bed, but at least now she could get to a bathroom. She sat up, running her fingers through her hair. Blood still stained some of the strands. Her head throbbed from where she'd been clobbered. Her foot ached, even though one of the men had the decency to pull the glass out, clean out the wound, and put a bandage on it.

There wasn't much in the room. A bed. A nightstand with a lamp. A small desk and chair. A wood floor with a rug. A tiny window that thankfully allowed in some sunlight. Under the window was a rocking chair with a plush pillow. There was a bathroom with an old-fashioned tub and shower. It was musty and made her congested.

Was this meant to be her cage… or her coffin?

Her stomach tightened and rolled. She needed food. All they had given her so far was a little bit of water and a turkey sandwich, which hadn't helped her morning sickness at all.

She wondered if telling her captors of her *condition* would help.

Probably not. But she wasn't opposed to begging for her release.

The door rattled.

Sitting up taller, she held her breath, waiting to see who walked through that door.

A tall, slender man appeared. He had shoulder-length brown hair with matching soulful eyes. He wore a tan shirt that came down to the center of his thighs and baggy dark pants. His feet were bare and dirty. "Good afternoon," he said in a gruff voice. He carried a tray of food. "I hope you like chicken and rice soup. It's home-made with fresh vegetables plucked right from my garden," he said with a smile.

"What I'd like is to be set free." She folded her arms across her chest and blew a puff of air out her nose. "You have no right to detain me against my will."

"That's not really what I'm doing." He set the tray on the bed. "I also made you some tea." He waved his hand over the food before easing into the rocking chair. He stretched out his long legs and folded his hands in his lap. "I'm sure you're starving. I apologize for my people and how they transported you here. Those were not the instructions they were given."

"Don't care." She reached behind her and tugged at the chain that tethered her to the bed. "This isn't any different." She cocked her head.

He laughed softly. "Behave and prove yourself worthy, and that will be removed." He pointed toward the door. "Continue to be good, and I'll keep that unlocked and you can be free to roam my house."

"I want to leave. I *demand* to leave," she said. "My

fiancé is a powerful man. I'm sure he's already out searching for me."

"Perhaps." The man nodded. "However, I'm not concerned with Lieutenant Commander Thor Mason Armstrong."

Her heart lurched to her throat. She tried not to gasp—tried not to have any reaction, but that proved to be impossible.

The man arched a brow and smirked. "Surprised I know his name?"

"You don't know anything." Tears burned her eyes.

"I know everything, Danni." The man rocked back and forth. "I know how you grew up in Wilmington, Delaware, and lived next door to Thor. How you've been in love with him since you were little, but him, not so much. It's one of the many reasons I'm not concerned." He leaned forward. "Given time, he'll get over you. He'll move on and find someone else. He'll get married and have babies because you were not meant to be with him. That is not your purpose."

"I'm not going to listen to this." She turned her head. She would not give this man the satisfaction of knowing just how much he had rattled her last resolve.

"You can't ignore the truth. It will always catch you."

She stared at the wall. If she didn't engage, maybe he'd go away, giving her time to explore the room and find a way out. She needed a plan. Thor always told her to be rational and think through things logically—and to plan.

She couldn't do that with this asshole spewing bull-shit in her direction.

"I know you, Danni. I know what you need," the man said. "I know it better than you do."

She wasn't going to take the bait.

The rocking sound stopped, and her heart jumped out of her chest. "Eat your food. I'll be back later. I'm sure you'll be chattier after you have a full belly."

"I don't want your fucking food." She swung her arm at the tray, knocking it off the bed and onto the floor. She'd never been the kind of person to use foul language on a regular basis. Nor did she condone violence of any kind to get a point across. But this man was holding her hostage, and dropping the f-bomb felt really good in the moment.

"Tsk-tsk, Danni. Tsk-tsk." The man stood over her. "You'll need to clean that up. You'll find supplies in the bathroom. No food now until suppertime." With that, the man disappeared behind the door.

Like hell, she'd clean it up.

She flung herself backward and covered her eyes with her forearm, fighting the tears. She needed to be strong. Flattening her hand over her belly, she sucked in a deep breath and waited for the sound of distant foot-steps to disappear. She jumped off the bed and raced through the room in search of anything that might aid in her escape.

She opened every drawer and found only more undergarments and dresses. In the cabinets in the bath-room, all that she could find were cleaning supplies, shampoo, soaps, and towels. Nothing sharp. Nothing she could use as a weapon or to make one.

The small window in the bathroom and the small bedroom were bolted shut. No way to open—not even for fresh air.

Defeated, she flopped on the bed, curled into a ball, and cried... again. She couldn't stop, nor could she control the violent trembling that overtook her muscles.

The food! There had to be a fork or knife. She could use those. Stab that asshole over and over again. Who could blame her for doing that? She eased to the side of the mattress and gasped when all she saw was a child's spoon.

More tears. Utter defeat.

This couldn't be the end.

---

Thor sat on the edge of his bed, fiddling with the matching wedding bands. This was supposed to be the happiest time of his life. He was marrying the woman he loved. They were about to start a family.

But some asshole snatched it away in a second.

"Hey," Moose said from the doorway. "Tim's team wrapped things up. The CSI unit is leaving. Tim said it would take a while for the prints they lifted to come back, but he put a rush on it. His partner is still interviewing the neighbors. One did say they saw a dark van parked down the street, but no one got a license plate number."

"Where's the rest of our team?" Thor glanced up.

"Kawan took it upon himself to check out Pearlman. Tim had a shit fit about that one."

Thor managed a chuckle. Kawan was a go-getter, and he didn't like rules. Believed they were meant to be broken.

"Lief and Jupiter are outside gathering as much as possible about the investigation. While Tim will keep us informed, his chief won't let us anywhere near it."

"I don't give a shit." Thor set the rings on his thigh, unclipped his dog tags, and put the rings on the chain before looping them back on his neck. "What about Sloan?"

"He went to go talk with Charlie."

"Once the cops leave, have everyone meet back here. I want to go over what we know and suspect and come up with…" He raised his hands and slapped them on his legs. Never in his life had he felt so fucking helpless. "I don't even know where to begin." He pointed to the laptop on the bed. "I've pulled up some of her old articles. Some of the things she's been working on. I've come up with five people or organizations that have a reason to be pissed at her and the least compelling is Origins of God. While she brought them into the limelight, she hasn't hurt their organization."

Moose rubbed his jaw. "Tim still believes it could be a random break-in."

"Why?" Thor jumped to his feet. "Because a television, a few paintings, and iPad were stolen? Or that her car was missing for like five hours but found fifty miles away? That's ridiculous. How could that be random? If all they wanted were things, why didn't they just kill her and leave her?" Thor choked on those last few words.

"I don't have those answers," Moose said quietly.

"I've got a theory on that." Tim appeared in the hallway. "But you're not going to like it, and I don't want you getting up in my business when it comes to this investigation. I will need you to let me do my job."

Thor rubbed the back of his neck. "What's your theory?"

"One of the neighbors did say they saw her vehicle drive away this morning about twenty minutes after she sent me and Charlie a text." Tim held up his hand. "They didn't notice who was driving the car, but they did mention that the van left the neighborhood at about the same time. If whoever took Danni was interested in robbing you, they would have loaded the van, but that car never came down your street."

"How can you be so sure?" Thor asked.

"Because Ben, your neighbor, was outside trimming his bushes. He's the one who saw Danni's car pull away. He only saw it after it pulled out of the driveway, so he couldn't see the driver's side," Tim said. "Which means, the kidnappers could only put so much in her small SUV. My best guess is that they wanted to stage this to look like a random break-in to throw us off what we're looking at, which is a kidnapping."

"No shit, Tim." Thor threaded his fingers through his flattop. He understood that talking through things helped bring insight. He and his team did it all the time. But it wasn't helping him cope with the situation at hand.

"We have the list you gave me from her computer. I will interview Pearlman myself. He's my first priority because he's close," Tim said. "I've put a call into the local police over in West Virginia. I've informed them of the situation here and how Danni was supposed to meet with Disciple Oliver. Because I can't be everywhere at once, a detective from that office will go ask some questions and poke around. I will head over there tomorrow." He held up a finger. "After I've spoken to as many people on the list that you've given me."

"I want to go with you." Thor planted his hands on his hips. "To as many as possible and I won't take no for an answer."

"You don't have a choice but to stand down."

"And what would you do if this was your wife?" Thor asked.

"I'd lose my fucking mind," Tim said. "But I'd stay away because I wouldn't want to botch the investigation and just having you there could call into question any interview. It could be the difference between taking a case to trial and not being able to make an arrest at all. I doubt you want that."

"Fuck," Thor muttered. "Fine. But I want constant updates, and you must understand, I can't sit on my thumbs."

"I won't say no to having you and the guys mull over the case, but I need you to trust that I'm good at my job," Tim said.

Thor nodded as he glanced at his watch. "Shit. Mine and Danni's parents should be here in the next half hour or so. I need to get this place cleaned up. I don't want them to see the blood." He held Tim's gaze. "You are done in here, right?"

"We got everything we need." Tim reached out and squeezed his shoulder. "I'll call you as soon as I'm done with Pearlman. I promise you that I will keep you and the boys in the loop."

"Thanks." Thor watched as Tim turned and disappeared down the hallway. He raised his hand and fingered his dog tags, and the matching wedding bands, dangling from his neck.

"I'll go start cleaning up in the kitchen," Moose said.

"I'll be there in a second." He lifted the picture off the nightstand. It had been taken the week they had gone to South Florida and gotten engaged. "I'm bringing you home if it's the last thing I do."

## 10

A WEEK LATER...

*D*anni stared at the food on the tray. Her stomach growled. It twitched and tightened. She allowed herself the bread. A few nibbles of the vegetables and fruit. Just enough to feed her baby. To keep him or her alive. That's all that mattered.

But she wouldn't be the good girl that this man expected her to be. The submissive woman he demanded, even if he was nice about it. She stared at the latest pamphlet on the dresser. The one that had been left for her to read and study. She'd opened it and glanced at the first page before tossing it aside. She wasn't going to play this game. She would not become one of them.

The door rattled and a young woman shuffled into the room and let out a long breath. "Sister Danni, you must eat."

"Tell that jerk I'll eat when he unchains me from this bed and lets me go." She yanked at the chain, her skin raw from tugging at it day in and day out. Dried blood clung to her damaged skin like a badge of honor.

"That's not how this works." The woman clasped her hands together, bowed her head, closed her eyes, and appeared to speak in tongues.

"Shut up," Danni yelled. "I will not listen to this. I do not want you to pray for me. If you want to talk about something, let's chat about how the leader of Origins of God has brainwashed you and this so-called community is a freaking cult." Danni sucked in a breath. "You want to help me, then stop that gibberish and untie me. What you are doing is not only illegal, but it also goes against every Christian value out there."

The woman gasped. "We are commanded by God through our Messiah and his disciples." With a shaky finger, the woman pointed to the pamphlet. "Please, Sister Danni, read that. It will help you understand."

Danni needed to change tactics. She needed to deal with this young woman as if she were conducting an interview. It would be a tall order, considering Danni was scared shitless. "Who are you?" she asked softly, hoping her voice didn't tremble like the rest of her body. "What's your name?"

"Sister Annabelle." The woman nodded. "I will bring you a fresh plate for lunch after you clean up. You need a shower."

"It's hard to do that being tethered to this bed." Danni yanked at the chains and winced as it dug into her fragile skin. "Please, untie me."

"I can't do that, and you are able to reach the bathtub," Annabelle said in a commanding tone. "When you are done with that, read from the doctrine. It is imperative you learn our ways."

"Fuck your doctrine and your beliefs." Danni swung her arm and knocked the food tray over onto the floor. The oatmeal landed upside down, splattering onto the wood.

Annabelle gasped and raced out of the room, slamming the door shut, muttering in the same tongues as before.

Danni heard muffled voices, but she couldn't make out the words. Seconds later, the man appeared, and Danni's heart dropped to her toes. This was only the second time she'd seen him.

Her only visitor had been Annabelle. Otherwise, it had been total isolation—total silence—for eight days. It was maddening.

"I understand that you're still fighting your purpose —fighting our ways." The man stood over her, staring down at her with his brown eyes boring into her like daggers of death.

"I have no purpose here with you. My life is with Thor, not chained to this bed. Let me go." She lunged off the bed toward the man, but he moved, and she fell to the floor and groaned.

He reached down, curling his long fingers around her forearm.

"Leave me alone." She jerked.

"I do hate to see you like this when it would be so much easier if you would simply open your eyes to what is around you. Listen to what our heavenly Father has commanded for you." He knelt. His breath landed on her skin like a cattle prod. "You belong here. This is your home. It's always been your home. You were created to be with us. It was predicted. It was written. You know that deep in your heart," he whispered, pressing his lips against her cheek.

"Leave me alone." She swung at him, catching the side of his face with the palm of her hand.

He laughed. "The devil is strong in you. We need you to fight him, not us." He stood tall. "Clean up this mess. If you choose not to, you won't get any more food. That is your choice. Or shall we say it is the devil's choice. Perhaps all we need to do is starve out the devil. We cast him out and you will see." He turned and left, leaving her on the floor next to the spilled oatmeal.

With what little resolve she had left, she pulled herself back on the bed and stared at the ceiling. She would not read their bullshit. She would not clean up that food. She would fight. She had to fight. She would not let him break her.

———

Thor sat on the porch of the cabin at The Refuge. He was no good to his family, his team, and he'd nearly gotten himself arrested yesterday. He needed to get his head on straight, and he had no idea how to do that. His entire world had crumbled.

Danni had vanished, and he was lost without her.

He stared into his coffee. His stomach revolted at the idea of even drinking it.

The sound of someone approaching caught his attention and he glanced up.

Brick.

Thor rolled his neck. Brick was a good man. He'd been through hell and had survived, though barely. He'd lost his entire team during a mission that had gone to shit in more ways than one. Thor had heard the story the first time he'd come to The Refuge, which had humbled him. He couldn't imagine what he'd do without the men on his team. He knew it would fundamentally change who he was and how he functioned if he lost even a single one.

But losing Danni would destroy him. Not knowing what happened to her was slowly killing him.

"Hey, man." Brick strolled up the steps. "How are you finding the accommodations?"

"Excellent, as always." Thor stood, stretching out his arm. He had spent time at The Refuge on a few separate occasions. Thanks to this place, his nightmares were few and far between, though his demons were always in the shadows.

"I'm glad we had space for you." Brick nodded as he eased into one of the chairs. "I understand you just wanted a little peace and quiet after what happened the other day. Some space to clear your head before heading to your parents'." He held up his hand. "But Henley wanted to stop by and speak with you."

Thor shouldn't be surprised by that. He'd spent some time with Henley, the resident therapist at The Refuge, the last time he'd been a guest. While he liked Henley, valued her services, he didn't want to spend any time talking through his emotions today. They were too raw, too real, and he didn't want to go down the slippery slope of… he had no idea.

He fingered the double rings dangling from his neck. His connection to Danni was still strong. She was alive. He knew it. He also knew that those fuckers at Origins of God had taken her, but he didn't know where. He didn't know exactly who inside that crazy cult had kidnapped her and what they were doing to her. His heart pounded painfully in his chest. It was worse than taking a bullet. Worse than any survivor's guilt he'd ever experienced.

There was no way he could survive this, and while he knew someone like Henley could help—he couldn't do it—not right now.

"Tell Henley I appreciate her concern and kindness, but I came here to stare at nothing but scenery and sky —to get away from the world for a minute before I did something so stupid there was no way I would recover from it."

Brick ran a hand over his mouth. "I know that feeling well. I also know you can't shut off your thoughts right now. While this is a place of healing and we'll do whatever you need, sitting around, alone, will allow those thoughts to fester—to bleed into darkness—and you'll be in a worse place than you were two days ago when you put your hands on that young woman." Brick arched a brow.

"I didn't hurt her," Thor grumbled. "I only wanted answers."

"That's not how you're going to get them. Not with

a group like that, and not with a young lady who was not only terrified of you but probably scared of the group she's living with." Brick pointed across the vast ranch. "Henley's already on her way. I thought it would be easier for you to chat here than in her office or anywhere else and especially not in a group setting."

"I wish you hadn't done that," Thor muttered. "I don't mean to be rude, and Henley is an excellent therapist. But it's not what I need right now."

"I don't believe you know what you need." Brick stood and rested his hand on Thor's shoulder. "I do know what it's like to have someone I care about disappear. I get the situations are different and I had intel that allowed me to act immediately. But that doesn't change what it did to me on the inside. You're only here for one more night. Talk to Henley. Doesn't matter what you choose to discuss, but you came here because you needed to do something for yourself. To heal something inside you to help you plant your feet so you can be the man Danni will need you to be when we do find the intel we need to get her back." Brick released his grip, nodded, and strolled off the porch and made his way toward Henley. He stopped for a few minutes, chatting, before continuing toward the main building.

Thor lifted his mug and took a long, slow sip of the bitter brew. His belly soured, but he needed the caffeine. He hadn't slept well since Danni had gone missing. When he did manage to get a few hours, it was filled with all the terrifying possible outcomes of what could have happened.

Beatings. Torture. Rape. Death.

Each one played out in his dreams like a horror show. He'd wake in a cold sweat with tears dribbling from his eyes like a waterfall.

"Hi, Thor." She held up a small bag. "I brought you a fresh blueberry muffin from Robert. It's still warm."

"Thanks. I appreciate it." He stood, taking the bag and pulling her in for an awkward hug. His chest tightened. His lungs burned. His mind went down a rabbit hole of excuses. But he was a guest at The Refuge. A paying one, but they'd gone out of their way to find him a room and give him the space he needed. He owed these men so much. The least he could do was humor Henley for an hour.

Maybe it would pull his mind from the darkness and that's what he needed before he went to his parents' house.

"Mind if I sit down for a bit?" Henley waved her hand over the handcrafted wood rocking chair.

He blinked, noticing her expanding waistline.

*Pregnant.*

"Please." He nodded. He hadn't told anyone at The Refuge that he and Danni were expecting a child. The only person who knew was Moose. Not even their parents had been told and he'd been grateful that she hadn't told them yet.

He did his best to ignore the gut-wrenching pain that gnawed at his psyche. He opened the bag and nibbled on the muffin. It was warm, sweet, and melted on the tip of his tongue. His stomach did a little dance, accepting the tasty treat and begging for more—he resented his body for wanting to be fed. "I'm amazed each and every time I come here. You all have done a spectacular job. Just sitting on this porch staring at the sun hanging in that blue sky helps ease the ache in my heart." That was a lie.

"Nice try," Henley said. "It's not stifling the pain in your soul. The questions that don't have any answers are swirling in your brain, screaming at you the second you give your mind any little opening to go down that rabbit hole." Henley shifted in her chair, facing him head-on. "You're not dealing with the aftereffects of trauma. Or suffering from a loss where working through the grief is the only way to get to the other side." She sucked in a deep breath and pushed it out harshly through her nose. "Every emotion your feeling is a sucker punch to your sensibilities. It's not even the not knowing. Not for someone like you. It's the not having a clear picture of where to turn. What enemy to fight and where to bring that battle. While you—because of your training—can thrive in chaos, you can't survive in the chaos that's created with no orders. No plan of action. No clear and present movement and that concerns me for you."

"Nothing like jumping right in." Thor stuffed half the muffin in his mouth. Anything to avoid having to share his thoughts on this subject. Henley was right. He knew it and he damn well understood it, even if he couldn't control what happened inside his head. The spinning of jumbled words and thoughts. The inability to focus. To push through any coherent course of action —because when he tried, he always landed on one fact.

They knew nothing about what had happened in his house that day.

JEN TALTY

All the prints had been from him, Danni, or someone on his team.

The only prints in the vehicle had been theirs. What few witnesses there had been, hadn't seen anything substantial. At least nothing that brought them any real leads.

No tips on the hotline.

Fucking nothing.

It was radio silence and there was nothing worse than that for a trained Navy SEAL.

He polished off the rest of the decadent treat and gulped down the rest of his drink while Henley twisted her hands in her lap. He couldn't figure out if she was waiting for him to say something or contemplating her next words.

Either way, the silence was starting to eat away at his nerves and the million and one questions that he didn't have answers for were threatening to hit his brain like a tidal wave.

"I want to ask you a question and I want a straight-forward honest answer," Henley said.

"I can do that." He hoped. He hated lying, but he wasn't so proud right now that he wouldn't resort to it if he had to.

"Why did you come here?" She held up her hands. "I don't want the standard response that everyone gives. I want that thought that happened right before you picked up the phone and called Brick's personal cell."

Thor pinched the bridge of his nose. "That if I didn't get away from my buddies, I might hurt one of them with the way they were calling me off the compounds. Off those fucking religious dirtbags." He tilted his head, catching Henley's gaze. "I know they have Danni. It's the only thing that makes sense. Every other story she'd worked on or had been working on where she pissed someone off, well, those people have all been cleared. They have alibis. But it's damn hard to give an entire organization an alibi, now isn't it?" Thor sucked in a deep breath. If one could feel their blood pressure rise, he knew his had moved to a dangerous level. His pulse vibrated in his throat. His jaw hurt from clenching it. "Cops and Feds couldn't get a full search warrant, so they couldn't really access every nook and cranny. She's on one of those ranches. They are—"

"Thor, I need you to take a breath." Henley placed her hand on his wrist. "I don't normally interrupt like this. You know that. But the rage that's inside you, it's toxic and it's not helping you or Danni. Your instincts to come here, even if only for two nights and to clear your head, were spot-on. But you need to find a way to channel this rage into something productive, or you're going to do something you'll regret."

Thor closed his eyes. He breathed deeply, holding his breath for the count of ten before releasing it. He blinked. "I know." He nodded. "I've never in all my life felt so helpless."

"Putting a label on that is a good place to start." She squeezed. "But you're not helpless. What you need to do is find a way to push through the rage so when you are given information, you can not only process the intel appropriately, but act in such a way that will ensure

129

Danni's safety and the safety of you and your team. Being reckless isn't—"

"You spoke with Moose." Thor shook his head. "I love that man like a brother, but he had no right."

"I haven't spoken to anyone on your team." She lowered her chin. "When you were here after you got shot the very first time, you spoke of Danni a lot and you constantly used the term… reckless when talking about getting involved with her."

"I did?"

Henley nodded. "I found it to be an interesting term to describe the possibility of a relationship with a woman you cared very much for." She held up her hand when he opened his mouth. "You believed you were being reckless with her life by even thinking about it because she was, one, younger than you, though not by much, and two, had yet to see the world. The only reason I used the word reckless a minute ago is because for you, life isn't always about right and wrong. It's about whether or not something is reckless. You hate it when others are reckless in the field or have no regard for human life." She arched a brow. "When you came here after the helicopter crash, you spoke about Danni and how you worried she wasn't being as diligent as she could be about her safety when it came to some of the stories she was working on."

"Are you suggesting I blame her for what happened?" He bolted to a standing position.

"No, God, no." Henley stood. "Though I suspect you blame yourself and that's normal. But what I'm trying to get you to consider is that for the first time in your life, you can't control the situation."

"That's not true." He raked his hand over the top of his head. "Most of the missions I've gone on have had something go wrong. We're always having to think on our feet—make adjustments in the field—do something different than what was in the so-called plan."

"You're good at that. You're good at assessing risk—making calculated decisions to minimize risk and optimize outcomes." Gently, she ran her hand up and down his arm. "Because you can't do what you're good at, what you've been trained to do all of your adult life and you're being forced to practically stand in the corner, you're acting out—being reckless. Because that's doing two things for you." She waggled her fingers. "First, it's giving you a false sense of doing something. You're active both mentally and physically. It's giving you an adrenaline rush and that's how you're built. I get that. But it's also allowing you to be out of control because deep down, you have nothing to latch on to. Nothing to anchor you."

Tears threatened to fall from his dry eyes. But he was not going to cry. Not today. Not in this moment. But Henley was spot-on. "What do you suggest I do?"

"I know you can't stay here. But I'm going to give you my private phone number. I want you to text or call anytime you need to talk. But especially when that rage bubbles to the surface and you want to take matters into your own hands in a way that's not beneficial." She placed her hand on his chest. "I don't mean helping the authorities or even doing what all of you do best, and that's taking the intel and saving Danni. I won't take that away from you because it's what men like you do. But you need to reground yourself. Refocus your mind. It won't be easy." She gave him a weak smile. "And talk to your friends. They care about you and will have your back no matter what." She pulled out a card from her pocket. "Promise me you'll call?"

He nodded. "Thanks, Henley." He swiped at his eyes. "I told myself I wasn't going to talk or even listen. But I heard you. I really did."

"Good. Now a group of guests are heading out for a hike. You should go."

"I think I'd rather go see Tonka and the animals."

Henley laughed. "He'd love that." She patted his shoulder and strolled down the steps and off toward the main building.

Thor rubbed the back of his neck. Going back to Delaware was going to be tough. Seeing Danni's parents, even tougher. But he'd manage. He had to.

## 11

A WEEK LATER...

*D*anni sat on the floor and cleaned her mess. She swirled the towel around on the floor with a huff.

Today should've been her wedding day. A day she'd dreamed about for years, and this freaking cult stole it from her… She sighed. Perhaps it was her own damn fault. She'd been chasing this story since high school. Everyone was right; she'd been obsessed with it and now it had cost her—everything.

No. She couldn't think that way. Thor always told her that if something wasn't working—try a different tactic.

Resisting wasn't working, so maybe it was time to soften. She wouldn't succumb, but she could pretend. Besides, she hadn't seen *the man* in the last three days.

She was tired of seeing Annabelle. If she was going to find a way out of this room, she needed to know who the man was, and she needed more information. That meant playing his game. It meant she needed to engage him in conversation. Maybe she could find his weak spot. Maybe she could exploit him because yelling, kicking, and screaming wasn't getting her anywhere.

She found it odd that he never raised his voice. The few times he visited, he always spoke in a calm, low tone. He would always offer up a prayer and a few times he quoted scripture, though it wasn't from any bible she'd read from before—and she'd read a few in her research.

Her stomach growled, reminding her she wasn't the only person suffering. She pressed her hand against her belly. None of this could be good for her baby.

The door rattled.

She sighed.

"Good afternoon, Danni," the man said. He wore the exact same thing every time he entered her room. "I'm glad to see you finally taking care of your space, though it hurts me that you keep doing this. It's not good for your body to skip even an occasional meal." He bent over, lifted the dirty rag, and placed it on the tray. He opened the door, set it on the floor, and waved to… someone… before closing it again. "I'll have Sister Annabelle bring you dinner early as your reward."

"Okay." She decided not to argue. It didn't get her anywhere. She sat on the side of the bed and folded her hands in her lap like she'd seen Annabelle do so many times before. Quickly, she smoothed down the front of her dress.

He waved to her head and spun a finger.

Reluctantly, she took the hair tie and made a ponytail.

"That's a little better, but braids are the proper way

for a woman to wear her hair. Please work on that." He smiled as he sat in the rocking chair, tapping his big, dirty toe.

She nodded.

"Let us start with a prayer," he said softly, bowing and closing his eyes. "Heavenly Father, thank you for showing Sister Danni how important it is for her to keep her space tidy. I pray she sees your light and wisdom. That she opens her eyes, her heart, and her soul to your will. It is only your will—through me—that she can be saved." He lifted his head, blinking. "You know, you were chosen from thousands of commoners. It saddens me that you continue to reject our ways. Your ways." He sighed. "What shall we discuss today?"

"How about you tell me your name?"

He chuckled. "Why is that important?"

"Because if I'm going to converse with you, I want to know who I'm talking with."

"That's an interesting turn of events." He leaned forward. "In the few times I've come to visit, you've turned your nose up at me, spat at me, even cursed me out. What's changed your mind?"

She tugged at the chain. "I want out of these, and I figured the only way to get out is to play nice."

"No." He shook his head. "The only way that is going to happen is if you behave, receive the word, and succumb to what you know deep down is in your heart is your place."

"I know you're not Disciple Oliver. I've met him. Are you Disciple Matt? Or maybe you're Disciple Louis."

"Hmmm. You think you know something of me and my people. But you haven't the slightest idea of who we are or how important you are to us."

She swallowed. She didn't like the sound of that. Pure crazy talk. "Are you going to tell me which disciple you are?"

"Sister Danni, I'm not a disciple. I'm the Messiah."

"You're Christopher Bently?"

He frowned. "Do not call me that. It's Messiah Christopher. Or simply Messiah. You refer to me as anything else, you will be punished." He glared at her with a menacing stare. One that sent a shiver up her spine.

She swallowed. That was the first time he ever used the word punished and she wasn't sure she wanted to find out what that meant. "I apologize." However, she couldn't bring herself to use the term he wished. Maybe later, but not right in that moment. Her stomach cramped. It twitched and tightened, and the pain went right through to her back.

Nerves. It had to be nerves. And fear. Every minute of every day she lived in a perpetual state of panic. It didn't matter that Annabelle was sweet enough—docile enough. Or that so far, no one had hit her or even slapped her across the face. Danni knew from the stories she'd heard and the documentaries she'd seen, it would happen.

It always did.

"Apology accepted." He nodded. "Now that you know sort of where you are, I have some interesting news for you."

"What's that?"

"While the police have not given up their extensive search for you, they haven't found you on any of my compounds, and I have granted them partial access, even when I legally didn't have to." Christopher waggled his finger. "They haven't come here." He leaned closer. "Because they don't know that this place exists, but I granted them access to the rumored ninth compound in Montana. I acted all concerned as I gave them a tour of the common grounds. My people have even fielded a couple of phone calls from your Thor."

She sucked in a deep breath. "You spoke to him?"

"Oh, no. Not me." Christopher waved his hands. "I can't be bothered. I don't want to hear his foul language or threats. From what I understand, he's a little unhinged. You're lucky we took you away from that. No telling what he might have done to you if—"

"You shut up about Thor," Danni said with a thick lump in her throat. "He's the kindest, sweetest, most gentle man I know."

"Really? Wow." Christopher shook his head. "This man who you say is so wonderful threatened one of my followers. A true gentle woman. A woman," Christopher repeated. "He called her a lying bitch and he grabbed her by the arms. Now, how can you say he's a sweet, kind, gentle man after that?"

"I'm sure he had his reasons."

Christopher arched a brow. "There is no reason to call a Devoted Woman a bitch." He closed his eyes for a brief moment and sighed. "Leaves a foul taste in my mouth just repeating it. But those are his sins, not mine

137

or yours." He clasped his hands together. "I feel as though we've turned a major corner here today. If we keep heading down this path, before you know it, we'll be able to take that chain off you." He smiled as if she should be so freaking grateful.

*Be logical. Solve the problem from the inside out.* Those were Thor's words and she'd been playing them in her head over and over again. While her biggest problem was finding a way out of her cage that was this bedroom, she'd learned enough about the Origins of God to understand that when it came to women, submission was key to survival—but not freedom.

When Krista—Marybeth—would push back, they tried to beat her into submission. What Heather witnessed was more of a bait and switch when it came to the doctrine. She had no idea what they would have done to her, but they did scare her, and Danni had found discrepancies between the two compounds.

A third girl had come forward, and her story was slightly different. They forced her into submission by isolation.

Again, a different compound with different rules.

Christopher wasn't anything like what she expected, though she wasn't exactly sure what she thought he would be like. She'd met and seen a few different cult leaders. Some ruled with an iron fist. Others were all hell and damnation. And others were just creepy as hell.

This guy reminded her of a hippy Jesus lover. Not anyone to be concerned about and that should terrify her all by itself.

"May I ask you a question?" She held his gaze. Her

belly cramped again. Harder this time. She was so hungry and tired.

"I might not answer but go ahead."

"As leader of your church—"

"It's not a church," he said. "You've been corrected on that a few times while writing those articles." He waggled his finger. "Which spew lies about us, but we can talk about those another time. Anyway, we are a spiritual community—the chosen community. When you use the word church or organized religion, it takes away the impact of who we are in the eyes of our heavenly Father."

This man was a nutjob. "Okay." She took a big calming breath. "But you are your community's leader, right? All nine compounds."

"We don't like to toss that term around. I'm the chosen one. The Messiah."

Right, because chosen one sounds better. It took every ounce of energy she had not to roll her eyes.

"I'm the vessel to which God speaks through to his chosen people."

"Does that mean the rest of us are forsaken somehow? Or tossed aside, and God doesn't care about us?"

Christopher stood, sauntered across the small room, and sat down on the bed. "Not necessarily and you, Sister Danni." He took her hand and kissed it. His lips were harsh. Cold. Scratchy. She wanted to yank her hand away, but instead, she bottled that emotion. Locked it up tight inside.

Like Thor said he did when he'd been on a mission. He told her he would save his feelings for when he was alone with his team. Or alone with his thoughts—and a picture of her.

She could do the same and she could muster an image of him in a nanosecond.

"Are not forsaken. You have a purpose with the chosen. God has spoken to me about it, and I know, in time, you'll hear it and want to follow his will."

"Why don't you tell me what it is."

"Hmmmm. I don't believe you're ready. You have not studied the doctrine." He stood. "I will make sure some food is sent up with a special piece of chocolate cake. I think you deserve a treat." He leaned in, his mouth so close to her skin she wanted to vomit. "You are special to my people—to me. Soon, I will show you just how special." He pressed his disgusting lips on her cheek.

She jerked.

He sighed. "Sister Danni, you must help us cast out the devil. I do not want to force this with you. God has a plan and know I will follow it whether you have come around or not." He stood tall. "I'll see you soon."

She clutched her gut as he stepped out of the room. Her stomach cramped again. This time she groaned, bending over. This no longer felt like hunger pains. She padded to the bathroom. Perspiration beaded across her brow. She gripped the sink as another wave of pain grappled across her stomach. "Oh God," she moaned.

Yanking down her undergarments, she sat on the toilet. "No. No. No. No," she cried, staring at the dark blood—too much blood. She opened the cabinet and found the feminine napkins that had been left there. She cleaned herself and curled up on the bed. This couldn't be happening. She couldn't be losing her precious baby. It was all she had to tie her to Thor. The only connection she had left.

She wrapped her arms around her middle. An hour ticked by as cramps tore through her midsection. She went back into the bathroom, and she'd soaked through the maxi pad. "I'm sorry, Thor. I'm so sorry. This is all my fault." She cupped her face and cried. She didn't know how long she sat there and shed painful tears, and it didn't matter.

But hours later, the pain subsided and perhaps the worst of it was over. But the emotional part would never end.

Not until she was in Thor's arms again.

And that would happen. She would make sure of it.

---

Thor stood on his parents' back patio on what should have been his wedding day. In his thirty-one years of life, he'd seen some shit.

But nothing he'd lived through could have prepared him for… this.

He lifted his wineglass and sipped. So many emotions filled his heart. Sadness. Pain. Loneliness. Anger. Rage. But the biggest one that settled on the top of his heart today was guilt.

Guilt for drinking her favorite wine.

Guilt for returning to Delaware—their hometown and where they had planned on getting married.

Guilt for letting her down and not finding her—yet. Because he knew deep down that she was still alive. He felt it in his bones. But he'd woken from his nap feeling a sharp pain in his temples and a weird sensation in his gut. He couldn't explain it, but he knew something horrible had happened… to her. It wasn't death. He knew that. He had to believe that.

But it was something, and it was killing him.

"Hey, son," his father said as he stepped out on the patio, followed by Nick, Danni's father. "How are you holding up?" His old man eyed the drink in Thor's hand.

"Okay." He swiped at his dry eyes. He'd never cried so much in his life. He woke up with tears in his eyes every freaking morning and he fell asleep with them dripping off his cheeks. He turned and eased into one of the chairs at the table, pouring himself more wine. He shouldn't get drunk, but he was halfway there, and he suspected no one would care. He had the week off and everyone told him to take the time.

Well, he'd stay at his folks' tonight. Maybe tomorrow. Spend some time with them and Danni's parents.

But then he was off to the races. He'd gone to two of those compounds and now it was time to visit the rest of those places. To speak to anyone and everyone he could—and he wanted to get his hands on that damn cult leader.

That fucker had gleefully allowed the cops onto all his compounds—well, the areas that weren't closed off to nonresidents. Except for the one in West Virginia.

That one the police had been given a partial search warrant—but they still found absolutely nothing.

Thor took three gulps of wine, ignoring the glares of his father and Danni's dad. "Are Mom and Alice back yet?" He leaned forward and fiddled with the wineglass, staring into the red liquid.

"No," Nick said. "I suspect they might be another hour or so." He sat down and his strong hand landed on Thor's shoulder. "The girls' travel hockey coach wanted to talk with Alice about possibly hanging Danni's jersey at the rink. I told her she should talk with you first about it."

"No. It's fine." Thor waved his hand. "As long as everyone understands anything they do isn't in remembrance, but in honor. Danni is still alive. She's out there, somewhere. I can feel it, here." He tapped his chest. "I'm not giving up."

Nick wiped his hand across his eyes. He choked on a sob. "I want to believe that too. I need to. It's just with every passing day, I—"

"No." Thor abruptly stood. "I will not give up. I will not let anyone else either." He took his glass, filled it to the literal brim, and strode across the patio. He stared out over the lawn. The same one where he used to toss a football with Danni when she was in middle school. Or play hide-and-seek with her when she was in elementary school. He sipped his wine, begging the tears to go away. Begging his heart to stop breaking.

His father came up beside him and looped an arm around his shoulder. "Not a single one of us is giving up hope," he whispered. "And we never will. Not while there is breath in our lungs. But it's not easy for us to see you like this—drinking like this." He reached inside Thor's shirt and pulled out the dog tags and with it the double rings. "We love Danni like a daughter." His dad glanced over his shoulder. "And her parents love you as if you're their flesh and blood. We're all hurting right now, especially today. But we need you to take a breath. Find your center and—"

"Dad, Danni is my center. Without her, I don't know who I am or what I'm doing."

His father took his wineglass from his hand and set it aside. "When we find her, she's going to need the best version of you, and this isn't it." His dad arched a brow. "Moose tells me you've been calling people at the cult, yelling at them. That you've driven to one of the compounds and nearly got yourself arrested."

Moose and his big freaking mouth. "It wasn't that bad and I'm not going to stop searching or showing my face at those compounds." He raised his hands. "But I will promise to keep these things to myself unless I'm given a real reason to use them."

"That's not making any of us feel any better and it was bad enough that Moose felt the need to call me." Nick pointed his finger over his head. "I don't want you to give up that fight, but getting yourself locked up isn't going to help Danni... or us."

Thor gripped the railing and lowered his head. The man he'd been the last fifteen days, his Danni would be ashamed of. He sucked in a deep breath and let it out slowly. "I'm sorry, but I can't sit around waiting for someone else to do something. That makes me crazy." He sighed. "And I'm unusually moody today."

"It's to be expected," Nick said. "We all are. Today should have been a joyous occasion."

Thor turned. "It's more than that." He fingered the wedding rings. "As strange as this might sound, I've felt a deep connection to Danni since we were kids. I remember when she broke her arm. I was sitting in biology class and felt this weird sharp pain in my elbow. It was the darndest thing."

His father laughed. "I remember when you came home from school that day, you kept rubbing it. You told me you thought something was wrong with it, until Danni came bopping through the front door with a cast on and the sensation went away."

"How about when she got appendicitis." Nick shook his head. "You were more pathetic than she was. I heard you came home from school with a tummy ache." He rubbed his belly and made a sourpuss look.

For a half a minute, Thor chuckled at the memory because it was funny, but then everything came crashing down. Tears filled his eyes. They hadn't gotten the chance to tell their parents she'd been pregnant and now wasn't the time.

That pain he'd have to own by himself.

"I'm sorry," Nick said.

"No, I'm the one who should be sorry." Thor swiped at his face. "I failed her, and I failed you."

"You did no such thing, son." Nick jumped to his feet. "All you have ever done is love my daughter, even if it took you a little while to get there. You've been the best thing that has ever happened to her—to this family. We are all going to get through this."

God, Thor hoped Nick was right, because if she wasn't found soon, Thor wasn't sure he'd survive.

---

Danni spent the next three days sobbing. No amount of food—or prayers—could ease her suffering.

"What has you so sad?" Christopher sat on the edge of the bed with his hand on her thigh.

She jerked. "Leave me alone." She kicked at him, trying to push him off the mattress.

"Now, now. That is no way to behave." He shifted, resting his hands on his lap. "Sister Annabelle tells me your monthly has visited you and I understand that often affects some women emotionally."

She scoffed, choking on another sob.

"Spiritually married women are often upset when their monthly visits because it means they weren't blessed with a child, so crying makes sense. But for you, I just don't understand."

"Maybe I'm crying because I'm being held like a caged animal." She pushed herself a little farther away, curling her knees to her chest, and glared at him. "You've ripped me from my life—from my family—from the people I love. You've held me against my will for close to three weeks. You've isolated me and the only interaction I've had is with some woman who brings me food and you. Any normal person would be sad about that."

He stood, strolled over to the desk, and lifted a stack of papers he'd brought. "You're looking at it all wrong." He eased back onto the bed and pushed the papers toward her, tapping his long fingers against them. "You've lived in the devil's world your entire life. You were raised in it. Raised to believe a certain way. The devil is powerful, and I can see his presence in you is still strong. But only because you refuse to release him from your soul and let in our heavenly Father. I know he's come to you. I feel him in this room trying to reach you and he's told me it's time to reveal your true purpose. Hopefully, you will receive his will, but if you don't, we'll have to work harder to cast out the devil."

A slow shiver crawled along her skin. Krista had told her about devil casting ceremonies. How the community would circle around someone who had been inflicted and how they would speak in tongues. How they would put the inflicted in closets for days. Weeks even. Until the devil had been banished.

"What are you going to do to me?" she whispered.

Christopher laughed. "I'm going to pray with you—and for you—to see God's plan." He reached behind her and tugged at the chains. "Life for you will be so glorious when you do."

"And if I don't want whatever *your* God has planned?"

His face hardened. He leaned closer. His longer fingers gripped her face, squeezing tight. "You will not reject our heavenly Father's plan." His nasty lips were less than an inch from hers. "Nor will you reject me. It is not written that way in our scripture. You will surrender.

One way or another, you will serve your purpose." His mouth brushed over hers. "Whether it is willingly, or whether I have to force it upon you, it will happen. It is the word of our Lord."

Her entire body stiffened. She closed her lips tight. She would not allow this man to take any part of her—ever. She would die first.

Pulling back, he stared at her with an unwavering gaze. "I will leave you to read the doctrine that predicted your calling." He dropped his hand and stood, towering over her. "This is your purpose in life. This is what you were meant to do. It's why you were drawn to my community in the first place—only you couldn't read the signs properly. The devil in the outside world influenced how you perceived us. But God will change that." He ran his grimy fingers through her hair. "I, the Messiah, will change that—and you will bring the second commander into this world." He turned, opened the door, and left.

With trembling fingers, she lifted the pages and stared at them with wide eyes.

*The coming of the commander. The second Messiah. The son of a commoner and Messiah Christopher.*

What the hell?

*It is foreseen that the Messiah will take his sixth and final wife from the devil's world. She will come to Origins of God in an unconventional way. She will be seen as an outsider. As a destroyer of our faith. At first, she will not be one of the trusted. She will need to be cleansed. The devil will have a strong hold on her beliefs. He will need to be isolated in order to be cast out. She will fight our ways, but no matter what, she will bring us our commander.*

Holy hell. She sat upright, gripping the pages. This was insane. There was no way this was predicted. This was utter bullshit. This man was making shit up as he went along. None of the people she'd spoken to ever mentioned it before. Nor did anyone ever say anything about a second coming or a commander.

They had mentioned polygamy, but it had never been proven.

*This commoner is the only vessel for the second coming. She is the creator for the commander. He will be conceived—whether she is a convert—or a sinner. That is foreseen and written. We must trust in God that he will show us the way. That he knows what is best for this vessel. We must take diligent care of her through this challenging time for her and for the spiritual chosen. We can only pray that she will be strong enough to cast out the devil and welcome her role.*

That was the end of the passage.

The rest of the pages were misquoted from other Christian bibles. Interpretations used to mislead and manipulate their followers.

It was all so disgusting.

She tossed them aside.

This was not going to be her fate. She would not let this man use her—rape her—so he could… She couldn't even finish the thought. Being submissive was no longer the way out of this hellhole. She would need to fight tooth and nail—or die trying.

Anything would be better than being Messiah Christopher's baby mama.

## 12

THREE DAYS LATER...

*D*anni had barely slept the last few nights. Her mind wouldn't shut down. The isolation had begun to drive her mad with desperation. While she spent hours contemplating different exit strategies, she also found her resolve slipping. The thought that if she caved to the cult's wishes, she'd be better off crept into her psychological makeup.

She pressed her hand against her belly and reminded herself of what these people had taken from her—from Thor.

Sister Annabelle continued to bring her food, water, and new material to read. Danni forced herself to consume the nourishment. She needed to keep her body strong because she wasn't going to let that man take any part of her soul. She would rather die before she surrendered—to him. She wouldn't be his vessel. She couldn't allow them to break her—which was what he wanted. Every time he visited, he told her with a smug smile that she would welcome him and her purpose soon enough.

He was confident he wouldn't have to take her—the hard way.

Tears burned her eyes. Her heart ached. Thor would understand. He'd have to. He wouldn't want her to give in passively to this crazy person.

She stared at the latest reading material. Everything they gave her to learn—to recite back—was so insane. Women were servants of God—through man. Boy children had more respect than elder women. They were the future of each compound, even if they were the lowest of all male callings. Girl children were groomed to be submissive to men—and boys. Their only purpose on the planet was to either bear children or to serve man.

It was disgusting, and yet women believed this of themselves.

The door rattled and Messiah Christopher waltzed into the room. "Good afternoon, Sister Danni."

"Nothing good about it." She yanked at the chains that bound her to this hellhole of a room. "When are you going to unchain me?"

He sat on the side of the bed, folding his hands in his lap. "The moment I know I can trust you." He reached out, palming her face.

She jerked, shoving his hand aside.

He chuckled, shaking his head. "It's time for you to accept your place." He waggled his finger. "Have you finished your studies?"

"That doctrine—the stuff you preach to your followers—it's utter crap. I won't ever accept anything about you or the Origins of God. I certainly don't plan on being your partner or the mother of any of your children." She folded her arms across her middle. "I will not accept that as what I'm supposed to be doing. My life is with Thor, not with you."

Christopher cocked his head. "No, my sweet Sister Danni, you are so very wrong." He sighed. "I need you to accept your fate." He shook his head. "What is it going to take?"

"I'm never going to succumb to your wishes. I'm never going to belong to you or be what you want."

He leaned closer and curled his fingers around her wrist. "Yes, you will." He squeezed tightly. He took his other hand and gently ran his fingers through her hair. "Our heavenly Father has commanded me to break you. He wants me to show you that you are mine. That you belong to me and this community. Today is the first day of your new life." He leaned closer. A slow smile spread across his face.

Her heart slammed into her throat like a baseball landing in a catcher's mitt after being hurled across home plate at ninety miles an hour.

His slimy lips pressed against her cheek.

"Leave me alone." She jumped to her feet. "You will not have me."

Slowly... methodically... he rose. He smoothed down the front of his long tan shirt.

Her pulse hammered in her chest. *Thump. Thump. Thump.* With every passing second, it got louder and faster. She couldn't swallow. It hurt to suck in even a shallow breath.

He inched closer. His smoldering eyes conveyed

anything but kindness. They were the eyes of a man who intended to take what didn't belong to him. His gaze glossed over her body like a snake before it struck its prey. This man was the devil.

"I will die before I allow you to touch me." She took a tentative step backward, holding up her hand.

"God has spoken to me." Christopher sighed, shaking his head. "I know he's spoken to you—he's told me so. He wants you to give yourself freely, but if you refuse to relinquish the clutches of the devil, then I'm to drive him out of you." Christopher grabbed her by the biceps, heaving her violently against his chest.

He was stronger than she expected.

She twisted her body, doing her best to shake from his firm grasp.

Tossing his head back, he laughed. "You can fight me—if you want—but that won't change your fate."

She narrowed her stare and spit on his face.

Shoving her back on the bed, he wiped the saliva from his skin. "You can try to rattle me by whatever means you feel necessary, but today is the first day of your new life. I've been patient long enough." He leaned over her with a hardened expression. "Do *not* make me hurt you because if that is what it takes for you to see the light... then that is what I will do." He climbed on top of her, wedging himself between her legs and holding her arms over her head.

She squirmed, wiggled, and thrashed. "You're not godly. You're not even a decent human. You're going to rot in hell because no God would ever condone this."

"You are mine," he whispered in her ear. His breath

tickled her skin, making the hair on the back of her neck rise on end.

She turned her head. "You disgust me." She kicked her legs and tugged at her hands.

All he did was laugh. "You can fight all you want, but all that will do is make this less pleasurable for you. Either way, your earthly role as the vessel to the commander is going to happen."

"I'll die before I give you a child." She jerked her head forward, smacking her forehead into his nose. Her eyes watered. A sharp pain vibrated from the center of her head right down to her toes.

But it was so worth it when he jumped off the bed, cupping his nose with blood dripping between his fingers.

He groaned. "You fucking bitch."

"Touch me again, I'll do far worse." She sat up tall, staring him down, mentally shooting daggers at him.

Quickly, he grabbed her by the neck, shoved her back, and squeezed… tight.

She curled her fingers around his wrist, gasping for air, but she couldn't suck in a deep enough breath.

"You do not call the shots," he said with a dark tone.

With a swift motion of her leg, she nailed him where it counted with her knee.

He doubled over, coughing. "You're going to… regret… that…" he managed with a ragged breath. He stumbled to the door, yanking it open. "Take her to the closet."

Two burly men appeared.

She swallowed. Maybe she'd pushed too far.

One of the men pulled her from the bed, while the other unlocked her from her restraints.

"Where are you taking me?" she asked with a shaky voice. She twisted her hands, grateful they were free, but no sooner did she revel in that than one of the men slapped a zip tie on her wrists.

"Lady, you shouldn't have pissed him off," the bald man said.

"You're not a believer, are you?" She blinked, staring at him—and his big gun.

"It doesn't matter what I believe," the man said.

"Why are you here? Why are you helping him keep me hostage if you don't believe his bullshit?"

"Lady, a paycheck is a paycheck," the man with the curly hair said. "And Christopher pays well."

"You don't care that he's holding me against my will?" She jerked her arms, trying to break free. "Or that he was about to rape me?"

The bald man stared at her with wide eyes.

The other man scoffed. "Like I said... money's money and I've known Christopher since we were kids. Now let's go." His fingers dug into her muscles as he guided her into the hallway. However, he wasn't as forceful as he could have been.

The other man opened a door. "I'm sorry," he whispered as the curly-haired man pushed her into the dark space.

The door shut and locked.

Darkness engulfed her as she reached out, flattening her hands against the door, then the three walls. The space was so small, there was barely enough room for her to sit down, but she managed to do so, leaning back against the far wall. She let the first guttural sob bubble up from deep in her gut.

She hugged her knees to her chest and cried… and cried… until there was nothing left.

*The next day…*

Danni blinked open her swollen, dry eyes.

Darkness.

She coughed. Her stomach ached. Her bladder hurt. If she didn't relieve herself soon, she'd explode, but she didn't want to do it in the closet.

More tears.

The isolation was too much.

The door rattled.

She held her breath, inching as far back as she could, holding her knees to her chest, ready to kick—but she feared she had no fight left.

Sister Annabelle appeared in the light from the hallway. "Come with me," she said softly.

"Where?"

"To your room." Sister Annabelle helped her to her feet and led her back to the confines of the bedroom that had been her prison cell for nearly a month.

"Please, let me go," Danni whispered as she glanced over her shoulder. The bald man stood guard—with his rifle. If she tried to overpower Annabelle, she would indeed be shot.

Annabelle said nothing.

The bald man took a pair of clippers, snipped the zip tie, and chained her to the bed.

"There is new reading material for you," Sister Annabelle said. "There will be no food today." She turned and left the room.

So did the bald man.

The door slammed shut. The lock clicked.

Danni raced to the bathroom. She sat on the toilet and cried… and cried. She had no idea how long she stayed there. It felt like hours, but it could have been less. She didn't know, and she no longer cared.

With no life left in her limbs, she padded into the other room and sank onto the mattress. For the first time since she'd been held captive, she gave up all hope and prayed for death.

*The next day…*

Danni bolted awake with her heart hammering in her chest. She blinked. It took a moment for her blurred vision to focus on the man standing over her with a scowl.

His nose was swollen and covered with a large piece of tape. Both eyes had black and blue marks under them.

A tiny bit of pride welled in her gut, but it wasn't enough because she wasn't free.

"Have you learned your lesson?" Christopher asked.

"The only lesson to be learned here is that you are a rapist and a criminal," she managed to choke out. "You'll pay for whatever you do to me. My Thor will make sure of that. He won't rest until you do."

Christopher leaned closer. "You fail to understand that I'm not doing anything to you that isn't commanded by God. Now, you will bathe so that when I return, you are clean and ready for me."

"I will not." She folded her arms across her chest.

He laughed. "If you don't, I will clean you myself, and then when we are done, you will go back to the closet." He waggled his finger. "However, you clean yourself and I can allow you to stay in your comfortable room."

"You might as well put me back in that closet because I will fight you." Her body trembled with every word. Her muscles were weak, and she knew it wouldn't be so easy to fend him off this time. If he wanted her, he would take her.

"I will be back." He stood tall. "I will bring those guards with me to tie you down if I have to." He smiled. It wasn't just any smile. It was a wicked, smug grin. "I understand a woman's cycle, and you, my darling newest wife, are ripe for the making of the commander. It is as the heavenly Father predicted. You can fight all you want, but you can't stop it." He stood tall, turned, and curled his fingers on the doorknob. "I expect you to be ready for me in an hour." With that, he disappeared into the hallway.

A few minutes later, the bald man tiptoed into her room. He held his rifle close to his chest. His gaze darted around the small room before he glanced out into the hallway. He raised his finger to his lips, making the shhhh sign. "What is your name?" he whispered.

"As if you don't know," she said, not being overly quiet in her response.

He glared. "If anyone knew I was speaking with you, not only would I be fired… I might be… Just tell me your name."

"Why?"

"Because I might be inclined to help you," he said softly, looking out into the hallway again.

"Get me out of here, that would help."

"That's not easily done at this moment," the man said.

"You have to." Her voice cracked. "Christopher is going to rape me when he returns in an hour if you don't."

"I've created a diversion for that." The man shook his head. "I won't let that happen today."

"I have no reason to trust you."

"No, you don't." He inched closer. "Is your name Danni Hagar?"

She gasped, covering her mouth.

The bald man closed his eyes and sighed. "I didn't sign up for this, but I owe Roger my life."

"Who's Roger?"

"One of the other guards here," the man said. "I'm Mo." He nodded. "I only started working here a week ago. I can't get into the details of why I can't just bust you out. It's personal and I don't have time. I need you to trust that I will do what I can over the next two days to make sure Christopher doesn't hurt you. I've set something in motion when I suspected you were that missing journalist." Mo spoke so quickly and softly that Danni wasn't sure she caught every word. She also wasn't sure she should trust anything that came out of his mouth.

It could be a trap.

But for now, she'd play along. What choice did she have?

"What should I do?"

"I honestly don't know. I can't tell if that freak gets off on you not falling at his feet or if it annoys the heck out of him. But for now, don't do what he says. Worst case, he'll put you in the closet. The good news there is I'm the one tasked in guarding you. I'm also the one giving him some false information on what the Feds and locals are doing regarding their search."

"Why and what are they doing?"

Nervously, he glanced over his shoulder again. "I have to go. Christopher won't be back today. That, I guarantee." Mo shuffled out of the door, closing it gently, locking it.

She swallowed. Did she dare to hope that she'd soon be free?

*One day later…*

Thor stood in the lobby of the local Park City FBI office. It had been twenty-five days since Danni disappeared, and no good lead had come his way. She'd vanished into thin air without a trace.

"Are you Lieutenant Commander Thor Armstrong?" a man asked.

"Yes, sir." Thor nodded, stretching out his arm.

"I'm Special Agent Raymond Olander. Feel free to call me Ray." He tucked a file under his arm.

"This is my colleague, Lieutenant Mark Adams." Thor nodded in Moose's direction.

"Everyone calls me Moose."

"I was told you brought your entire team," Ray said. "Where are they?"

"Out in the parking lot." Thor jerked his thumb over his shoulder. "I thought it might be a little aggressive if five Navy SEALs descended upon this office."

"Wouldn't be the first time." Ray chuckled, opening a door to a small office with a single wood desk with two chairs. "Though it wasn't SEALs the last time, it was three Snow brothers. Delta Force." He shook his head. "I worked with their mother on a couple of cases. I don't know who frightens me more. Those three boys or her."

Moose eased into the chair closer to the wall, and Thor took the one by the door.

"I've only spoken to Phoenix Snow on the phone." Thor rubbed his thighs. "Seems like a decent guy."

"He and his family are the best. His mom saved my life once. So, when she called asking me to poke around, it was the least I could do."

"I take it you found something, and that's why we're here," Moose stated the obvious.

"I have some information for you on Christopher Bently." Ray nodded.

"Must be good intel if you wanted me here in person—and with my team." Thor leaned forward, resting his hands on the desk. His leg rattled uncontrollably.

"It's twofold." Ray leaned back in his chair and flipped open the file. "Let's start with the background I learned." He wet his finger and turned the page. "Christopher wasn't born into the cult he leads. But he was raised in a strict fundamentalist religion. One that has had numerous run-ins with the law in this state."

"What kind of run-ins?" Moose asked.

"Mostly polygamy. Child endangerment. Tax evasion. There have been stories of abuse, but nothing we've been able to make stick when it comes to that. Women don't often leave or come forward. When they do, it's to run and run fast. They don't want to press charges or talk about it. Frankly, I don't blame them." He tapped his fingers on the file. "Christopher became estranged from his family when he was sixteen."

"Why?" Thor asked.

"Turns out, he rebelled against the religion he was raised in." Ray arched a brow. "He was arrested as a minor for drugs, illegal weapons, and assault. But those records were sealed. It's why your local detective didn't know about them. Why no one did. But when the case came across my desk at the urging of Phoenix's mom, I did some digging. I was able to get a judge to unseal the records and it was eye-opening."

"Jesus," Thor muttered. "Did he serve time?"

"He spent a year in juvie and a year of probation." Ray flipped a page. "He was excommunicated from his church and from there, he fell off the radar." He handed Thor a piece of paper. "Except, I've since learned that two women filed restraining orders against him in the state of Utah when he was twenty and twenty-one. I've obtained those records and I've spoken to one of the women."

Thor glanced at the sheet in his hands. "This states the woman accused him of rape."

"Accused is the operative term because it was never proven." Ray shook his head. "It still amazes me how much victim shaming goes on when it comes to this kind of shit, but the DA didn't have enough evidence to take it to court. No rape kit was ever taken. It became her word against his and with his record being sealed, they had nothing to go on."

"You mentioned you had the chance to speak with this one." Thor raised the paper. "What did she say?" He sucked in a deep breath. He needed to approach this situation as if it were a mission. He needed to take the emotion out of it. Remove the personal parts and do what was necessary to save an innocent.

It was what he did day in and day out.

Ray ran a hand over his mouth. "She had a lot to say about how Christopher planned on creating his own community—one he didn't want to call a religion—but that it was a cult. She used those words." He glanced toward the ceiling. "She told me that his goal was to be a quiet, but powerful leader that brought about a different understanding of the Lord. She mentioned how charismatic he could be and how easily people fell for his charm—at first. But when women—his wives, and I guess he has like five now—don't follow his commands, he uses force, much like he did with her."

Thor growled. It was deep and it vibrated in his chest with a violent wave.

"This woman left long before his so-called community expanded to more than one compound," Ray continued. "Christopher left Utah a long time ago, but five years ago, his father died." Ray arched a brow. "His old man owned a large ranch outside of Park City."

"How did we not know this?" Moose asked.

"Because all the other properties are listed under an LLC, for one," Ray said. "And also this property isn't listed under Christopher Bently. It's deeded to Gina, his sister."

"Has anyone gone out there to check it out?" Thor's hands trembled. He was scheduled to be deployed next week for ten days.

"I've been there many times." Ray nodded. "It's like Fort Fucking Knox over there and I've had no probable cause to enter without a search warrant."

"My fiancée is missing!" Thor jumped to his feet. "She's been working a series of articles about cults, mostly about Origins of God, which should be enough."

"All that gives me is enough to ask questions." Ray raised his hand. "But I might have more shortly."

"What does that mean?" Thor glared.

"I got a call from a man by the name of Mo—just Mo. He wouldn't give me his last name. He says he works security over at the Bently place and he wants to meet me and talk about something. He wouldn't give me the details over the phone."

"When is this meeting taking place?" Thor paced in the small office. He itched to do something. Anything.

Ray glanced at his watch. "In two hours and no, you're not coming. At least not visibly."

"That's bullshit," Moose said. "We're not sitting on the sidelines. You called us here. You're using us."

"I didn't say you couldn't be there. You just can't be in eyesight." Ray pressed his hands on the desk and rose. "I'm meeting him at a park. There will be lots of places you and your team can be hidden. I just don't want you spooking this guy in case he does have good intel. However, the reality is, he could be there to send us— me—on a wild goose chase. Christopher knows every law enforcement agency known to man believes he had something to do with Danni's disappearance. We must face the idea that this guy Mo is being sent to give us faulty information."

"What about comms," Thor asked. "I want to hear everything."

"I can't have an earpiece." Ray shook his head. "I didn't have to tell you I was even meeting with this guy." He lowered his chin. "I did it because if I were in your shoes, I'd be losing my mind, and if things go sideways, well, I'll have backup when my department is more than stretched thin and this case is colder than the majority of the ones sitting on my desk right now. Don't make me regret giving you this courtesy."

"I'm sorry, but right now it doesn't even feel like a bone," Thor muttered, planting his hands on his hips. "But I'll take it."

"Good." Ray nodded. "I have a few things I need to do before we head out. Why don't you and your team go across the street to the diner and grab a cup of coffee and a bite to eat. I'll be over in about forty minutes with the details."

"How about you give me the—"

"I'm not going to fuck you over," Ray interrupted Thor, waving his hand to the door.

"Fine." Thor and Moose shuffled out of the office, into the lobby, and out the front door. Once outside, Thor made a beeline for the rest of the team. "Jupiter," he called. "I need you to run your magic and find out everything you can on—"

"Moose already texted me." Jupiter lifted his head. He held a tablet in his hands. "I've found a local security company—Taft Security—run by an ex-military guy named Roger Taft. What's interesting about Roger is that he grew up here in Park City and he has listed as one of his clients..." Jupiter turned the tablet. "...Gina Bently." He arched a brow. "I sent a quick text to Phoenix and his mom to see if they can connect Roger to anyone by the name Mo."

"Fucking needle in a haystack." Thor ran his hand across the back of his neck.

"Unless they served together," Jupiter said, snagging his cell, holding it up. "And according to Phoenix, Roger served four years with a guy by the name of Maricio Ortiz. He even sent us a picture of the two men together."

Thor snatched the phone from Jupiter's fingertips. "If this is the guy Ray is meeting with, I want to get to him before Ray does."

"Jesus," Kawan said. "Why would you want to do that?"

"Because the Feds will want to call in hostage negotiators." Thor's heart rattled around in his chest like a dog trying to get out of a cage. "They will want to talk to Christopher. They will waste time doing stupid shit instead of acting. If she's on that ranch, we'll be able to plan and execute an extraction much faster than they could make a fucking phone call."

Lief placed a firm hand on Thor's shoulder. "You're not thinking. You're letting your emotions—"

"Don't tell me to back down." Thor shrugged Lief's hand off his body. "Are you with me or not?"

"Of course we are," Sloan said softly. "But we don't even know where this meeting is."

Thor pointed to the diner. "When Ray comes and tells us what park he's meeting Mo at, we'll have to go there first for recon. He knows that. We'll cut Mo off before Ray knows what hit him. We'll find out what we need to know. In the meantime, we need to find out all we can about that ranch. How to get on the property. What the house is…" Thor started to pace. "How big is that security company?"

"I don't know." Jupiter lifted the tablet. "This isn't sufficient time to figure out what we're up against. I think we need to split up. How about if Moose and Kawan head over to the ranch and do a little recon there. I'll continue to see what I can find out here through all my tech and human resources at the diner while we wait to head to the park. If this Mo has good intel, we'll regroup and go from there."

"It will have to do." Thor paused and nodded. "If any of you don't want to—"

"We're not leaving you." Moose held his gaze. "But you're going to have to listen to what we have to say when it comes to the execution of this mission."

"I can live with that." For the first time in nearly a month, Thor allowed his hopes to be raised.

anni stared at the door. Her only visitor had been Sister Annabelle, who brought her bread, water, and reading material. Danni drank, ate, and read. She decided that if she ever did get out of this room, she needed to consume the knowledge. She knew she would need to write—to tell—her own story.

She wished she had pen and paper because if she didn't make it out, she wanted someone else to write it. Her story needed to be told.

Once again, the door rattled, and she held her breath with her heart beating in her throat. Mo had kept his promise. Christopher had not come to her, but that didn't mean he wouldn't.

She braced herself to fight. She was proud of herself for holding on to what little sanity she had left for so long. Thor had told her stories about how hard being deployed had been and all the tricks he used to keep his mind and body sharp. She used every single one, but nothing could have prepared her for captivity. She knew it could have been so much worse, but for twenty-five days, she hadn't sucked fresh air into her lungs. She hadn't felt the sun on her face. And she hadn't held the man she loved in her arms.

Wrapping her arms around her middle, the weight of what she lost tormented her soul.

Mo slipped into the room. "You need to know I'm leaving the house today for a few hours," he whispered. "I've done what I can to keep Christopher away from you. I don't know what will happen while I'm gone."

"Where are you going?" She hugged her knees to her chest and stared at him with tears in her eyes.

"Hopefully to find us both a way out of this," he said softly. "Christopher has a meeting with elders for the next couple of hours. I'm hoping I'll be back before that ends." He pulled something shiny from his pocket. "If he comes to you, fight him off." He handed her a large knife. "If he doesn't, this will be part of our plan. Hide it where you can get it easily." He gave her a weak smile. "Stay strong." He turned and left her sitting on the bed with the knife in her trembling hands.

Finally, she had real hope.

---

Thor cracked his fingers one by one. He hated that noise. He hated it when anyone did it in his presence. But he needed to do something and pacing in a park would only bring attention to himself, something he couldn't afford.

"Your one o'clock," Lief said over the comms.

Thor shifted his gaze and saw Mo strolling into the park. "Got him and approaching." He took long strides, constantly looking over his shoulder. Ray sat on a park bench around the bend, out of sight thankfully. "Excuse me," Thor said.

Mo paused, staring at him with narrowed eyes.

"I know you're here to meet with Special Agent Raymond Olander—"

"I have no idea what you're talking about." Mo took three swift steps.

"I don't want to stop you from meeting with him," Thor continued. "But I have an invested interest in this meeting. Danni Hagar's my fiancée, and I believe she's being held at Christopher Bently's ranch against her will."

"Dude, I'm sorry about your girl, but I seriously have no idea what you're talking about." He waved his hand.

"My name is Thor Armstrong. I'm a decorated Navy SEAL." Thor pulled out his military badge for impact, which he never did. He held it up so Mo could examine it. Then he pointed to where Lief stood in the distance and then Sloan. "Those are two of my teammates. I've got two more doing recon at the ranch. We've surmised that you work for a friend at a security company at the ranch. I believe Danni is being held there." Thor spoke succinctly and quickly. "I also believe you contacted Ray because you have intel on Danni. I want that information before you give it to Ray."

"And do what with it? Storm the ranch?" Mo let out

a long breath. "That might get Danni out, but that doesn't help me."

Thor cocked his head. "What do you need help with?" He stuffed his badge back in his pocket.

"Two things," Mo said. "The first one is I want to make sure I have immunity for this shit." He ran a hand over his bald head. "I didn't know what I signed up for when I agreed to this security detail. If I had, I would have said no, only I owed Roger and that brings me to the second thing." Mo's eyes grew wet. "They have my wife."

"They're holding your wife hostage too?"

"No," Mo said softly. "She's currently working in the kitchen at the ranch. She took the job the same time I did. Three days in, we both saw things we didn't like, though she hasn't seen the same things I have." He wiped his eyes. "I haven't told her everything I know about your Danni, but she knows that place is bad. Roger doesn't care. All he cares about is that Christopher pays him a hefty sum."

"Dumb question here, but if you and your wife don't believe, why didn't you just walk away? Or have her leave?"

"I wanted her to." Mo nodded. "She was going to, but once you're there, it's fucking *Hotel California*. You can check in, but you can never leave."

"What's your wife's name?"

"Reena."

"You tell me and my team where on that compound Danni is and how many guns we have to deal with, we'll make sure Reena gets out safely too."

"How do I know I can trust you?"

"Same way I'm trusting you." Thor stretched out his hand. "But you can't tell Ray what we're up to. He's going to want to do things the long, hard way."

"What the hell am I supposed to tell him, then?"

"Very little," Thor said. "You go meet with him, and then we'll devise a plan. We'll go in tonight. You make sure Reena knows we're coming. We're going to need your help on the inside. Are you willing to do that?"

Mo nodded.

Thor swallowed. "Have you seen Danni? Is she okay?"

"Your Danni, she's a fighter." Mo reached out and squeezed Thor's biceps. "I can't say she's unfazed, or even unharmed, but he hasn't hurt her—not in the way I can tell your mind has gone."

All the oxygen in Thor's lungs flew out like a flock of birds. She's alive. That's what he needed to focus on.

"I've done what I could to protect her," Mo said somberly.

"Thank you for that," Thor managed. "You better go chat with Ray before he loses his shit."

Mo took a tentative step before turning and glancing over his shoulder. "I had loyalty to Roger because he saved my life. We were brothers-in-arms. I thought that meant something. It means something to me. I watched too many good men die in battles that made no sense. This is even more senseless to me. You have my loyalty —my trust. I will gladly walk into battle with you. A man who loves as deeply as you and for a woman who has as much fight as Danni does is a man I want to know." He turned.

"Hey, Mo," Thor said. "I've been lucky in my career not to have been betrayed by my brothers, so I can't imagine what that's like. However, I will always take a man on my team who values, honors, and respects what we face when we're deployed and not just on the battlefield, but when we leave our loved ones behind. Thank you for taking the risk and coming forward. I owe you everything."

"You owe me nothing but to make sure we get Danni and Reena out of that hellhole."

## 14

*T*hor adjusted his earpiece, checked his weapon, and held his cell in a death grip in his hand. He stared at the house illuminated by the glow of the moon and the stars hanging in the night sky. "Everyone in place?"

"Copy," Moose said.

"I can see the front door," Kawan said. "Two armed guards, just like Mo said."

"I've got a visual on the east entrance," Sloan said. "One guard."

"One guard on the roof," Lief added. "One more at the gate."

"I'm ready to take out the one making rounds," Jupiter said. "Mo said once we make it inside, it's just him and Roger."

"Can't do anything until… wait. Hang on." Thor's phone buzzed. He glanced down at the text.

**Mo:** *Go.*

"Mission is a go. Take out the guards. Moose, you're

with me. We enter through the west side. That should be the kitchen. Reena should be there. She'll guide us up the back stairs." Thor tucked his cell in his pocket. The plan wasn't a complicated one.

Christopher was in the meeting room with some elders. They would methodically remove the guards, slink into the house, take Danni and Reena, and get out. Once that happened, they would call the Feds and let them make the arrests. It was unconventional, but it would work. They had witnesses who would testify—at least, he knew his Danni would.

God, he hoped she wasn't too broken.

Twenty-five days in captivity—even he wasn't sure he could survive that, and he was trained for that shit.

"Man on roof down," Lief said. "Going after the guard at the gate."

One by one, Thor's men took out the guards. It was swift and quiet. And no one died.

"Let's roll," Thor said. Time to get Danni.

---

Thor entered the kitchen. A woman stood in front of a staircase. She stared at him with wide eyes. "Thor?"

He nodded.

His men entered the house through different entrances. They had all checked in, stating something was amiss. Things were too quiet.

"Where is everyone?" Thor whispered.

"Main meeting room, which is in the front of the

house." She pointed. "Roger is standing guard there. Mo is upstairs."

"You need to come with me."

"I know," she said. "Mo gave me the instructions. I'm to act like you've taken me hostage."

"I won't hurt you." Gently, Thor curled his fingers around her arm. "I thought there would be more women milling about."

"Something strange is going on," she said as she guided him up the stairs. "Christopher ordered everyone to their rooms."

"But not you?"

She shook her head. "I'm supposed to bring that tray of food to them in about a half hour. But that wasn't the original plan. Mo is worried."

"We'll get Danni, and we'll get out. Don't worry." Thor continued up the stairs. He tapped his earpiece. "Be on high alert. Something is very wrong."

"Copy that," Kawan said. "I'm near the meeting room, but no visual on Roger. That doesn't seem right."

"Let's stick with the plan," Jupiter said. "We've got your back, Thor."

"At the top of the stairs now. Watch the kitchen and the main stairs. Let me know what the best way down is." Thor held his weapon at the ready as he inched down the hallway. His heart hammered in his throat.

If Danni wasn't in that room, he would hunt Christopher down and squeeze the life out of him with his bare hands.

Mo waved.

Thor moved faster. "Something's wrong," he said. "I'm afraid we might get ambushed on our way out."

"Why do you say that?" Mo shifted his rifle.

"Everyone's been ordered to their quarters," Reena said. "Last I saw Roger or Christopher, they went to the main meeting room."

"But Roger isn't standing guard," Thor said.

"The outside guards are supposed to check in…" Mo glanced at his watch. "…every half hour. They might know we're here. We better get a move on."

Thor nodded as he gripped the door handle. No emotion. Nothing but training.

At least that's what he told himself.

---

Danni sat on the bed, fingering the knife. Christopher had not come. That was both a blessing and a curse. Her thoughts had turned dark. Darker than she ever could have thought possible. She wasn't a violent person. She never wanted to bring harm to anyone.

Justice and truth.

That's all she'd ever wanted.

Not destruction and death.

But for the last few hours, she could only think about taking this sharp object and driving it right through Christopher's heart. Visions of his blood trickling from his body danced in her head like sugarplums.

It both electrified and horrified her at the same time.

The house was eerily quiet. Not even the wind howled. She stared at the door, willing it to rattle.

But nothing.

Then the doorknob turned.

She swallowed her breath and pulse. Inching to the side of the bed, she held the knife, ready to strike. No one could blame her.

The door flung open, and she sprang to her feet, waving the knife around like a wild woman. "I'll fucking kill you if you come near me."

"Danni," Thor's voice rang out loud. "It's me," he said. "Put that down." He held up his hands.

Her ears and eyes were playing tricks on her. That man—it couldn't be her Thor. She wanted it to be. Needed it to be. But how could he be standing there in dark pants and a black shirt, holding a gun?

She lunged forward, jerking the knife left and right.

The man dodged and ducked. "Danni, sweetheart, it's me. Put that thing down."

"Danni, it's him." Mo stepped into the room. "I forgot I gave her that thing, and you didn't want me to tell her you were coming, which was the dumbest part of this plan."

"I couldn't risk Christopher overhearing it," Thor said, holding her gaze.

"Thor?" She dropped the knife. It landed on the floor with a thud, one inch from her bare feet. "Thor?" she repeated.

"You're okay, babe. I've got you."

She flung herself at him, wrapping her arms and legs around his thick body. The chain that held her to the bed rattled, smacking him in the side.

He groaned.

179

She let out a guttural sob. The tears came hard and fast. She buried her face in his neck and breathed in his rich, musky scent. "I lost our baby," she mumbled into his skin. "They took that from us."

His body stiffened and he tightened his grip around her waist. "Get these chains off her," he commanded.

Someone… it had to have been Mo… slipped a key into the cuffs and her hands were free.

She hugged Thor harder. Cried harder.

"Let's get out of here," Thor said, and he moved swiftly.

She didn't dare open her eyes. Nor did she release her legs and arms from his body. He carried her down the hallway, down a set of stairs, and out a door. She heard voices.

Moose, Jupiter, Kawan, Sloan, and Lief.

They were muffled and she couldn't make out anything they said, and she didn't care. She was in Thor's arms.

"Drive," Thor said as he shimmied them both into a vehicle.

Again, she didn't even blink until the sound of the door slammed shut and panic set in. "I can't breathe," she whispered, pushing herself away from her beloved Thor. She gripped and clawed at the door. "I have to get out. Let me out."

"It's okay. You're safe. I've got you," Thor said.

"I can't be in here." She pounded on the glass.

"Roll down the window," Thor said softly. "Look at me, babe." Gently, he placed his thumb under her chin. "Can you do that?"

She turned her head, taking in a deep breath.

"That's it. Just breathe. One breath at a time. Focus just on me." He held her gaze with warm loving eyes. "No one is going to hurt you."

"You don't understand." She turned and stuck her head out the window. Her hair flew across her face. She sucked in a deep breath. The fresh air filled her lungs. "Please, stop the car and let me out."

"Kawan, pull over," Thor said in soft but commanding voice.

Seconds later, she bolted from the vehicle and ran around it three times. Her legs felt like she'd been underwater for months. Or maybe in outer space. They could barely hold her, but she needed to move. To feel the air across her skin. She paused, glancing toward the sky, and stared at the moon and the stars. Her chest heaved up and down, but the panic hadn't left her body.

"She hasn't been out of that room in twenty-five days," a familiar male voice said.

Mo.

"Confined spaces are going to be hard," she heard Sloan say. "Did you call Brick at The Refuge?"

"I did and he has a cabin ready and waiting for us. All I have to do is get her there." Thor stood in front of her, his hand on her forearm. "Danni?"

She blew out a puff of air. Tears burned her cheeks.

"Are you going to be able to get back in the car? Because if you can't, it will be a long walk to New Mexico," Thor said.

"The Refuge," she said softly. "You've always loved

that place. You said it helped you expunge the demons from your missions."

He palmed her cheek.

She jerked. "I'm sorry." She lowered her gaze.

"You have nothing to be sorry about," he said. "Can I try that again?"

She nodded.

He touched the side of her face gently, tilting her head.

"I thought if I ever got out of that room, I'd be fine. He didn't beat me. He didn't hurt me. I—"

"Danni," Thor said so sweetly. "I know how hard you fought. Mo told me, but that doesn't change that you were held in that room for twenty-five days. That will change even the strongest of people."

She clenched her fists at her sides. "I lost our baby because of them," she said with such thick emotion she thought she might choke on it. "Is he dead? Did you kill him? He doesn't even deserve to rot in prison."

Thor glanced over his shoulder.

Kawan shook his head. "Ray texted a few minutes ago. Compound was empty."

"Shit," Thor mumbled.

"What does that mean?" she asked.

"Nothing you need to worry about right now."

She grabbed Thor's shirt, pounding her hand against his chest. "Tell me. I need to know."

"He must have gotten wind we were there. My priority was getting you and Mo's wife out safely," Thor said. "Christopher must have slipped away. But the FBI will find him, and he will pay for what he did." Thor cupped her face. "Your only focus right now is healing and the best place to do that is at The Refuge."

"He's going to come for me." Danni's heart twisted. "He thinks my purpose is to give him a child."

"The Refuge is a safe place. They have security and I won't leave your side. The team will come too."

"Damn right we will," Kawan said.

"And if we're not there, we will be tracking that asshole." Lief stood next to Thor. "He'll never get to you again."

Danni leaned into Thor's arms. "I thought I was going to die in that room because there was no way I was ever going to let that man have me."

Thor pressed his warm lips on her forehead. "Close your eyes and keep your arms around me. We'll talk about happy times and things that bring you joy."

"You're going to put me in that car, aren't you?" She sighed, knowing she would have to let him help her through this as her heart began to race again.

"Don't think about it. Think about our wedding, because we're still going to have one. Think about that dress that I still haven't looked at that's hanging in our guest room, or the stupid speech that Moose will make at our wedding." He lifted her into his arms and climbed into the back of the SUV.

"Moose can't give a speech unless I've approved it." She closed her eyes tight. "I'm so sorry, Thor. I lost our baby on what was supposed to be our wedding day."

He tangled his fingers in her hair and kissed her cheek. "It's not your fault," he whispered. "None of this is your fault."

"Do you still lo—"

"Forever and always, I will love you. That hasn't changed and it will never. Don't you ever forget that."

"Loving you was the only thing that kept me going."

"Me too," he said. "You're going to be okay. We're going to be okay."

For the last twenty-five days, she whispered to herself that if she got out, everything would be all right the second she saw Thor again.

But the truth was, nothing was okay. Everything was upside down and she wasn't sure she'd ever be the same person again.

---

## 15

*T*hor decided stopping for the night and staying in a hotel wouldn't be a good idea. Danni struggled in the SUV, especially if the windows weren't rolled down. Thankfully, she slept for a few hours, even if it was fitfully, and a nightmare jerked her awake… more than once.

But now they were at The Refuge. The vastness of the property would give Danni the space she needed to feel safe. The people at The Refuge would give her the tools she needed to rebuild and reshape her life.

Thor rubbed his dry eyes as he guided Danni up the cabin's porch steps. Outside of her panic attacks, she'd been unusually quiet—for her—but he didn't press for her to talk about what happened. While he wanted to know every sordid detail, he understood that she needed time, space, and professionals.

His job was to love, support, and give her whatever she needed.

Only, he had no idea what that was or what he

should be saying or doing. He was at even more of a loss than when she'd been missing.

He wanted to race from The Refuge and search for Christopher, but his team and Brick and everyone else wouldn't let him leave. They thought he was too hotheaded and would do something he would regret.

They were probably right, but what difference did it make? Christopher had robbed him and Danni of so much.

Danni stopped at the front door and glanced at him with wide, fearful eyes.

"It's going to be okay." He rested his hands on her shoulders and squeezed. "It's bigger than it appears. It has a small kitchen. A nice-sized family room. A huge bathroom with a bathtub and the bedroom is a decent size. It's a nice night, so we can open a window and leave the door open—for now." He leaned in and kissed her cheek.

He worried about even doing that, but it was more for him than for her. He'd been without her for nearly a month—which felt like a lifetime. He needed to be reminded that she was alive. Her heart beat right next to him and Christopher hadn't hurt her—not in all the ways that played out in his mind.

"All right." She inhaled sharply before blowing out the air with a big puff and crossing the threshold. She hadn't spoken much on the car ride. Mostly, she stared out the window, holding his hand as tight as she could.

Or she hugged him as if he were a life raft and cried until she slept.

"There's that group session Brick mentioned when

we checked in," Thor said softly as he tossed his rucksack on the sofa. "We can go together, or if you prefer, I can sit outside and wait." He turned and gently rested his hands on her shoulders. "Henley runs the sessions. She's an amazing therapist. You're going to love her."

"So, you and the guys keep telling me." She slipped from his grasp and scurried toward the front door. Her movements were quick—jerky. She folded her arms across her middle and stared out at the vast ranch that stretched on forever. "It's beautiful here. I always understood how you needed a little space after some of those missions to deal with the things you did, saw, experienced." She swiped at her cheeks. "I never took it personally or felt hopeless, as if I couldn't help you through those times. I knew you needed people who had lived it." She turned. "Has anyone here been through what I have?" She held up her hand. "Because it's hard to put into words what's going on in my brain and about how I'm processing what happened."

"Everyone who has ever experienced the kind of trauma that sits in your soul forever goes through that." He opened the front door and waved toward the chairs.

She eased into one, keeping her gaze on the horizon, her arms firmly locked around her middle, as if to protect something. Only, that something wasn't there anymore.

Thor felt that loss deep in his core, but this moment wasn't the time to experience or express it.

He took her hand and kissed her palm. "It's not my place to tell anyone's story and everyone here—including those who work here—have one. We don't compare trauma. No one person's pain or emotional torment is worse or less than someone else's. All you need to do is give yourself permission to heal. Trust that everyone here wants that for you. Open up to them. This is a safe place."

"You haven't asked me too many questions." She turned, catching his gaze. "Why?"

His heart dropped to his toes.

The horror that lived behind her sweet blue eyes filled his gut and twisted. No matter how strong she was —being held captive for as long as she had could break anyone.

"Are you afraid to hear it?" Tears dribbled down her cheeks.

He reached out and wiped them away. "No. It's not that at all." He squeezed her hand. "I'll be here to listen whenever you're ready to tell me." He scooted his chair closer. "However, I want you to understand that right now, it's more important that you work through it with people like Henley. She's the professional. But I'll be right by your side every step of the way. I'm not going anywhere."

"What about the Navy? I'm not your wife and I know they—"

"Shhhh." He pressed his finger on her lips. "I have time accumulated, and we can change your status as my wife anytime we want." He arched a brow. "We have a marriage license and if we need to do that so I can get more time, we will, and we can still have that big ceremony you want on a later date. I'm here for as long as it takes for you to be able to put this shadowy demon in a box."

"I don't know if I can do that with Christopher Bently still out there. I still feel as though I'm being held captive while he's roaming free."

He shifted the chair to face her head-on. He took both her hands, rubbing his thumbs over the top, while he searched for the perfect words to ease her aching heart. "Mo—the man who worked for Christopher but was key in us finding you—he's with the FBI agent, giving him all the information he can on Christopher, his sister, and Roger, the owner of the security firm. My team is working with the Snow brothers and their mom, along with all her contacts. We've built a small army. We will find Christopher and he will pay for what he's done. I promise you that."

She shifted her gaze back to the sky, squinting at the bright sun. Her forehead crinkled and she pursed her lips. This meant she was deep in thought.

"What is it?" Thor asked.

"I spent twenty-five days in that room, and I learned nothing of that cult. I saw only two believers. Christopher and Annabelle. Although, I'm not sure Christopher believes his own shit, but Annabelle totally does." Danni sucked in a breath and let it out in a choppy pant. "While I read the material I was handed, my only focus was on figuring a way out. I tried fighting. I tried being passive. I tried being combative. But what I didn't do was learn." She turned. "I should've been learning. I should've done whatever he wanted so I could've roamed that house and… and…" She choked on a sob.

"Babe, you know what would have happened to you if you became submissive," he said tenderly. He resented the tremor in his voice. He tried desperately to mask it. He didn't want her to mistake it for sadness or even trepidation. The only reason it was there was because of the rage that coursed through his veins.

And the fear that he could kill a man in cold blood, because if he were left alone in a room with Christopher Bently, or even Roger Taft, he was terrified of what he might do.

It didn't matter that they didn't beat her—or worse. They stripped her of everything that made her who she was, and they took away their family.

For that, he'd never rest until justice was served— only he wasn't sure what justice looked like anymore.

"You don't understand." She jumped to her feet. "How can I help anyone who is being held there against their will or afraid to leave because of their ridiculous doctrine if I couldn't even do it for myself?"

He ran his fingers through the top of his flattop and rose. She was right… he hadn't a clue and was at a loss for how to help her sort through any of this. Brick and Tiny—another owner at The Refuge—had warned him that he might need to take a step back and allow them to step in. That his role would be to help her get through the nights and those moments when no one else was around. To show her all the love and support he had in his heart.

Just like he'd been doing when she'd been missing.

How he'd never given up hope—or the search.

She needed to know that he'd always carried her in his soul.

Tentatively, he wrapped his arms around her body. She'd lost weight. Too much weight. She was physically and emotionally weak, and yet she still thought about others.

He loved that about his Danni.

"I won't pretend that I know what you went through," he whispered. "But I do know that you're not alone in what you're experiencing."

She turned and faced him. The tears had dried and all that was left were bloodshot eyes and a hardened expression. One that showed him her resolve hadn't been completely destroyed.

He tucked a few stray strands of hair behind her ears. "You need to focus on you right now. You need to deal with what you went through and by doing that, you'll help others. Expressing that here at The Refuge will help those that are walking through their demons. It's how I was able to come back to you a whole man after some of the stuff I went through on those missions."

"What I need is to stop Christopher from continuing to destroy lives." She palmed his cheek. "Do you remember when I first interviewed Krista?"

He nodded.

"The man who beat and raped her was Christopher."

Thor stiffened. His blood ran cold. "How do you know that?" All he wanted to do was wrap his fingers around Christopher's neck and strangle that man until he took his last breath.

"The words Christopher used when he told me he would make me succumb to him and his crazy world were similar to what Krista had used. She told me she'd never seen that man before. I didn't make the connection until the last week of my captivity. Until after I lost our baby. Christopher believed that was the start of my cycle and his cue for… for…" She turned away, lowering her gaze and sucking in a deep breath before lifting her chin. "Christopher raped Krista, and I bet there are other women he did that to. I have to stop him."

"You are the most amazing human I know." Gently, he brushed his lips over her mouth. God, he had missed her so much. He loved her with every ounce of his soul. "I know how important this is and what it means to you. I don't want to stomp out your desire to take this man down." He pressed his finger over her lips. "But right now, it can't be you."

She pounded her fist into his shirt. "I can't sit here in this cabin and stare at the walls or talk about my feelings with a bunch of strangers. I'll lose my mind."

He wrapped his arms around her trembling body and heaved her to his chest. Her mind was already fractured. She was half in the present, and half still in that room chained to that bed. "Do you trust me?"

"Yes," she whispered.

"Let's walk down to the group session. You don't have to say anything. All you have to do is sit there and listen. After that, we can talk more about what you can do to help Ray find Christopher."

She glanced up. "I don't just want him to pay for what he's done," she said. "I want to expose Origins of God for what they really are and it's a lot more than a cult." She glanced over her shoulder. "I'm going to need a notebook, a pen, and my computer."

"Danni, you need to spend some time dealing with—"

"I can't turn off what's happening in my brain. It won't stop." She gripped his shoulders. "What happened to me will happen to someone else—for all we know he's holding some other woman captive as we speak." She jerked her thumb toward the cabin. "I understand that I'll struggle with small spaces and will have nightmares. I spent enough nights with you thrashing about while you tried to protect me from your demons. But what did you do a few weeks later?" She covered his mouth. "You went right back out there when you got deployed and did it all over again because it's who you are and what you do. I'm an investigative reporter. It's who I am, and I just became the story. I can't sit idle. You can't expect me to hike and enjoy the scenery while that man is out there doing dreadful things to innocent people."

"I will get you all the things you've asked for as long as you promise me two things."

"What's that?"

"You will go to the group session, and you will speak with Henley one-on-one. You need to take care of yourself." He cocked his head. "You are strong, and I can see that resolve and spark in your eye. I'm glad it's there and you can use that to heal. But trust me when I say if you don't deal with the trauma of the last month, you won't be doing yourself—or anyone else—any good."

"Okay." She dropped her head to his chest and sighed. "I lost my engagement ring."

"I'll get you a new one." He smoothed his hand down her spine. "I can go to town tomorrow and buy it."

She chuckled. "You don't have to do that."

"I want to." He tilted her chin. "I love you so much, Danni. My world stopped when you disappeared. I wasn't sure I could go on without you. You're my compass."

"Sounds like you're the one who needs group therapy," she said with a teasing tone.

He allowed himself a weak smile. "I have my own sessions set up with Henley," he admitted. "While what I endured wasn't anything like what you suffered, it was still pure hell, and I have my own demons to wrestle with because of it."

"I'm sorry."

"Hush." He kissed her. Not hard, but it was the kind of kiss that reminded them both of the love they shared. "You have nothing to apologize for. You didn't do anything wrong. I, however, almost got myself arrested while you were gone."

"I can't imagine what it must have been like for you." She shivered. "Every time you were deployed and were late coming home, my mind went to dark and dangerous places."

"I know." He threaded his fingers through hers and tugged her down the steps. "I've always hated that for you."

"But it's our life and I've never wanted you to stop being a SEAL. I'm proud of who you are. I love you."

"I love you, too." He would never tire of those three little words, and he would say them as often as he could.

———

Danni slipped from the group meeting minutes after it began with her heart hammering in her chest. She tried sucking in a deep breath the second she stepped outside into the fresh air, but she couldn't get enough oxygen.

She had forced Thor to leave because if she had chosen to participate, she didn't want him to hear anything she had to say—not yet anyway.

Now she wished she hadn't sent him away because he was nowhere in sight. He'd mentioned something about finding Kawan and Lief in hopes of getting an update.

A large man approached her with a kind smile. "Hi," he said. "Are you okay?"

She managed a nod between gasping breaths.

"Let's go sit over here." The man waved to a log. "My name's Tonka."

"Interesting name," she whispered as she lowered herself onto the log, taking in more breaths.

"Group sessions can sometimes be overwhelming." He stretched out his legs, picked up a stick, and fiddled with it. "Took me a long time to be able to open up."

She breathed in through her nose and blew it out through her mouth. She'd never had a panic attack before being held captive, but she knew that's what she was experiencing.

Worse, she knew what had set her off.

Henley.

It would be impossible to keep her promise to Thor if she couldn't even be in the same room with the therapist.

"I'm usually an open book," Danni admitted. "Thor used to tease me that I don't even need a glass of wine to tell someone my life story."

"Trauma will change people, and while those demons might be with you forever, they don't have to change you completely." Tonka spoke softly and in an even tone. It was calming, and she enjoyed the sound of his voice. "I struggled for a long time. I still do, but I've learned that there are people I can trust and lean on. You've already got the love of a good man." Tonka smiled. "I've known Thor now for a few years." He laughed. "I remember the first time he came to The Refuge. He was contemplating so much about his life after the first time he'd been shot and dealt with a mission that had gone sideways. But what he really struggled with was his feelings for you."

"He wrote me a letter while he was here." Her heart swelled in her chest at the memory. "I was in college. He was so hung up on our age difference."

Tonka dropped his head back and laughed. It was throaty and full and vibrated from his chest. "We all thought that was funny since four years is nothing, but he got over that."

"He sure did." Her heartbeat calmed. The panic eased.

But the pain of her loss did not, nor did the rage that circled her soul. In all her young life, she'd never experienced such an intense and extreme sensation. Not even her love for Thor was this... she couldn't even put a word to it because she couldn't compare them. Loving Thor was easy. It was natural. It calmed and grounded her, giving her a sense of peace. But the moment she thought of what Christoper stole from her—from Thor —a burning desire to seek revenge seeped into her bones like a disease.

"It might be good for you to speak with Alaska, Brick's girl. She was held captive and struggled with confined spaces."

Danni turned her gaze toward the building. While she'd had a difficult moment the second they closed the door, she managed because she knew she could get out. She had sat near the exit, testing the door at Thor's urging and it worked. Simply knowing she was in control and could leave at any time gave her the courage she needed to plant her butt in that chair.

Until Henley strolled in wearing an oversized shirt, doing her best to hide her expanding belly. However, the second the petite woman sat down and adjusted her clothing, the baby bump had been exposed and panic gripped Danni's body.

"That's not why I left," she whispered.

"Oh. I see," Tonka said. "Do you want to tell me what happened, then?"

Danni pressed her hand over her stomach and closed her eyes.

"This is a safe space and whatever is discussed between you and me is private. You have my word."

She blinked, staring into Tonka kind eyes. He seemed like a sweet man. "While I was being held, I lost my baby."

A warm, firm hand gently squeezed her shoulder.

"I'm so sorry," Tonka said. "Can I be totally honest with you?"

"Please."

"Henley tried to cover that up, knowing it might trigger you, but she's far enough along that it's hard."

"I promised Thor that I'd do my best to take care of myself and see this through, but I don't know how I'll be able to sit in a one-on-one session with her and not freak out. I'm more worried about that than trying to sleep in a bedroom, because at least there, I know I'll have Thor to help me through it."

"Perhaps Thor can be in on that first session."

"I don't want him there."

Tonka arched a brow. "Why not?"

"Don't get me wrong, I love Thor, and I know he loves me, but he's barely acknowledged the loss of our child. His focus is on me healing." A flare of anger hit her gut. It had been an unwelcome and unexpected emotion, but it festered in her muscles like a rabid dog chewing on a bone. "It's like it doesn't matter."

"I know that's not true, but me telling you that isn't

going to change how you feel about it," Tonka said. "And feelings are important. Expressing them even more so. I've learned that the hard way. I've spent most of my life with animals because I trust them more than I trust humans. In some ways I still do. But one thing I know for sure is that when you love someone, you can't let a feeling like that go without telling them it's there and this is one of those things that needs to be done now."

"The pregnancy wasn't planned." Why she told Tonka that, she had no idea. He was a complete stranger and not a therapist. Hell, all she knew about the man was that he was one of the owners'… Crap. He was the one married to Henley. "I shouldn't have told you that."

"No, it's okay. You can confide in me." Tonka took her hand, squeezed it, and smiled. "We're all in the same boat here at The Refuge. If you can't talk in there, you find someone whom you can share with. If that's me, I'm happy to listen."

"It's just that Thor and I had wanted to be married for a year or two before we had kids, but I got pregnant, and I thought he was happy. When I told him I lost the baby…" She let the words trail off. "I don't know. Everything happened so fast. I just thought he'd be as devastated as I was, and he hasn't shown much emotion."

Tonka took both her hands and held her gaze. "Thor has spent the last twenty-five days trying to hold it together. He's been a shell of a man, and now that he's found you, he's doing whatever he can to be strong for you. While I can't be totally sure of what he's thinking, I'm guessing he believes if he falls apart, it won't be helpful to your recovery and right now, he cares only about two things." He held up his fingers and wiggled them. "He wants to make sure you're going to come through this on the other side and the asshole who took you gets what he deserves. That's a tough line for a man like Thor to walk. On the one hand, he wants to be here, with you. But on the other, he wants to be out there, serving down the hand of justice." Tonka lowered his chin. "We had to practically force him to stay with you because we're all afraid of what he might do to Christopher if he finds him before that FBI agent does."

"I was prepared to kill him if he came at me again," she whispered.

"That's different. It would have been self-defense. Self-preservation. What Thor would be doing is cold-blooded revenge—because that man not only took the woman he loves, but he took his family from him." Tonka arched a brow. "So, don't think for one second that Thor isn't hurting over that. He's just not showing it. And now I'm going to ask you a big favor. One that I have no right to ask, but I believe it will be good for you and Thor."

"What's that?"

"Talk to him about this—about how you're feeling. Ask him to get his emotions out. It won't be an easy chat, and I can get Henley involved if you want, but I know Thor and I'm sure he's up at the main lodge talking with his team and working on a plan. While we all want to take down Christopher, it can't be a destroy mission."

"You really think Thor would go that far?"

"I'm afraid he's been pushed to his limit." Tonka jerked his chin. "Here he comes. Do you want me to get Henley?"

"No." She shook her head. "This one I believe Thor and I need to do on our own."

## 16

T hor hightailed it up to the main lodge in search of Kawan and Lief. Jupiter, Sloan, and Moose had left The Refuge to chase down a few leads. They would hopefully be back by nightfall—or at the latest, by morning. Thor had wanted to go, but everyone told him that Danni needed him more. Deep down, he knew that, and he wouldn't have been able to leave her side if he tried. But it was killing him not to be part of the hunt.

He wanted five minutes alone with Christopher. That's all he needed to kick the crap out of that man.

Kawan and Lief were perched on a picnic table outside with Tiny, Brick, and Spike—another one of the owners.

"Hey, man." Kawan waved. "I thought you were going to group."

"Danni didn't want me to stay." He joined the men at the table and sighed. "I don't know if it's because there are things she doesn't want me to know yet about what happened to her, or if she's not ready to talk and plans on sitting there with her arms folded, waiting to bolt."

"How are you holding up?" Brick asked.

"About as well as you'd expect." Thor rested his hands on the table. "The hardest part is I honestly don't know how to help her outside of talking her off a cliff when she has a panic attack."

"That's something," Brick said. "It might be all she needs from you right now."

"If that's all she needs, plenty of people can give her that here," Thor muttered. "What I need is to be out there doing something to put the asshole who did this where he belongs."

"And where's that?" Spike asked with an arched brow.

"Six feet under." Thor held his gaze.

"That's one of three reasons you're not leaving this ranch." Brick tapped his fingers against the wooden top.

"What's the other two?" Thor dared to ask.

"You really need to ask that?" Lief glared.

Thor knew the answer, but he did need to hear someone else verbalize it. Otherwise, his brain and heart wouldn't hear it or compartmentalize it. He understood himself well enough that if he tried to remind himself what he honestly needed, he'd have a case of selective hearing. "Yeah, I do."

"I'm happy to drill the points home if you're too stubborn to reach inside and do it yourself," Brick said. "For starters, Danni needs you."

"I'm aware." Thor folded his arms across his chest.

"But she also needs professional help. That I can't give her."

"Maybe not, but she needs more than that." Brick cocked his head. "If you walked off this ranch right now, she'd feel abandoned and that's not an emotion she could process on top of everything else she's going through." He held up his hand. "And then there's you. Whether you want to face it or not, you suffered your own brand of trauma and still are. This cloud that's hanging over your head is full of rage. The kind of rage that changes a man—the kind of change that someone doesn't come back from if they were to act on it. You need to find a way to dump it, or when we do find out where Christopher is and execute this plan, you won't be coming with us."

Thor jumped to his feet. "This is my team. My plan. You don't call the shots." He wagged his finger.

Kawan pressed his hands on the table and slowly rose. He inched closer to Thor. Kawan was a tall man at six-three, and he towered over Thor, who wasn't short by any means. Kawan was the oldest on the team and he had a gruff look about him. Almost menacing. If Thor met the man in a dark alley, he'd be terrified, but once you got to know him, you learned he was a big teddy bear.

However, looking at him right now, Thor wanted to turn and run.

"I love you like my own flesh and blood," Kawan said in a deep tone. "I respect you as my team leader. In fact, I've never had a better one. I would walk through fire with you—for you—but I will not let you do something that will not only endanger yourself, but the rest of us. You're not thinking clearly right now, and until you get your head on straight again, we all decided for this civilian plan—because right now we're not doing an op for the government—Moose is in charge, and he agrees that you need to stand down."

It was as if a dagger went right through Thor's heart. He'd known Moose since bootcamp. If he had a best friend, it would be Moose. Heck, he'd chosen Moose to be his best man at this wedding. While all the men on his team were his ride or die, Moose was the man who was always right on his tail. He was like an appendage that couldn't be removed. They did everything together.

Thor blinked. He didn't need to call Moose to find out if what Kawan was saying were true because not a single man on his team would lie to him. Thor nodded in acceptance.

Kawan eased back into his seat. Silence overtook the men for a long painful few minutes.

"Can I ask you a difficult question?" Tiny clasped his hands together and rested them on the table.

"I might not answer," Thor said.

"Fair enough." Tiny nodded. "When you and your team went in to get Danni, you were on point—focused. I get that seeing the aftermath of her being in captivity for twenty-five days is a lot for anyone to take in, but what has you seeing red? What has you going down this dark and dangerous road of revenge over justice?"

Thor's pulse increased. His blood boiled. His skin prickled. He couldn't see straight. He turned and glanced down toward the building where they held group sessions and saw Danni sitting outside with Tonka. "I gotta go," he said.

"What? Why?" Brick asked. "You can't avoid this. It's not healthy. You know that."

"I'm not avoiding." Only he was, but right now, that didn't matter. "Danni left group, and she needs me." He pointed. "Or maybe it's Tonka who needs saving." He tried to make a joke, but it fell flat and no one laughed. "Let me know if you hear anything." He turned and took off at a half jog toward Danni. He did his best to leave what the guys described as his cloud of rage behind.

He'd known something bad had happened to his Danni on the day they were to be married. He'd felt it deep in his core, and he wasn't there to help her through it. He'd been robbed of his child, robbed of his grief, and robbed of his wedding.

He swallowed the emotions and shoved them deep inside. He did exactly what Henley always told him not to, but he didn't know what else to do. Danni didn't need to deal with his pain.

Sucking in a deep breath, he slowed as he got closer. "Hey, Tonka. Hi, babe." He tried to smile, but he suspected it looked as if he swallowed a lemon. "Is everything okay?"

"We were just having a nice little chat." Tonka stood. "Come visit the animals anytime."

"Thanks. I'll do that." Danni nodded, taking Tonka's hand. She raised up on tiptoe and kissed his cheek. "I appreciate you taking the time to sit with me."

"My pleasure." Tonka disappeared into the building.

Thor inched closer, taking Danni into his arms. "What's wrong?"

"I don't want to talk about it here," she said so softly he barely heard the words. "Can we go back to our cabin?"

"Of course." He took her hand and guided her toward the path. A million questions ran through his head, but he didn't ask a single one. He walked in deafening silence until they reached the porch. "Do you want some tea?"

"That would be nice."

"We can sit outside."

"No." She shook her head. "While I only lasted a few minutes in group, I do need to work on being in closed spaces. I need to feel normal and that would be a normal thing to do."

"So would sitting on the porch, enjoying the sunset."

She chuckled. "You're a sweet man." Tentatively, she stepped inside, glancing around. "I didn't really notice how nice this cabin was before."

"It's the one I stayed in the first time I was ever here." He smiled. "I wrote you that letter sitting at that desk." He waved his hand before heading to the small galley kitchen. He found a mug, filled it with water, and shoved it in the microwave. While he waited for the water to heat, he snagged a soda from the fridge and a tea bag from the cupboard.

Danni made herself comfortable on the sofa, curling up in the corner, staring at the open door, and picking at her thumbnail. He hadn't seen her do that in years. She used to do it when she'd been in high school and was nervous about something. He'd seen her do it a few times in college when he'd come home, but since they'd been a couple, he'd only seen her do it once or twice when she'd been working on a tough article.

He grabbed the mug from the microwave, dunked the tea bag in it, and brought it to Danni. "I don't mean to pressure you, but you're scaring me a little with this silence." He sat beside her and sipped his beverage.

"I don't know how to bring this up so I'm just going to blurt it out." She shifted, palming the mug with both hands. "Being held captive by that crazy man was hard."

"Danni, I—"

"Let me finish, please."

"Okay." He nodded.

"What happened to me was utterly horrifying. He kept me locked in a room for twenty-five days. I barely saw anyone. I was isolated and alone. It's crazy to think that I was lucky he didn't beat or rape me. But the truth is, I am lucky that it didn't happen. I hold on to that and as strange as it sounds, it keeps me sane. It's probably why he couldn't break me. I don't know why he waited or what he was trying to do. Maybe he wanted me to be willing. I have no idea."

Every muscle in Thor's body stiffened. He took a hefty swig to keep from opening his mouth. He understood the need to purge, but damn, he didn't want to hear this. Not this way. Not when she was diminishing what she went through. However, he needed to let her get through it her way.

"But on the day we were supposed to get married, everything changed. That was fifteen days into my captivity. When I lost our baby, I decided that I would rather die before I let Christopher make me his vessel for his commander. I would have done anything to ensure that didn't happen."

"Danni, what are saying?" He set his soda aside and wrapped his arm around her, tugging her close to his body. "Are you telling me you didn't think you had anything to live for?"

"I lost our baby," she said softly. "On our wedding day. That man took our child and... and..." Her hands trembled, and the hot tea dribbled over the mug and sloshed onto her hands.

He took it and set it aside.

"Sweetheart—"

"Why don't you care that he took our child?"

"Oh, Danni." He pressed his lips to her temple. "Of course I care," he whispered, squeezing his eyes shut. Every demon lurking in his mind's shadows taunted him, begging to surface. "I want to strangle him until his last breath slips from his lips. I want to feel his heart beat one last time until it stops and there is no life in him at all. I want to watch him die a slow and painful death... at my hands... for what he took from us." The words tumbled from his lips and filled his soul. He pushed her aside and jumped up from the sofa. "I felt you lose our baby." He paced in front of the coffee table. He trembled from the inside out. "I knew something had happened. Just like when you had appendicitis. It was deep and gut-wrenching, and I couldn't do a damn fucking thing about it." He swung his leg, kicking the side of the couch. "I never felt so damn helpless in my life." He pointed toward the door. "I want off this ranch. I want to find him, his damn disciples, and that Roger asshole, and kill every single one of them because they took away the two most precious things from me." He pounded his chest. "They robbed me of my child. They took away my ability to grieve it with you. They forced you to cope with that pain all alone while I was…" He blinked.

Danni stared at him with wide, horrified eyes. As if she didn't even know the man standing in front of her. She clutched the necklace dangling from her neck that he'd given her at her high school graduation.

"I care," he said softly. "But I don't want to feel because I'm not capable of setting aside what's necessary in justice and what I want in revenge." He turned and stormed out the door. He shouldn't have. This shouldn't be about him. Danni needed him more than he needed a temper tantrum. His emotions shouldn't matter. He should be able to compartmentalize. He should be able to set them aside and be the trained Navy SEAL and good fiancé that Danni needed.

Not that broken man that twenty-five days without her had created.

She was the one who had suffered.

Not him.

He gripped the sides of the porch railing and breathed deeply. Tears scorched his cheeks. He'd wanted that child. He'd loved that child. And now they were gone.

The door creaked open and slammed shut. A warm hand ran up his back.

"I'm sorry," he managed as the cobwebs began to clear and rage gave way to grief. God, that hurt. It grabbed hold of his heart and squeezed it so tight he wasn't sure it would beat again.

"Don't be. I've had similar thoughts."

He jerked his head. "You're the kindest, sweetest, most forgiving human I know."

"Not anymore." She rested her head on his shoulder. "Your words both scared me and touched me."

"They frightened me too." He wrapped her in his arms and kissed her temple. "I'm sorry I didn't give you the reaction you needed when you told me about the miscarriage." He cupped her face. Tears still rolled down his face. "I struggle thinking about anything you went through during those twenty-five days, but especially that. I wasn't there. I should've been there."

She tilted her head. "I blame myself. If I hadn't been so obsessed with this story. If I hadn't chased it so hard, maybe I wouldn't have been taken and I wouldn't have lost our baby. It's my fault and—"

"No, Danni." He kissed her tenderly. "And don't ever for one second believe that I could blame you, because if that's what you're thinking, I need you to stop. Our loss didn't happen because of a choice either one of us made. My friends are going to catch that asshole, and he'll pay. They will make sure of that. Our job now is to heal. Both of us. We'll get through this because we've got our whole lives ahead of us. When we're ready, we'll try for another baby."

She shifted her gaze toward the cabin, then back at him. "I've missed you, Thor."

He cocked a brow.

Tugging at his hand, she pulled him back inside.

"Danni, what are you doing?"

"It's time to go to bed."

"It's only"—he glanced at his watch—"seven."

"I want to lie down with my future husband." She paused at the bedroom door. "Does the sofa open into a bed?"

"It does."

"Can we sleep in the family room?"

"We can," he said. "But we don't have to do anything. All I need is to hold you in my arms. It can be like the first few times I visited you in college."

She chuckled. "I was so afraid to tell you I was a virgin."

"I have to admit, that was a bit of a shocker." He tossed the sofa cushions aside and pulled out the sofa bed. Danni helped with the sheets, and they undressed for bed, though Danni slipped into his boxers and a tank top.

"But you handled it well enough." She climbed under the covers. "I thought for sure you might break up with me."

"Never." He pulled her close. "I like knowing I'm the only man you've ever been..." He swallowed. Christopher might not have raped her, but the thought that he could have—would have if Thor hadn't found her when he did—stormed through his system like a freight train.

He held her tighter.

She ran her hand across his chest. "Don't go there," she whispered. "Neither one of us can afford to let the rage out of the cage. I think we're both dangerous that way."

"For someone who left group without participating, you sound like Henley."

"I didn't even speak to her," Danni said softly. "And honestly, I fear that might be hard. She's pregnant and I don't know how I'll react to that one-on-one."

"She's a good therapist. We should do that together."

"I'm afraid to talk about some of this with you." Danni rested her chin on Thor's shoulder and gazed into his eyes. "I've never seen you that enraged before. I understand it because it's in me too, but you're trained for things I'm not. You're capable of things I know nothing about. I'm scared—"

He hushed her with a kiss. "My team isn't letting me off this ranch while my head is that far up my ass." He ran his hand up and down her back. It felt so good to have her in his arms. To have her lie down next to him again. His world had been so empty. Some of that ache in his soul had been filled. "Twice today I've been made aware of the demons that have surfaced. The darkness that's lurking. I'm coming into the person I was before you were kidnapped. It will take a little time and I'm in the right place for that. We both are. I trust my men— Brick's men—to do what I can't right now. Don't worry, I'm not going off the deep end." He kissed her nose. "Please don't shut me out. I promise I won't do that to you again—I thought I was protecting you when I closed off how utterly I broken I was—am—over what we lost. I didn't want you to suffer more than you already have."

"I just needed to know that you didn't blame me and that you had wanted our baby."

"I love you, Danni. You're my world. I'm lost without you in it."

"I love you, too." She smiled. "Now, are you going to make love to me, or do I have to beg?"

Thor rolled to his side, holding her close.

His eyes burned with desire as he took in the sight of her, his heart pounding at the thought of peeling them away. "No begging required," he murmured as he tangled his hand in her loose hair, drawing her into a searing kiss that set their nerves on fire. "But are you sure? You've been through so much, and with this, I can be a patient man."

"I need you… I need this," she whispered. "The mere thought of being in your arms again is what kept me going during those long days and nights."

His breath hitched, and Danni's eyes darkened. Thor's hands found the edge of her shirt, brushing against the soft skin of her stomach before he pulled it over her head, leaving her in just the boxers that were far too big. He kissed a path from the base of her neck to the clip of her bra. His hands shaking slightly, every nerve alert to her soft sighs and quiet moans, he unhooked it and tossed it to one side.

The sight of her laid bare to him made his heart clench in his chest. The emotion was raw, open, and it had everything to do with how much he loved this woman.

"You're beautiful," Thor whispered hoarsely as his gaze raked over her bared skin. She pressed herself into him as if seeking reassurance.

His mouth moved lower, trailing kisses down the valley between her breasts, across the flat plane of her stomach, until he reached the band of his own boxers that she wore. Hooking his fingers under the waistband, he pulled them down her legs, revealing every inch of her body to his hungry gaze. A red flush spread over Danni's cheeks and down toward her chest, but instead of pulling away, she leaned into him further. This show of trust melted Thor's heart even more.

Quickly, he shed his pajama bottoms. Lying naked next to each other rekindled a fire he thought they would never feel again. The need to reassure each other of their love, desire, and place in each other's lives.

Thor sank his fingers into her soft hair, pulling her closer to him. Their lips met in a fiery kiss that ignited a desperate heat between them. A heat that had nothing to do with revenge or vendettas.

"I want you, Danni," Thor whispered between trailing kisses down her throat. His hands found the curve of her hips, pulling her closer until she was straddled over him.

"Yes," she breathed, running her fingers through his short-cropped hair as she angled herself over him. They moved rhythmically against each other, relearning and rediscovering each other's bodies.

Danni's fingers dug into his shoulders as his movements became faster and more intense. Any sounds in the cabin were swallowed up by their lovemaking, their bodies craving the connection only they could provide for each other.

The cabin was filled with the intoxicating scent of them, a mingling of sweat and desire that clung to the heavy air. Their shared passion echoed off the walls, a testament to their deep love for each other as they lost themselves to the pleasure of their joining.

When they finally came down from their high, they collapsed onto the bed, panting heavily and holding each other close. Thor brushed a stray lock of hair from Danni's face, his touch featherlight as he traced her cheekbone with his thumb. Her skin glowed in the dim light filtering through the open blinds, her eyes soft as she looked at him.

"I love you," he whispered, pressing a soft kiss to her forehead.

"I love you, too," she murmured back, snuggling closer into his chest. They lay in silence for a while, both lost in the comfort of their shared warmth, the rhythm of their heartbeats syncing as they drifted off into a peaceful sleep.

Later that night, Thor woke up to find Danni sitting up in bed, staring blankly into the darkness. He propped himself up on one elbow and touched her shoulder gently. "Babe? What's wrong?" he asked softly.

Danni swallowed hard before turning to face him. "I was just thinking," she began hesitantly, "about what happened earlier... about our conversation."

"Is there anything else you want to talk about?"

Thor asked gently, caressing her arm to provide some small comfort.

"No." Danni shook her head slowly before leaning into his touch. "I just... I just needed some time to process it all."

Thor pulled her close, pressing a soft kiss to the top of her head as he wrapped his arms around her. "We can take all the time we need, okay? There's no rush."

They fell silent once more, just holding each other in the darkness. Despite the chaos that swirled around them—the hunt for Christopher, the unresolved pain from their loss—for this moment, they had each other. And somehow, that seemed to be enough.

As Thor held Danni close, feeling her heartbeat against his chest, he knew without a doubt that he'd do anything to keep her safe—even if it meant facing his demons head-on.

ive days had passed since Danni had come to The Refuge. She spoke to her parents every day and she could hear both pain and relief in their voices, but she wasn't ready to go home yet. She spent most of her days with the animals or hiking with other guests. Nights were spent in the arms of the man she couldn't live without. Their lovemaking was raw and wild, and she couldn't get enough of Thor. She desperately needed him to touch her in ways he never had before. She needed to be loved and desired by him. The intensity of those feelings was overwhelming and sometimes she didn't know how to cope except through sex.

At first, Thor didn't mind, but last night, he mentioned that perhaps she was avoiding something and her appetite for all things sexual was her way of dealing with things. She dealt with that one by seducing him, and he hadn't denied her, so there was that.

Then, this morning, when she woke with her period, her heart dropped to her toes. The pain of all she'd lost crashed into her heart. It was as if she'd been catapulted into that room and chained to the bed. Thor had been as understanding as he could be when she crumpled to the floor and cried, but he couldn't comprehend her true emotions or how it was as if she were reliving the loss all over again.

Thor had again pushed for her to speak with Henley privately. He knew she'd skipped out on the last scheduled visit, and she felt bad about that, but only because she'd broken her promise to him. The hardest part about that was that it had caused a fight. Not a big one, but for the first time since they'd been reunited, they argued.

She pushed it aside and focused on Tonka. She liked Tonka and was comfortable in his presence. He had this quietness about him. She could sit with him for a whole hour and say absolutely nothing and feel as though the weight of the world had been lifted from her shoulders.

When she did choose to speak, he listened intently and without judgment.

However, today, he sported a perplexing and confusing crinkle on his forehead as he watched his family of squirrels enjoy their meal.

"You're always asking me if I'm okay," she said nervously. "Today I feel the need to ask you that question."

Tonka ran a hand over his face and sighed. "I'm fine." He nodded, lifting his gaze. "You've avoided two sessions with Henley and while that's none of my business and I understand the trigger, being around a pregnant person isn't something you're going to be able to avoid for the rest of your life." He waved his arm. "I don't pretend to know anything about women and things. I only know that loving Henley has been an easy thing for me and that's shocking all by itself."

"Why? You're a good man. You're kind and sensitive." She inched closer on the log and smiled. "You're handsome too."

"Why, thank you, ma'am." He chuckled and quickly sobered. "I'm also a bit broken and just a few years ago, I could barely be in a room full of my friends and not feel like I didn't belong with the men and women who saved my life." He tapped his fingers on her knee. "I've listened to you in the group and you're so willing and so open. Not only do you want to push past what's lurking in the darkest places of your soul, but you also want to help people. That's an incredibly unique thing." He sucked in a deep breath. "But you refuse to do the one thing you need the most. That Thor needs the most."

"I talk to Henley," Danni said with a tinge of defiance in her tone. "She does run the group sessions, and she's incredibly good. I like her."

"You avoid the topic of your loss." He held up his hand. "I understand why. I did it for years. Grief is a tricky thing and there is no right or wrong way to go through it—as long as you do."

"Thor and I are managing."

"Are you?" Tonka arched a brow.

"We're doing it together." She folded her arms and glared at the man she'd come to call friend. Over his shoulder, a figure appeared—two actually. She swallowed. "Tonka, what have you done?"

"What I thought was right for someone I've grown to care about." He took her hand and squeezed. "And what Thor asked me to do because he's worried about you." Slowly, he rose and walked away.

She stared—more like glared—at Thor, who stood next to Henley. "I told you I need to do this my way."

"All I'm asking is that we have a conversation—with Henley. We don't have to do it in her office," Thor said softly. "We need to do this for us. Please, I'm begging you, Danni. You've made so much progress, but if we're going to survive this, we must face it head-on and that goes deeper than what we've done. We need help. This morning showed me that."

A surge of anger bubbled in her throat. She closed the gap between them and poked him dead center in the chest. "You don't know anything. You don't know what it was like to be alone and lose my only connection to the outside world—to you." She heaved in a breath and held on to the tears. She would not shed another one. "I had no one to hold me. No one to cry with. No one to tell me it was going to be okay. I was all alone while I bled and bled. Not a single person knew what I was going through because no one even came into my room for days while I went through the single worst moment in my life, so don't you dare tell me what I need to do because you don't know the utter emptiness I feel inside and how I can't fill that space." She turned her gaze to Henley and waved her finger at her rounded belly. "You have life growing in you. That space is filled. Mine was taken from me and this morning, I was reminded of… of…" The tears burned her eyes. The searing pain filled her soul. The rage engorged her heart. She wanted everyone in her wake to feel her wrath. She didn't want a single person to go untouched by her fire.

And then the sheer madness of it all wrapped her body like an ice cube in the frozen tundra.

She cupped her face and sobbed.

Strong arms circled her, and Thor whispered something, but she couldn't quite make out the words over her guttural moans. He held her for a long moment, running his hands up and down her arms and back. His lips landed on her temple. More soft words. Sweet words. Loving words.

He was her rock, and he loved her, she knew that with all her heart.

He cupped her face, kissing her lips softly.

When she glanced up and caught his gaze, she saw a combination of sadness and rage behind his soft brown eyes. She knew he struggled to keep that fierce anger in check. But it was that sadness that struck a different chord in her body. A deeper connection.

He understood.

Really understood.

He felt it too. It was different for him. She could see the guilt over not being there to comfort her. To protect her. The anguish over losing his child. The pain over spending twenty-five days not knowing what had happened—to her. She couldn't imagine. That would have killed her in a different way.

In her heart, she'd never truly been alone.

"I'm sorry," she whispered.

"You have nothing to be sorry about." Thor ran his

thumbs across her cheeks. That seemed to be his mantra lately. "Do you want me to stay while you talk with Henley?"

"Not this time, but maybe we should schedule one before we leave."

"Sounds like a good plan." He kissed her nose. "I'll see you back at the cabin." He hugged her tight, as if he didn't want to release her, before strolling off down the path, glancing over his shoulder a couple of times.

Henley perched herself on the log and said nothing. She sipped her water and waited.

That drove Danni crazy. She could take silence from Tonka, but not from Henley. She didn't know why, and she supposed it didn't matter. She chose to sit on the stump across from Henley, grateful the therapist didn't ask to step into her office. While Danni had made great strides about being inside buildings, she still struggled in small spaces, including not being able to sleep in the bedroom.

She also worried that she might not be able to return to her and Thor's home, to which Thor decided they would look for a new place. Maybe even buy a home. He even offered for them to go back to her parents' house for a bit. It would be hard since he only had so much time before having to be deployed and that meant she'd be alone.

Staying at her parents' might be a good idea.

"So, what did Thor tell you?" Danni asked, staring at the little squirrel house that Tonka had built.

"One thing you can count on from me is honesty." Henley folded her hands in her lap. "He mentioned how you talked through your concerns with him over his reaction, or lack of reaction when you first told him and how you were worried he might blame you for the miscarriage. His concern now is he feels you're not dealing with your emotions over the loss. That you're hyper-focused on overcoming panic attacks about small spaces and jumping back into work and life as a couple." Henley cleared her throat. "And he might have mentioned that you could be a little too vigorous in that last part."

"He spoke to you about our sex life?"

"Not in so many words," Henley said.

"Whatever words he used, he shouldn't have done that." She huffed out a puff of air.

"He came to my office at what was supposed to be the end of your session yesterday because he wanted to take you for a hike. When you weren't there, he asked if I had time to talk, so we did. I don't normally tell others what was said in a session, but he's given me permission and if he were here, he'd say it."

"I'm afraid he and I will have words later."

"Maybe." Henley nodded. "Thing is, Thor would do anything for you and he's at a total loss for what you need, and that's hard for him because he's felt like for your whole life, he's always known exactly what you need, even when you weren't a couple. He knows he loved you long before he accepted that emotion. He had feelings for you when you kissed him that first time." Henley smiled. "I remember exactly when he told me about that kiss at your high school graduation." She touched her lips as if she had experienced it for herself.

"He told me it was the single most powerful thing that had ever happened to him and that it stuck with him for two years. That when he'd been shot, it's what he thought about and he worried that if he died, he'd never be able to get back what he might have given up."

Danni laughed. "He's always been a bit of a dork."

"Agreed." Henley smiled, leaning forward. "I'm going to say a few things and I want you to let me finish. Some might sound harsh, but I think this is all important for you to hear so you can heal this part of you. You're one of the strongest women I've ever met here at The Refuge. You have grit, resolve, and fierce determination to get better. You want it. You don't want to be held captive by these demons. You and Thor share that. It's a unique trait." She waved her hand toward the main building. "The men who built this place, they have it too. Some of them, like my Tonka, it took them longer to get there, but that desire to be better, it's there. Yet they have to fight it every day and you know that and because of it, I believe you're holding on to this one piece, perhaps the biggest piece, so that you never forget —never stop feeling—deep in your core what happened. Because once the panic stops, once the sensation of being in a closed room stops, what else is there?" Henley lowered her chin. "And then there is that empty feeling you have. The piece of Thor that was stolen from you and now you desperately want that back. Being with him isn't enough. You're trying to replace that and this morning your hopes of doing that were gone."

Danni gasped. "Are you trying to tell me that in the

last couple of days, I was trying to get pregnant again? That's crazy."

"It's not crazy," Henley said softly. "Not only did you lose something precious, but you also had to do that alone and in the worst of conditions. It's normal to try to fill that void by any means possible. But it becomes a problem when we do it as a way to avoid and that's what Thor's concerned about. Honestly, so am I. I've seen the way you work through things logically in group. I've watched you push through panic attacks. I've helped you tackle tough emotions when it comes to some of your rage. But holding this so close to your heart is only going to be the thing that keeps you from truly healing all of yourself." Henley held her gaze. "What is keeping you from honestly opening this door and allowing yourself to feel all of it? To share all of your feelings with anyone, whether that be me or Thor?"

Danni swallowed. Hard. "I don't know what else there is to share. I lost the one thing I wanted more than life. More than Thor. I wanted to die after I lost my baby and there's nothing I can do to change what happened." She swiped at her cheeks. If she said exactly what she was thinking, her entire world would flip upside down.

"Danni, you're holding back on me," Henley said softly. "You can't deal with this demon unless you face it. There is no judgment here. This is a safe place. All I want is to help you get to the other side."

"You don't understand." Danni's heart hammered in her chest, gripped in panic. "My entire adult life has been about chasing down this story. Thor has said a million times my passion is why he loves me, but if I had never pursued this story so hard, I would have never been targeted, and that's what happened. They came after me. They planned this attack. They were watching me. They waited until Thor was deployed and snuck into my home and took me. Thor can say he doesn't blame me for what happened, and maybe right now he doesn't, but he will. How could he not? I brought them to our doorstep and let them destroy everything. How can Thor ever look at me the same again?"

"Is that what you really believe?"

"Yes. No. I don't know." Danni raised her hands and then slapped them on her thighs. "It's crazy talk because my heart tells me otherwise. He shows me every day how much he loves me." She wiggled her ring finger. "He went out and bought me this the second say we were here. He's so thoughtful and I'm the luckiest woman in the world to have him, but I'm terrified I'm going to lose him." She sighed. "First, I thought it was because he hadn't wanted the baby, but then he showed me how heartbroken he was over it, and I wish I hadn't pushed him to do that. Now, I fear if I don't give him another baby, the blame will fester in him, and it will come crashing down and it will be all my fault." Her eyes burned, but no more tears fell. The well had dried up. The words had been said. The emotions had been purged.

The work was far from over.

She was broken in ways she wasn't sure she could recover from and admitting that didn't feel good—but it didn't feel bad either. Actually, it was freeing.

"This isn't your fault," Henley said. "No more than it's Thor's fault that you were kidnapped." She cocked her head. "And if you think for one second that thought doesn't cross his mind every second of every day, you're sorely mistaken."

"How on earth could that be his fault?"

"He left," Henley said matter-of-factly. "He didn't take things more seriously. He didn't have Tim check up on you more diligently. I could name ten more reasons, and while they wouldn't change anything and none of them are valid, he beats himself up over them. He knows logically, it wouldn't change anything, but it doesn't stop him from slamming his fist on my desk and getting angry at himself."

"Seriously?"

Henley nodded. "You have to know Thor doesn't want to change you. We've all watched him fall in love with you. He's come here after missions where he's lost men, or things went to shit, and he needed to clear his head so he didn't bring that crap back to you. While he was here, he'd talk about his amazing Danni and her drive and determination. He'd tell us how proud he was of you and all the work you'd done with your articles. How you were going to write a book. The things that you believe got you to this horrible point are the very things that he admires most. He doesn't and couldn't ever blame you, Danni. And you can't blame yourself. What happened to you is terrible. I'm so sorry for your loss. I have no doubt that you will work through the grief. I'm here for you."

"Is it bad that I want to try for another baby right away?"

"No." Henley shook her head. "But I do think that's a conversation you need to have with Thor."

"I'm sorry I've avoided you."

"You're not the first one." Henley laughed. "It happens more than you think."

"It wasn't you, so please don't take it personally."

"I never do." Henley stood, smoothing down the front of her top, showing off her belly.

"Are you feeling the baby move?"

"I am." Henley nodded, smiling weakly. "All the time now."

"Can I feel?"

"If you'd like."

Tentatively, Danni stood, inching closer. She placed her hand over Henley's stomach and waited. A few seconds later, her belly danced. "Oh my." Her lips curved upward. "That's amazing."

"It is pretty wild."

Danni tilted her gaze. "Thank you."

"For what?"

"Letting me feel life again."

## 18

*F*our days later, Thor was on an airplane from New Mexico back to Delaware. He hated leaving the safety of The Refuge. Besides not feeling as though Danni was ready, even though she'd given everything she had to heal herself—and them— her mental state was still weak, and he wished she had agreed to stay a little longer, but he understood her desire to be with her family.

But with him and his team having to report to the base for a few days, he would have preferred her to stay where he knew she would be protected.

Thankfully, Brick and Pipe had the time and the ability to come to Delaware. He hadn't asked for their services, but he wouldn't say no. Danni needed protection. Christopher was still out there—somewhere— waiting to strike. He knew that.

The flight was uneventful. Danni didn't have a single panic attack, though she was on edge. She constantly looked over her shoulder as if Christopher was going to jump out from a corner and kidnap her again.

He'd asked both parents not to meet them at the airport. He thought that might be too much commotion, so he rented a car service for him, Danni, Brick, and Pipe.

"Are you okay?" He squeezed Danni's thigh as they pulled into the neighborhood.

"I don't know why I'm so nervous." She stared out the window. "I've spoken to my mom and dad numerous times on the phone. Same as your parents. But I'm terrified I'm going to break down. I don't want to do that. I'm tired of doing that."

"It's going to be emotional, that's for sure." Boldly, he took her chin with his thumb and forefinger. "Remember what Henley said. They experienced something too. Far different from what you did, but it was hard on them."

"I know. I can't imagine what they suffered worrying about me. I hate that they went through that."

"You're always concerned with everyone else." He arched a brow. "Don't use that to—"

"Thor, I'm not. I'm honestly past doing that. Really, I am. It's just that I know our mothers and they will cry and be all weird. I don't know if I can deal with that. I know it's selfish, and while I know I need to feel everything, I can't deal with them sometimes. Yesterday, my mother started sobbing on the phone. It was all I could do not to start yelling at her to shut up. I got so angry, and I did bottle it because it wouldn't have been fair to unleash it on her, but she was being ridiculous. Like when I had a concussion and she wouldn't stop checking on me. I swear, when we become parents, I will not be like her."

Thor bit down on his tongue and did his best not to laugh, but a soft chuckle rumbled in his chest and rolled into his throat. "I'm sorry, babe, but you're already a little like Alice."

"I am not." Danni folded her arms. "I love my mother, but she's overbearing and insanely overprotective. Did you know that she told me the dress I wore to my high school graduation would get the attention of the wrong kind of man and that it was childish of me to even try to use that to get you to see me."

Thor couldn't stop the fit of laughter now if he tried. He tossed his head back and roared.

"And why is that so funny?"

He cleared his throat. "Your mother wasn't entirely wrong. If all I saw was the body in the dress, I'd be the wrong man." He leaned in and kissed her cheek. "It wasn't the dress, Danni. It was you. It's always been you."

"I looked hot in that dress."

"Not denying that." He winked. "Then again, you look hot in anything."

"That might get you laid tonight."

He rolled his eyes. "What is it with you and doing it in your parents' house?"

"Maybe it's because that's the first place we had sex." She shrugged. "Or maybe it's because I like watching you blush having coffee next to my dad and his shotgun the next morning." She rested her head on his shoulder as they turned into the driveway. "Thanks for getting a second car for Brick and Pipe. I like them both, but I wish it could have been Tonka who came. He's got a special place in my heart."

"I think he feels the same way about you, but he couldn't leave Henley and their other kid. Brick and Pipe are good men. You'll barely know they're here, other than you will be protected and safe while I'm gone." He let out a heavy breath. "I wish I didn't have to leave you while he's still out there. But it's not a deployment and since we're getting married next week, the Navy is giving me a little more time off."

"I know it's not the wedding we planned, but I don't want to wait. Your team, our closest friends, and our family will be there. I just wish Tonka and Henley could have come."

"I do too." He kissed her nose. "It will be a special day."

"But no real honeymoon," she whispered.

"We'll do that when Christopher is behind bars. I promise you."

She glanced up. "I'm sorry. I shouldn't have said that because I honestly don't care about that anymore. I just want to feel safe again, and I can't until he's been caught."

Thor shifted in the seat as the vehicle rolled to a stop in front of Danni's childhood home. "I can have Brick and Pipe take you back to The Refuge. I know I'd feel better if you were there."

"No." Danni shook her head wildly. "I refuse to live

my life in fear. We don't know how long this will take. It could be days, or it could be weeks or even months. I can't hide there forever." She palmed his cheek. "I spoke with both Henley and Alaska at length before I left. They both agree that perhaps working on my book might be cathartic for me, and Henley said I can call her anytime I feel I need to talk through tough emotions. Tonka even offered."

Thor chuckled. "When I first met that man, he barely spoke to humans. He'll be a great…" Thor's smile faded. His eyes filled with sadness. "I'm happy for them."

"But you're sad for us."

"I am." He nodded. "But we're still young and you have an appointment in a couple of days with your old doctor here. I'm sure everything is okay with you, and we can try for another baby when all of this is over."

Danni sighed. "I don't want to wait. I know Henley believes we need time to process and maybe that's true. Maybe I am trying to fill the emptiness that's been left behind after everything that's happened, but lots of other people try quickly after having a miscarriage."

"I'm not opposed to trying again." He kissed her softly. "I just want you to see a doctor. I need to know you're okay."

"All right," she agreed.

A tap at the door startled him. He turned his head to see Brick and Pipe standing outside the car. "Come on. I'm sure our parents are standing by the door dying to hug you."

"I'm so ready to see them, but not ready for their tears."

He took her hand and helped her from the vehicle.

"Something doesn't feel right," Brick said, glancing around. "I know you mentioned that everyone would wait inside, which I don't understand, but my hackles are up."

Thor reached in his back pocket and pulled out his cell. "I texted our parents when we landed. I got a normal response. And like I said before, I didn't want them storming the car and I've asked them to give us a little space as we enter. Danni's still—"

"I'm fine," she interrupted, squeezing his hand. "They all went through something too. I don't have the right to take away those feelings from them just because I still struggle to be confined in a small space or panic over the thought of people coming at me all at once. They're my parents and future in-laws. They aren't going to hurt me."

"We should do a sweep," Pipe said. "Check everything out."

"I gave my dad a code word if anything was wonky. He didn't use it." Thor waved his cell. "You two can walk the perimeter of both houses. I'll do a check of Alice and Nick's place once inside. I'll get you the keys to my parents' place, which is where you'll be crashing anyway. We'll regroup after that."

"Okay." Brick nodded with his hands on his hips as he continued to scan the cul-de-sac. The man was almost always on high alert. He and the men at The Refuge had been through some shit—both in the military and lately in civilian life. Brick was a kind and decent man—but a deadly one too. He would do whatever it took to protect those he called family.

Somehow, Thor and his team had become just that —family.

He valued and appreciated those relationships and would walk through fire for those men and their loved ones. Not out of obligation—because Thor didn't do obligation anymore. That was a wasted emotion in his book. It tied you to someone in such a way that only led to resentment and bad judgment. Thor would do anything for Brick and the people at The Refuge because he cared about them the same way he cared about his parents, Danni's parents, and Danni.

They had become part of who he was as a man. They had shaped him, saved him, and more importantly, they believed in him.

"You ready?" He kissed Danni's temple.

"Let's do this." Danni tugged at his hand and walked slowly, at first, toward the front door. By the time they were halfway up the stone path, she was running.

Her mother, Alice, flung open the wood door and held open her arms. Danni jumped into them, tears flying from her eyes like rain pouring from the skies. But they were happy tears and Thor let out a long sigh of relief.

He'd brought Danni home.

His father slipped past Alice and Nick, who were both hugging their daughter, while his mom stood in the background, cupping her cheeks, smiling and crying.

"Hey, son." His dad rested a strong arm on his shoulder. "It's good to have you both home."

"It's damn good to be here." He wrapped his arms around his old man like a small child and hugged him—hard. They had never been the touchy-feely kind of father and son, but Thor had never lacked for attention. His dad had always been there for him. He helped coach his hockey teams and offered sound advice on anything and everything, including Danni—especially Danni.

Thor would be lost without the love and support of his parents.

His dad gripped his forearms and took a step back. "This has been a long, hard road. But I feel as though we are all back on track now."

"We're getting there." He glanced over at Danni, who wiggled and squirmed, trying to break free from the death grip the moms now had on her.

Danni glanced over her shoulder with wide eyes.

Thor raced to her side. "Give her some room," he said softly, not wanting to startle anyone, but he could tell Danni was close to a full-on panic attack. Kudos to her for doing her best at keeping it at bay, but as he curled his fingers around her biceps, he noticed her chest heaved up and down as she struggled for breath. "Do you want to step outside?"

"No," she whispered. "Can we go into the family room, please? And can I have some water?"

"I'll get that," Nick said.

Alice and Thor's mom took a step back, confusion etched in both of their faces.

237

"She just needs a little space." Thor nodded.

"I'm sorry," his mom said. "I momentarily forgot all you said because I'm just so excited that... that..." His mom hiccupped.

"It's okay, Helene," Danni said. "I hate being this way." She smoothed her shaky hands down her jeans, and with her head held high, heaving in deep calming breaths, she made her way past everyone and into the family room.

Thor couldn't have been prouder.

"At The Refuge, after group sessions, people often approach and hug. I struggled with that. Henley, the therapist, told me it's because for those twenty-five days, I had almost no human contact, and what little I did— well, it was fear-based. I don't want you to think I'm afraid of you, because I'm not. It's just this sense of being surrounded with no way out."

"Sweetheart, we understand." Nick handed his daughter a glass of water.

Just then, Brick and Pipe entered the family room sporting all business faces.

"Everyone, this is Brick and Pipe. They are two of the owners at The Refuge."

"Oh my. It's so nice to finally meet you," his mother exclaimed. "We've heard so much about you and The Refuge over the years from Thor. We can't thank you enough for all that you've done."

Brick nodded. He was a proud man, and he reveled in how much what he'd created with his buddies could do to help those in need. But he was also a humble man. "I'm glad The Refuge was there to serve," he said softly. "However, I need to discuss some things with Thor."

Thor stiffened his spine. The timbre of Brick's voice sent a shiver across Thor's skin. "Why don't we go into the kitchen," he said.

"Is something wrong?" Danni asked with a shaky voice. "If there is, I want to know about it. Being in the dark would be worse than not knowing. I can't handle that."

"We don't know there's anything wrong—yet," Pipe said in his British accent that could calm anyone, but looking at the man would terrify most. It was one of the reasons Thor was grateful Pipe had volunteered to come. However, of all the men at The Refuge, Danni hadn't warmed up to him. She much preferred Tonka over all of them. He was the only one she didn't back away from immediately. The one she felt free to talk about her feelings and felt safe with. "However, we have a… concern."

"If that's the case, we'd all like to know about it," Thor's dad said.

"We're all on edge." Nick inched closer to Danni, wrapping a protective arm around his daughter. "The man who kidnapped Danni is still out there and what scares us all the most is that it's radio silence. The FBI agent in charge of this case—Raymond Olander—he's told us that he doesn't have a single lead on where that man has gone. It's like he's vanished. Most of his disciples have gone underground as well and no one is talking. Those damn compounds are locked up tight since the initial searches after they found Danni and according to him, without some kind of lead or tip, he has no reason to keep hounding them, though he says he's been sending agents to each one every day and keeps coming up with nothing."

"We've been keeping up with what they've been doing," Brick said. "Dina and Lois Snow, both former CIA agents, along with their three sons, who are former Delta Force, have contacts in places Raymond doesn't. So do we, but he's right about one thing. It's radio silence and if I'm being totally honest about that—it makes all of us more than nervous."

Danni sank into the sofa, clutching her water glass. It wasn't as if she hadn't heard all this before. Thor had made a promise that he'd been honest, and he'd been painfully truthful about everything. He worried it hindered her progress with her own PTSD, but Henley assured him that it was okay for her to know. That she needed to know. Keeping her in the dark could be more damaging to her psyche than knowing the truth about what she possibly faced.

Especially with Thor having to report for duty and there was no avoiding that—unless he wanted to be court-martialed.

That wasn't an option.

He couldn't help her if he was in a military prison.

Needing to be near Danni, he sat on the edge of the couch and took her hand. She shoved her father to the other side of the sofa and yanked Thor closer, practically sitting in his lap.

"Brick, please tell us what's bothering you," she said softly. Her leg rattled. She set the water glass on the table and lifted her finger to her mouth, nibbling on her nail. Her nerves were frazzled, but she was determined, and Thor could see her resolve shining through.

"When we drove into the neighborhood I noticed work vans," Brick said.

"I saw them." Thor nodded. "One was parked at the front gate. It was an internet company. I noted the logo. It's the same one that everyone uses in this hood. The second one was for the local electric company parked around the corner."

"At first glance, it might not seem odd," Pipe added. "But we didn't see any workers lurking around, so I called Ry back at The Refuge. I asked her to open her computer and investigate work orders placed in this area." Pipe lifted his phone. "She got back to me when we were doing our sweep and there are none."

"Shit," Thor mumbled, holding Danni a little tighter as she trembled in his arms. "This might be a dumb question, but how does Ry know anything about computers or how to find that out?"

"That's a long story, mate, and not what's impor- tant right now," Pipe said. "I've asked her, much to Tiny's dismay, to hack into both home's security systems. She's doing that as we speak, among other things. This girl is ridiculously talented in what she can do behind a screen that it's a little terrifying. It's got Tiny on edge. He's standing over her, watching her every move."

"Ry saved Jasna and aided in so many other things. Her lie about her name is immaterial at this point." Brick let out a long breath. "Whatever she can do with that computer of hers to help us find this asshole, I honestly don't care how she does it."

"I'm not arguing that point," Pipe said. "Once she's into the system, we'll be able to not only monitor both systems remotely, but she'll be able to see if they've tampered with anything."

"That's it, I'm not going back to the base. I don't care what happens. The Navy can—"

"No," Brick said sternly, interrupting Thor. "No rash decisions that will jeopardize your career. We have your back and you'll only be gone for a few days."

"You wouldn't leave if this were Alaska." Thor stood, puffing out his chest.

"I'm not still in the military and I would if I was facing a court-martial and if I had an entire team willing to stand in my place." He lowered his chin. "Besides, we don't know anything yet."

Pipe's phone blared. "It's Ry," he said. "I'll put it on speaker." He tapped the screen. "Hey, Ry. You've got me, Brick, Thor, and his family here. Tell me what you know."

"It's not good," Ry said softly. "Someone's watching. I'm working on stopping the feed, but whoever did this, they were good."

"What do mean, watching?" Nick asked.

"Someone hacked the security system and are live streaming the cameras. I did the same. I can see you, but I can't hear you. Well, I can, because we're on the phone."

"You mean someone is watching us right now?" Danni jumped from the sofa, knocking over her water glass as she leaped across the table, tumbling onto the floor, face-planting with a *thud*. She groaned.

Thor and Nick were at her side in a flash, trying to help her to her feet, but she thrashed her arms about, pushing them aside. A combination of panic and anger flared in her eyes as she hobbled to her feet and glared at the phone in Pipe's hand.

"Yes," Ry said.

"We should act as normal as possible." Brick eased into the rocking chair in the corner. "If Ry can't hear us, then neither can whoever else is watching. Ry, don't shut them down. Not yet. Everyone, take a seat and let's just talk as calmly as we can. Danni, I know this is hard. Maybe we can get a message to Henley and get her on the phone to help—"

"No. I'm fine." Danni took a chunk of hair and twisted it through her fingers. "I'll manage." She glanced at Thor. "Really, I'll be okay."

He took her by the hand and guided her back to the sofa and let out a long breath.

Someone was watching.

That someone was fucking Christopher.

"Ry, this Thor. Is it possible to find out where that transmission is going?"

"Yes, but it will take me some time," Ry said. "Whoever this is, they know what they're doing. They are pinging it to various locations across the country. But I could shut it down right now."

"It's too late for that," Pipe said. "Whoever it is knows we're here—knows Danni is here."

"But we could leave." Alice glanced around the

room with a horrified gaze. "We could find a safe place to hide."

Thor turned and stared at Brick and immediately knew what the man was thinking. They'd never been in battle together before, but it didn't matter. They were cut from the same cloth. "No," Thor said. "All that will do is delay the inevitable."

"I don't think I like what you're insinuating, son." Nick stood. "Because it sounds an awful lot like you want to bring this asshole right to my doorstep."

"Nick, he's already here." Thor let out a long breath. "I'm sure they hacked into my system back in Virginia too. They might not have known we were at The Refuge, but they knew we'd surface eventually, and I knew he'd come for her at some point. I'd rather do this battle before I leave." He glanced at his watch. "That means we don't have much time. I'll put out an SOS to my team and they can get here in a couple of hours. That should give us enough time to set up a plan, get mine and Danni's parents to a safe place—"

"Moving them will tip them off," Pipe said. "Ry, what else have you done with that computer of yours?"

"I've really only just begun," Ry said. "I know they started this stream two hours ago. There are cameras in every room."

"That's impossible." Nick shook his head. "I only have cameras on the outside, in the garage, and facing the doors, which are only activated when we are gone."

"Jesus, that means they've been in the house," Thor muttered. He snagged his cell and sent a message to his team, along with one to Ray and Dina. "Moose and the guys will have landed in Virginia a half hour ago. They can charter—"

"I'll get them a plane," Brick said. "But as soon as the sun goes down, we need to be prepared. They've seen us. I'm sure they might suspect we're preparing for battle but let's not give them any ammunition."

"Speaking of which," Nick said. "I'm a bit of a gun nut. I've got a few weapons locked up in a closet in the basement."

"Ry, are there cameras down there?" Brick asked.

"There's one by a door in the hallway, but I don't see anything in a basement," Ry said. "But there could be motion detectors set up to trigger them."

"What else do you keep down there?" Pipe asked.

"I have a wine cellar with some vintage bottles I was saving for the wedding," Nick said. "I could go down there to grab a couple bottles."

"That's a good idea." Brick nodded. "Your daughter returning is reason to celebrate. Ry will tell us if anything triggers, and we'll know if we can use that space to plan."

To Nick's credit, he rose slowly and made his way to the basement door.

"This is impossible," Alice said softly. "I can't act normally. I don't know what to do."

"You're doing just fine," Pipe said reassuringly as he leaned against the doorjamb between the family room and the hallway. "Whoever is watching probably has a good idea that we're on edge now, but that's okay. The key here is that they don't know we'll be ready when they storm."

"I'm sorry, but that doesn't make us feel better," Thor's mother said, clinging to Alice's hand. "You all have done this for a living, and we just got our sweet Danni back. This is all too much."

"Mom, it's going to be okay." Thor knew his words fell flat, but what else was he supposed to say. "I texted Raymond, the FBI agent, along with Dina Snow, the retired CIA agent we mentioned before. Everyone knows what's happening here. We're going to be protected." While he had reached out to both Ray and Dina, he hadn't given Ray the full picture, and both Brick and Pipe knew that because he'd copied them in on the text. While he needed the proper law enforcement present for the arrest, he couldn't have them fucking up whatever plan they put into place. He needed to have that first before the Feds moved in.

"Okay," Ry's voice boomed over the phone. "There's one camera on a motion sensor down there, but it doesn't cover the entire basement. I sent Pipe screenshots of what I could see. I hope that helps. Also, I was able to find out they've hacked into two computer systems. Nick's and Mason's. They have full access to everything on those systems."

"Fuck." Thor raked his fingers across the top of his head. "Can you see what they've accessed?"

"Yes and no," Ry said. "I see browsers and email opened on both computers… oh shit."

"What is it, Ry?" Brick sat up a little taller.

"It looks like they knew Danni was coming home," Ry said. "There's an email from Thor to his dad about that and how he has to head back to the base, but that email stated you're leaving tonight—with Brick and Pipe. Did you do that on purpose?"

"I did." Thor sucked in a deep breath and blinked his eyes slowly, turning his gaze from Danni for a moment.

"How long have you been worried they might be looking at your correspondence?" Danni asked with a hardened tone.

"I didn't know, nor did I suspect." He shifted, facing her glare. "But Jupiter thought lying in any written correspondence might be a clever idea. You know how Jupiter is with all things techie, and he's got mad computer skills. To him, if it's out in the airwaves, it's hackable and available to anyone who wants to find it. He figured if I put anything real out there, it would come back to bite me in the ass. But putting out false information might work to my benefit."

Danni turned and stared at his father. "Did you know anything about this?"

"I knew he lied in that email, and I understood why, but I didn't expect this to be the outcome."

She folded her arms across her chest. "You should have told me," she said in a harsh tone. The same one he'd gotten used to before she'd been taken from him and she'd been pissed at him over something silly like forgetting to mention he'd invited the entire team over for dinner.

His lip twitched into a half smile. It shouldn't, but it did because that was his Danni. "I'm sorry I didn't tell you, but this is why Brick and Pipe are here." Thor arched a brow.

Nick appeared in the family room holding two bottles of wine. "Well, I don't know about any of you, but I sure could take the edge off with one glass."

Brick lifted his cell. "Your team is in the air. Let's take this party to the kitchen while Pipe goes over those images to see if he can get those extra weapons. Ry?"

"Yeah. I'm still here," Ry said.

"Any chance you can find out if those vans are still in the area?" Brick asked.

"Oh, yeah. They are," Ry said. "I've learned a couple more things since you all have been talking and I've been doing my thing."

"We're listening." Pipe held the phone up as everyone shuffled into the kitchen and Nick and Alice went about pulling down wineglasses and opening bottles.

"Okay. I've tracked that the feed is going to one of those vans. The one parked down the street, so whoever is watching is close. Not sure about the second van, though. Could be backup, could be nothing. They're also monitoring the computer, so you could use that to your advantage. Maybe send a message to someone to throw them off."

Pipe sat down on one of the stools in front of the island. He swiped at the screen and then waved Nick over. "Explain to me where these images are in the basement in relation to where the closet is with the guns."

Nick went about pointing and quickly giving Pipe the lowdown. Thor glanced over Pipe's massive shoulder. "We should be able to retrieve them, as long as our backs are up against the wall," he said. "It will be tricky, but if Ry talks you through it as she's watching, it can be done."

"All right." Pipe nodded. "Where's the bathroom?"

"Right across from the basement door," Nick said.

"Ry, do you think you could cause static or something on one of the cameras?" Pipe asked. "I don't want to make them too nervous, but something that would give me just enough time to get across the hallway and into—"

"Oh my God," Ry said. "I don't know why I didn't think of it before, but I could do a loop for maybe five minutes. If everyone sits in one spot and drinks and chats, I could play that over and over for a few minutes. It can't be too long and there can't be too many sudden movements."

"Why do I get the feeling I've seen that somewhere before," Alice said.

"Because it's in that movie *Speed* you love so much." Nick chuckled. "We can do that."

"Pipe," Ry said. "You'll need to be in the bathroom. I'll tell you when you can leave. Everyone else sit down. I'll record for five minutes. Someone set a timer. We'll have to make sure that when I reboot, you are all doing exactly the same thing as when I started. So, the beginning will be doing nothing but with your hands around your glass. That will be for the first thirty seconds. The last thirty seconds will be the same. Because I will be on the phone with Pipe, you won't have anything but that timer to go by. It's got to be precise."

"We got it, Ry," Brick said. "Everyone get ready."

"It will start as soon as Pipe is out of the frame. He'll be able to yell at you to start that," Ry said.

Pipe nodded as he headed down the hallway.

"Okay, Pipe. You're out of the frame."

"Start the timer," Pipe called.

"Go," Ry said.

Pipe disappeared and Thor was left with his heart in his throat. He'd done countless missions that had him doing some crazy things, but none of them prepared him for this one.

## 19

*F*ive minutes ticked by... and it was the longest five minutes of Danni's life.

If they screwed this up, she had no idea what might happen. They all sat around that kitchen, not talking about much of anything, making no sudden movements, and doing their best to ensure the last thirty seconds matched the first.

Her breath flew out of her lungs when Pipe appeared—though he didn't have the weapons. Ry's voice boomed over the phone, letting them know that all appeared good, whatever that meant.

"Everyone, you should know that the van has moved to the end of the cul-de-sac," Ry said.

"How do you know that?" Nick asked.

"GPS systems have trackers, and they are using theirs so I'm tracking them," Ry said softly, as if what she was doing wasn't the greatest thing since sliced bread. "They've stopped four houses away. I think the other van is right behind them, but I can't be sure."

"Why do you say that?" Thor asked.

"I'm hacking into their system. It's taking a little doing, but I'm... wait a second... yes... there it is. I'm in," Ry said. "Holy shit."

"What is it, Ry?" Pipe asked.

"They are using a computer to text and I'm able to read it," Ry said. "I'm going to screenshot it and send it to you."

Pipe swiped at his screen and then glanced up. "The email that you sent said you were leaving tonight at seven, right?"

Thor nodded.

"And your car is at your parents' house?" Pipe asked.

"I left it here when I flew to Utah when we learned that's where Danni was being held, why?" Thor asked.

Danni grabbed his hand. "Can you please just spit out whatever's going on?"

Pipe set his cell on the table. Danni leaned over and glanced at the screenshot that appeared.

*The bomb has been planted in the car. He won't get out alive. We can snatch the girl as soon as it explodes.*

She gasped, covering her mouth.

Thor had the nerve to laugh.

"It's not funny." She glared.

"No, it's not, but we can use that." He tapped his fingers on the counter. "Ry, can you see inside my parents' garage?"

"I can," Ry said.

"Shit," Thor mumbled. "I don't want it to go off inside my parents' house, but if I can find out what kind of bomb it is or where the trigger is, I can have it go off down the street and they can think they've killed me."

"Are you crazy?" Danni lifted her wineglass and gulped. "That's about the most insane thing I've ever heard."

"Not really," Brick said. "But if they can see inside that garage, they will see you trying to figure out where that bomb is and if they're smart, which we know they are, it will either be a starter trigger, setting it off the second you hit the ignition, or they will have the trigger in their hands."

"So, set it off in my house." His dad raised his drink and shrugged. "It's just a house. We can fix a house."

"Now that's crazy." Thor shook his head. "A bomb would do a ridiculous amount of damage."

"Yeah, but it would control when they come to us, and we'd be prepared." Pipe glanced at his watch. "Your team will be here by the time you said you'd leave. We can communicate with them while they are in the air and en route on what we need. We can pull Raymond and the Feds into the plan as we need them. We might even be able to contain the blast."

"Oh my God." Danni reached for the bottle and poured more wine. "I can't even listen to this because someone—Thor—has to be in or near that car to set the bomb off. He'll be injured or, worse, die. I'm not letting you do this."

"Babe—"

"Don't fucking babe me." She took a large sip of her wine with a shaky hand before turning and glaring. Her nerves were fried. The fear she'd felt for twenty-five days bubbled in her throat. But the sheer terror of losing Thor tormented her soul. "It's a bomb. A goddamn bomb."

"Hang on," Ry said. "If the trigger is remote, I might be able to find it."

"How?" Brick said with an amused look on his face. "Bombs aren't that high-tech. They're made of C4 and they go boom."

"Yes, but if there is a remote switch that triggers it from a separate location, that's digital, and that can be hacked. Anything digital can be hacked," Ry said.

"My God, is there anything you can't do?" Pipe asked.

"Yes," Ry said. "Give me a few minutes."

"Please don't do this," Danni pleaded before turning to Mason, Thor's father. "You can't let him blow himself up with your home."

Mason reached across the counter and took her hand. "If I thought for one second he was walking into a suicide mission, I'd stop him."

"But your home?" Danni stared at Mason with tears in her eyes.

"It's just a house that can be replaced." He smiled weakly. "We thought we lost you, but here you are. We won't take the chance of losing you or him ever again. Whatever it takes to make sure that happens, we'll gladly do it. Right, Helene?"

"That's right." Helene nodded. "Even if it means blowing up… I can't believe I'm saying that, but yes."

"You people have all lost your marbles." Danni

dropped her head to the counter. How could this be happening?

"Okay," Ry said. "I'm sorting through a bunch of their messages and computer stuff. I've got a few other things in front of me... and there... oh, that's interesting."

"What, Ry?" Brick asked.

Danni jerked up tall. She swallowed her pulse.

"Well, I've got information on the bomb," Ry said. "It's set on a three-minute timer from ignition. No remote trigger."

Thor ran a hand over his mouth. "That wouldn't get me past their van. It's barely enough time to get out of the driveway."

"That's probably the point," Brick said. "What's in that garage?"

"Three cars. Mine, my mom's SUV, and my dad's sports car. Mine's on the far right. All backed in, making this slightly easier." Thor placed his hand on her shoulder.

She tensed, shrugging it off. It wasn't that she didn't appreciate the gesture, she did, but when her heart raced like this, when she fought her demons this hard, being touched actually hurt.

Thor sighed, but he backed off. "Ry, can you hack into my parents' smart home pod and make sure the lights in the garage don't go on when I step into the space or open the garage? My dad's got the lights out there set up on a motion detector."

"I can do that," Ry said. "I'm on it, but it won't

make you invisible, not when it's still light outside and some will filter through that window on the door."

"Maybe we can create a diversion." Thor waved his cell. "The Snow brothers are twenty minutes out. I was shocked to get their message. I had no idea they decided to hightail it down here earlier today, but I won't say no to their help."

"Janelle's husband is on his way here?" Danni had interviewed Janelle for a follow-up piece she'd done on a different religious group and her story had made the hair on the back of Danni's neck stand on edge. However, the woman's courage to come forward and put an end to her father's crazy cult was nothing short of amazing.

Not to mention her willingness to help Krista in her time of need. But it hadn't gotten Krista's brother out of the cult—not yet anyway.

"Read the text." Thor pushed his phone across the counter. "You'll get a kick out of it."

She tapped the screen and pulled up Phoenix's name.

**Phoenix:** *My wife is literally boot-kicking me and my brothers out of the house. She told me if I didn't get my sexy ass down to Delaware, she'd go instead. Now, my wife's a badass, but she's about to pop with, good Lord, a second set of twins, so yeah, you're stuck with me.*

Danni smiled, chuckled, and then sighed, trying to cover a gut-wrenching… she wasn't sure what was about to bubble into her throat, but she was tired of all the negative feelings over everyone who had the good fortune of being pregnant—especially Janelle.

Thor leaned in and kissed her cheek. "We'll get there, babe. We'll be done with this craziness tonight. We're getting married next weekend, and we can start on... well, you know," he whispered.

God, she loved that man.

"Thing is," Thor said loudly, "those goons out there don't know who the Snow boys are and all we need is one or two of them to get in the way. Stop and ask for directions. Be a pain in the ass for less than two minutes so I can rig the accelerator, slip under my mom's SUV, and watch my brand-new truck burn safely in the middle of the cul-de-sac."

"I can't believe I'm going to ask this." Danni heaved in a deep breath. "But then what?"

Thor growled. It was deep, low, and it made her shiver.

"What on earth was that?" she glared.

"He's reacting to the part of the plan he knows is inevitable but is still trying to figure out how to change." Brick waggled his finger. "Everyone has to come running out of the house. We need them to try to take you again. It's the only way."

"Why?" Helene asked. "Why can't they just arrest who's out there?"

"Because we don't know if Christopher is in that van." Thor took Danni's hand and squeezed, hard. "It's possible he's sent others to do his bidding. If that's the case, we can't prove they did anything wrong."

"But what about that Ry girl and all that hacking she did?" Thor's mom waved her hand over the counter.

"What she did was highly illegal and wouldn't stand

up in a court of law, I'm afraid," Pipe said. "If Christopher is out there, it's game over. We take him down. If he's not, we take those suckers out of the equation and we use them to find out where Christopher is. "

"One thing I did learn during my time there is that the security people don't seem to be followers," Danni said.

"I would bet that if those people out there aren't devote, they will roll over on that jerk to save their own asses." Thor squared his shoulders. "Where are those weapons?"

"In the bathroom," Pipe said. "It will be tricky to hide a weapon on you."

"My rucksack is in the hallway. I'll manage to get something in there. The hard part will be getting it out while I'm making a mad dash for it without being seen, and I don't think using the Snow brothers to cause a diversion is a good one. I'm going to have to fly under the radar on this, literally."

Danni glanced at the time, taunting her from the stove. "I need a word with Thor before all this takes place."

"We don't have much time," Brick said. "We need to have our own discussion with him and the team."

"Come on." She hopped off the stool and tugged Thor into her father's den, closing the door, being careful not to search for the hidden cameras. "What if something goes wrong? What if you can't make it out of the car? Or they storm the house before you even get the chance to try? What if Ry has the bomb thing all wrong and it goes off the second you hit the ignition button?" She exhaled before heaving in another breath. She had a million more questions, but they all had the same possible answer.

Thor would be dead, and she would never have the chance to be his wife—much less the mother to his children.

All this would have been for nothing.

Thor inched closer. He cupped her face, tilting his head, and kissed her, hard. It was the kind of kiss that reminded her how much he loved her—but it didn't make any of her fear dissipate.

She fisted his shirt, gripping it tightly, pounding her hand into his chest. Tears welled in her eyes.

He dropped his forehead to hers and sighed. "I know you cry every single time I'm deployed," he whispered.

She gasped.

His strong fingers danced up and down her back. "I wanted so many times to tell you that it was okay to do it in front of me or while I was walking out the door, but it was Brick who said to me one day while I was at The Refuge that I should let it be. That you most likely didn't want me to see those tears because deep down, they weren't about your fears of what might happen to me because you absolutely accepted who I was—am—as a Navy SEAL. That it all came with the territory of being in love with me, so I said nothing and I let you deal with my deployments your own way." He dug his fingers deep into her muscles. "Much like I had to deal with leaving you and coming home on my terms and you never once asked me to change that. But now that you're expressing—quite loudly—your fears, I'm going to address them."

"Do I want hear this?"

"Probably not." He pulled her to his chest, resting his chin on the top of her head. "Every single mission I go on, I worry I might not return. I have Moose pick me up so I can write you a new letter on the way to the base."

"What?" She tilted her head.

He held her gaze. "I give the letter to a girl who works in the administration building. I tell her that if I don't make it back alive, she's to make sure you get that envelope. Every single time I hand it to her, she glares at me like I've grown ten heads and tells me that she hopes she never has to meet you, and I better return so she can rip that sucker up." Thor chuckled, shaking his head. "I believe she gets half a dozen letters a day from men like me and I don't want to think about the ones she's delivered. What I do is dangerous, but what you must know, trust, and believe, is that me and the boys—we're damn good at what we do. I'm not being arrogant, and I don't say that lightly. I know that on any given day, I could die. I've been shot. I've been in a helicopter crash. And I've had good men die in my arms. I know what's at stake, even if me and the boys poke fun at it sometimes. We have to do that or we'd go crazy. I've loved you for longer than I knew I was in love with you. I'd give up being a Navy SEAL if you asked me to."

"Thor, that's not what—"

He hushed her with his finger. "I know." He nodded. "I'm just saying that if it ever got too much, you're always more important to me than a job. However, right now, it's my skill set that will get us out of this mess and I need you to trust me, even if it feels like I'm doing the most insane thing in the world." He arched a brow. "What I need to know is if you're going to be okay with the plan once it's executed. It means you'll have to run into the danger, not away from it or hide from it."

She blew out a heavy puff of air and nodded. "I want my life—our life—back. Yes, I can do this. My parents will be with me… Brick… that massive, tattooed man, Pipe will be nearby. That alone should make me feel safe." She smiled. "You know, he's kind of cute."

Thor chuckled before pressing his lips against hers and God, he tasted so good.

A knock at the door startled her and she jumped.

"Thor, we to talk strategy." Pipe's voice echoed through the door.

"I'll be right out." Thor stared lovingly into her eyes. "Are you going to be okay?"

"Yeah. I'm good," she said. Well, she was as good as she would ever be considering the circumstances.

---

## 20

*E*very mission came down to a few key things. Timing, planning, the people…

But two always stuck out in Thor's mind—what you controlled and what you didn't. Thor and his men were a well-oiled machine. He knew exactly what they would do—before they did it. He understood what they were thinking, without looking at them. If things went to shit —like they often did—and their backup plan fell apart, Thor knew intuitively that his men would do exactly what he expected. On the rare chance they didn't, Thor could pivot, following their lead, improvising alongside his men, because that's what they did.

However, this was different. This was personal.

He stood at the side door of his future in-laws' house, cupping Danni's cheeks and staring into her beautiful, loving eyes. "Everyone's in place. Remember to do your best to act like you think I blew up in that car and stay as close to Pipe as you can. Hold on to his arm as you race outside. We'll move quickly once they show their face, and we know exactly who and how many we're dealing with."

She blinked and gave him a short nod. "Be safe, Thor, and I love you with everything I am."

"I love you, too, babe, and please, whatever you do, listen to Pipe and don't take matters into your own hands." He cocked a brow.

"I would never." She pursed her lips.

"Time to go, mate." Pipe stepped into the hallway. "No reason to push this off any longer."

"Take good care of my Danni." Thor stared at Pipe. He was an intimidating specimen of a man, but deep down, he had a heart of gold.

"You know I will." Pipe nodded. "Your dad and Brick will walk you across the lawn. Moose and Jupiter will have eyes on you, and everyone else has eyes on either the house or the vans."

"What about Ray?" Thor asked.

"Still in the dark, and he's with Dina about ten miles away. She's in contact with her boys, so she'll know when to tip him off." Pipe shuffled him down the hallway where his dad and Brick stood with pensive faces. Pipe opened the side door. "Keep your head down, mate."

Thor swallowed his pulse and focused solely on the plan—on what he could control and that was doing his fucking best to get that car out of the garage without killing himself—then helping his buddies surround a bunch of assholes without a single bullet flying.

If they did have to pull the trigger, he hoped only the enemy suffered.

He hugged Alice, then his mother, just like he'd done a million times before. He shook Pipe's hand and hugged his future father-in-law before stepping out into the evening air. His heart felt heavy in his chest. Heavier than when Danni had been gone—but a different kind of weight.

When his world had stopped, that heaviness had caused paralyzing fear. He couldn't breathe, much less work through even a simple mission.

Not that this was simple, but it wasn't overly complicated either.

This pressure he sensed in his chest was from the responsibility of it all. When he went into war, he was responsible for his men. He was their leader, and it was his job to make the kinds of decisions that made the probability of their safe return greater than zero.

Good men died in battle. It was a reality that Thor had accepted. He had to or he'd never be able to do his job. His men signed on to be Navy SEALs. This, too, was their world.

But his parents, Danni's folks, didn't belong in it, and that's why he had this crushing mass sitting at the center of his chest, making it impossible to shed the extra pounds, to properly compartmentalize the pieces of the mission.

"I don't like my dad coming over here at all," Thor mumbled.

"It would have looked weird if only I did it." Brick kept his gaze forward, never looking over his shoulder. They had eyes everywhere for that. "I've got your dad. You worry about getting out of that truck and staying out of sight during the chaos. All we need is for them to come at us and Ray and his team to cover us when we need them. It's a good plan, Thor. We've got this."

"I just want it over with." He pushed open his parents' side door, adjusting his rucksack. All he had loaded in it was a few random items and one of Nick's rifles. It wasn't his sniper rifle, but it would do the trick. He also had a handgun in a holster on his ankle. "Let's do this." He turned to his dad. "Get in the bathroom." He squeezed his father's shoulder, knowing a camera pointed at them and whoever had hacked the system was watching.

But so was Ry and she was feeding Pipe their every move. She'd tell him exactly what was going on inside that garage, right down to the vehicle rolling into the driveway.

"I love you, son." His dad nodded and quickly disappeared down the hallway, leaving Thor standing there with Brick.

"If anything happens to me, I need you—"

"Nothing's going to happen." Brick gave him the same look that Moose often gave him. It was that look that said, *yeah, I hear you, but get the job done so I don't have to.* "Checking comms," Brick said.

"Reading you loud and clear," Jupiter's voice boomed.

Thor had never been so grateful for Brick and Pipe's preparedness in bringing an extra few earpieces. Otherwise, Thor might have been flying blind, and he hated that. He'd done it before and it sucked. He opened the garage door. He pushed all thoughts of family out of his brain. He'd spent a lifetime training. A lifetime going on one dangerous mission after another—a few of which he shouldn't have come back alive. He knew the drill. He understood the risks.

But it didn't change the facts.

This was *his* family.

This was his turf, and he resented the hell out of this war being dropped in their laps.

He opened the rear passenger door behind the driver's seat and dropped his rucksack, reaching in and grabbing the small weight and rope. He'd had three minutes from the time he started the car to duck, roll, and get his weapon all while making sure the car eased out into the street... slowly. It wasn't an easy task, but it wasn't impossible. He had the tools. Now all he had to do was set it in motion.

Once behind the steering wheel, he reached down and rigged the gas pedal... loosely. He'd tighten it when he was ready to roll. "Hitting the garage button," he said. It hummed to life.

"On your ready," Moose said in his ear.

Thor sucked in a deep breath. He wasn't a bomb tech, but he knew enough about them to know he didn't like them. Not one bit. His finger hovered over the start button. He swallowed hard as he pressed it. The engine roared to life. He put the vehicle in drive, tightened the rope, secured the weight, reached behind the seat, and gripped the rifle, all while mentally counting the seconds that had ticked by.

Quickly, he opened the door, rolled to the cement floor, and slammed the door shut as he took cover under his mother's SUV. He watched his pickup ease into the driveway and into the center of the cul-de-sac. He held his breath and peered over the top of the rifle, searching for movement. "Fifteen seconds to boom, if my calculations are correct."

"We're ready," Moose said.

*Kaboom!*

Thor resisted the urge to move—to race out into the street and protect those he loved from the danger that was certainly heading his way. But the second he showed his face, was the second whoever planted the bomb ran.

Screams and shouting echoed in his ears.

Brick and his father ran past him through the garage.

"Two men slinked from the first van, carrying weapons," Jupiter said. "Three men from the second."

"Let's take these motherfuckers down." Thor rolled and hopped to his feet. "Get my family inside, now."

"On it," Pipe said.

*Pop! Pop! Pop!*

Gunfire erupted from… first from the rooftop and then from everywhere else.

"Where's my dad?" Thor raced through the street. He blinked.

*Pop!*

"Fuck," he muttered as a bullet tore through his shoulder—from behind him. He dropped to the ground and rolled. "I'm hit—someone's behind us."

"I got him in my sights," Jupiter said.

*Bang!*

"Are you okay?" Brick's hand came down on his side as he dragged him behind the fiery blaze.

"Fucking dandy." He glanced at the wound, wincing. "Where'd that asshole come from?"

"Another vehicle," Kawan's voice echoed in his ear. "But we took care of them."

"Good." Thor scanned the area. Bodies lay sprawled out on the pavement.

Pipe raced across the front lawn, glancing over his shoulder, ducking down, dodging left and right, as if danger still lurked in every corner. Nick was right behind him, weapon at the ready.

"We've got a problem, mate." Pipe blew out a puff of air.

"What?" Thor's heart landed in his throat like a brick.

"Ry's still got eyes on the inside of Danni's house." Sirens blared in the distance. "Christopher managed to get by us."

"Who's inside?" Thor asked.

"Just Alice, your mom, and Danni," Pipe said.

"Shit." Thor handed the rifle to his dad. He reached down and checked his handgun before letting out a long breath. "Does anyone have a visual on Christopher?"

"I'm on your parents' roof, and negative," Kawan said.

"I'm in the side yard and I can see Danni, but not him. If someone can get him in front of the window, I can get a shot off," Moose said.

"All right. I'm going in." Thor rolled his neck.

"You're bleeding everywhere." Brick ripped off his

shirt, tore it into pieces, and tied it around Thor's shoulder. "I'll cover the front window. Get one of us a decent shot."

"Or maybe I'll strangle that asshole with my bare hands." Thor marched off toward the front door. It was time to put an end to Christopher.

"Thor," Nick called. "What do you want us to do?"

"We're minutes from having fire trucks and locals here." Thor put some pressure on his wound. "Stay here and deal with them." He turned to Brick. "Help Nick and my dad with that. Pipe, cover me. They could have more firepower out here."

"You got it."

"Let's roll." Thor didn't wait another second; he took off running.

---

Danni held on to her mother for dear life. Watching Thor's truck explode had been too real. It was all she could do to hold it together, but panic surged when Pipe wrapped his arm around her and tossed her like a sack of potatoes back inside the house. She trembled from the inside out. It was as if she were frozen in time—unable to move or speak.

Until she saw *him* slink into her parents' home.

She swiped at her eyes—as if that would make the vision disappear.

But it didn't.

There Christopher stood with a large weapon and a smug grin.

"You can't prevent God's will, Danni," he said, staring at her—and only her. However, he pointed his massive weapon at... Helene, who stared at it with wide eyes as she inched backward, reaching for Danni's hand.

Pipe and her father were outside.

The gunfire had ceased, and it had become eerily quiet. Too quiet. She hated quiet. All it did was remind her of being in captivity, where all she had was the thumping of her heart and the sound of her breath.

"You're mine, Danni. You belong to me and God, and if I have to kill a hundred men to make sure you serve your purpose, I'll do it." Christopher cocked his head.

She tilted her chin. She refused to let the tears come. "Did you kill Thor? His friends? My dad?" she managed.

"I underestimated that so-called man of yours." Christopher laughed. "But I doubt he escaped the car bomb, and if he did, he didn't escape those bullets." He pushed his weapon into Helene's chest.

She gasped.

"So, unless you want me to kill two more innocent people, you'll come with me now, freely and willingly."

The front door flew open, and Thor marched into the family room. "No one is going anywhere with you," he said, holding up his hand. "The cops will be here in less than five minutes. This is your cue to leave." He cocked a brow. "Unless you don't want this one and only chance I'm giving you to get away."

"I'm not walking out that door without what belongs to me." Christopher shifted his weapon.

Danni gasped, covering her mouth.

Thor stepped to the right, his hands still high in the air.

Christopher moved with him. "I have only one regret," he said softly. "That she's going to have to witness me killing you."

"No," Danni screamed.

---

"Stay back, Danni," Thor said harshly.

As Christopher glanced over his shoulder, Thor realized he couldn't wait for him to be lured into full view of the window. He had to take matters into his own hands, and this might be his only shot.

Quickly, he used his good arm to smash the semiautomatic weapon.

*Pop! Pop! Pop!*

Thankfully, the bullets flew past Thor, landing in the wall over his shoulder. He lunged forward, knocking Christopher off-balance and slamming him into the ground. He kicked the weapon out of reach just as Pipe bolted through the front door, panting, waving his weapon, ready to fire.

"Get my mom, Alice, and Danni out of here." Thor stared into the eyes of what could only be described as pure evil. He pinned him down with the full weight of his body, his knee jammed into the man's throat, and cocked his good fist, smacking it into Christopher's cheekbone.

His head twisted, and blood spewed from both his

cheek and his mouth, but the fucking asshole laughed as if to egg Thor on—and it did. All Thor saw was red. He wanted this man dead. He didn't want him to suffer. That was too good for him. He wound up his arm and landed a second punch in the center of Christopher's nose. Thor heard the cartilage crumble under the full force of his blow.

Thor grabbed Christopher by his hair, preparing to slam his head into the wooden floor, but a firm hand touched his shoulder. "Mate, stop." Pipe's voice rattled around in Thor's rage-filled mind. "You're better than this—better than him."

Thor stared at the man who had taken twenty-five days from his life, stolen his child, and ripped away their wedding right from their fingertips. Thor loathed this man. He wanted to destroy him and everything he believed in—and it wouldn't be with his fists. No, he wouldn't do that because the pen was often stronger than the sword.

"You will pay for what you've done in more ways than one." Thor released his grip just as Raymond and his Federal agents stomped into the house and barked orders. Slowly, he rose. The pain in his shoulder registered in his brain.

"Thor!" Danni flung herself at his body, wrapping her arms around his waist.

He groaned, catching her with his good hand.

"Let's get you away from all this," he whispered, pressing his lips to her temple.

Raymond slapped the cuffs on Christopher, who said nothing while they read him his rights.

"Mom? Alice? Are you both okay?" Thor maneuvered through the hallway and out onto the front lawn.

What a bloodbath.

"We're fine," his mother said. "But you're bleeding."

Danni gasped. "Oh no," she said. "Over there's an ambulance. Come on." She tugged at his good arm.

"I hate riding in those things," Thor said.

Moose, Jupiter, Kawan, Sloan, and Lief milled about the front yard, chatting with the local firemen, law enforcement, and a few of the neighbors.

"But you need to be seen by a doctor." Danni ran her delicate fingers up and down his biceps. "And if it were me, you'd be insisting, so I'm... insisting."

"I'm not arguing about going to the hospital, but it doesn't have to be in an ambulance." He waggled his finger.

"Well, you can't go in that." Pipe pointed and laughed but quickly cleared his throat.

Thor sat down on the back of the ambulance and winced as one of the paramedics undid the makeshift tourniquet. He hated getting shot, but the icing on the cake was that he wouldn't have to report for duty, at least not for a bit. He could spend time with his Danni —with his family.

"There's an exit wound," the paramedic said. "We're going to need to—"

"Not my first rodeo, boys. I know the drill—but no drugs. I don't want anything that's going to make me loopy and stupid." He took Danni's hand and kissed it. "She's riding with me."

"Oh my God. Danni?" the paramedic said. "It's been a long time."

"Jeramy?" Danni smiled. "Wow, I haven't seen you since prom and graduation."

Thor glanced between his fiancée and the guy washing out his bullet hole.

"Dude, that's my girl. In fact, we're getting married next weekend, so—"

"You must be the badass Navy boy." Jeramy raised his hands. "I spent that prom date listening to her talk all about you and how one day she would get you to notice her and marry her." Jeramy laughed.

"A man would have to be dead not to notice my Danni." Thor cocked a brow. "You're not dead, so…"

"Wow, he's a possessive one." Jeramy chuckled.

"He can be." Danni squeezed Thor's hand. "It's been a long night."

"I can see that," Jeramy said. "Let's get you both inside. I'll radio the ER. My girlfriend is a resident and is on call tonight. I'll make sure he's seen right away and has the best care."

"Thanks, Jeramy." Danni nodded.

"My pleasure." Jeramy tucked them inside the back of the ambulance before jogging around to the front.

"Thor?" Danni whispered.

"Yeah, babe?"

"I was so scared when your truck exploded."

He opened his mouth, but she hushed him by covering it with her hand.

"And then when the gunfire erupted, but the most terrifying part of the night was when you started hitting

Christopher. I knew you were capable of beating the life out of him."

Thor curled his fingers around her wrist and let out a long breath. "You know I've taken human life before."

"On the battlefield." She nodded. "But that felt different. Maybe it's not, I don't know, because there is a small part of me that wished you had killed him."

He took both her hands and brought them to her lips. "Every decent man or woman is capable of killing and I don't say that lightly. But when everything we hold dear has been threatened and pieces of them have been destroyed or altered, it's not an abnormal response. But Pipe was right. Had I not contained the beast inside— the one that was part created by the career I've chosen and part created by the situation I was put in—I would have regretted it, no matter how justified it might have been."

"Do you think you would have been able to stop yourself had Pipe not intervened?"

"I honestly don't know. I'd like to believe so, but I'm just damn glad he did because that's not something our mothers—or you—needed to see."

She smiled. It melted his heart. "I also didn't need you to go all jealous fiancé on me over my old prom date."

"I remember my parents telling me about that guy and how he was hanging out at your pool and practically groping you all the time. I was too stupid to admit I was jealous ten years ago, but I'm not today." He winked. "You know, the Navy's going to give me a little more time off now because of this bullet hole in my arm and that means we can take our honeymoon." He waggled his brow. "Where do you want to go?"

"Maybe we can go back to The Refuge for a couple of days before heading off, say to Santa Cruz? You know how much I love the wine that comes from that region."

"I do and it sounds like a plan." He winced. "I might need to take some of those drugs I hate so much."

"Lie back and rest." She palmed his cheek. "I love you, Thor."

"I love you, too, babe." He swung his legs back on the gurney and closed his eyes. No matter what happened next, he had *his* Danni.

She was all he'd ever need. She healed his soul, saved his heart, and mended all the broken pieces.

## 21

A YEAR LATER...

*D*anni paced in the living room of their new home. They bought it two months ago and were still unpacking and buying furniture. It's more like arguing over what to purchase and where to put it, but they'd get it all organized and figured out soon enough.

They always did.

She still struggled to be alone when Thor was deployed and often chose to fly back to Delaware and stay with her parents... or sometimes went to The Refuge.

But Christopher was not only behind bars—where he was going to stay for the rest of his life without the possibility of parole—and his so-called community had crumbled. Many of his followers—especially the women—had turned on him. Some of his elders and disciples had done the same thing. The things law enforcement had learned were utterly horrifying.

Krista's brother was grappling with the fallout, as many of her siblings were, but she was rebuilding some of her relationships while they began living outside the confines of being controlled. It was a start, a new beginning, and everyone was hopeful.

Danni groaned, rubbing her massive baby bump. She wasn't due for another week, and both her mom and mother-in-law constantly told her that first babies came late. Well, these damn false labor pains were killing her and had kept her up half the night. She'd woken up Thor twice, making him time the contractions —if what she was even feeling were contractions—but they were so erratic she told him to go back to sleep.

He hadn't, so now he was in his study, reading the final revision of her book before she turned it in to her editor.

The release date was in six months, and it just got optioned for a documentary.

Crazy.

"Are you done yet?" she asked, unable to take a deep breath. She sat on the edge of the new leather sofa and rubbed the top of her belly. Thor had to have the expensive leather one and right now, the way it felt soft and cool against her bare legs, she appreciated that decision.

"Reading the last page now," Thor called.

Her stomach was as hard as a rock. She opened her mouth, but all that came out was a grunt. Or maybe a groan. She rubbed the sides of her belly and panted, waiting for the pain to subside. Helene had told her that for weeks before she gave birth to Thor, she had false labor pains.

Wonderful.

Thor strolled into the living room. "Danni? Are you all right?" He dropped to his knees.

She nodded, still panting.

He glanced at his watch. "Should I be timing this?"

"Maybe if another one hits me," she managed as the pain subsided. "Wow, that was a big one." She continued to massage her stomach. The tightness had eased up, but not completely. "I've loved being pregnant, but I can't wait for this kid to be out of me."

Thor chuckled.

She glared.

He lowered his gaze and cleared his throat.

"So? What did you think of my book?" She winced as her stomach contracted again—this time faster and harder than the last time.

"I'm speechless. It was amazing. I'm so proud of… Danni?"

She rubbed her belly, panting and blowing air until a burst of warmth flowed from between her legs. She glanced down and stared at the pool of water that landed on the couch and floor. All the pain that had surrounded her midsection shifted into a sudden urge to… She held her breath, thinking she might be able to control it, but she couldn't. Staring into Thor's wide eyes, she pushed with all her might.

"Danni?"

"Phone," she managed. "Ambulance," she said in more of a breath. "Baby… coming… now." She sucked in a deep breath through her nose and blew it out loudly.

"Are you serious?"

She nodded, sliding to the floor, holding her knees to her chest. "Might have to get these biker shorts... oh God. Here comes another one and I want to push, Thor. I want to get it out."

"Jesus. Don't do that." He yanked his phone out and tapped the screen.

"Nine-one-one, what is your emergency?"

"My wife's about to have a baby right here on our living room floor," Thor said. "She's pushing and I don't know what to do."

"Sir, first, what's your name and address?" some woman said.

Thor rattled off the information while he helped Danni out of the bottom half of her clothes, and she bore down like her life depended on it. This kid was coming and there was nothing they could do to stop it if they tried.

"Okay, now tell me what you see," the woman said.

"Oh my..." Thor whispered. "It's a head." He glanced up, catching Danni's gaze. "You doing okay, babe?"

"Just dandy." She nodded.

"The ambulance is ten minutes away," the woman said. "But not sure that baby will wait. My name is Cassandra. Now, Dad, I know this is scary, but you've got this."

"Right. Yeah, sure." Thor rested his hands on Danni's knees and squeezed.

"Mom, next contraction, big push," Cassandra said. "Dad, be on the lookout for the cord around baby's neck. It's not all that common, but we need to look for it. Once the head's out, we'll need to rotate baby and prepare for the shoulders."

Danni barely heard anything this woman said as another contraction built deep in her gut. She lifted her legs and moaned.

"The baby's head is almost out," Thor said so calmly and Danni focused on that because she was anything but calm. She expected labor to be long and slow. And she thought her child would be delivered at a hospital by a doctor.

Not her husband and some girl who sounded like she was barely twenty.

"Come on, Danni. You've got this," Thor encouraged.

She wanted to tell him, *you don't have a uterus so your thoughts on the subject don't matter.* But she refrained. There was no one else to take over at the moment.

"The head's out," Thor whispered. "No cord around the baby's neck."

"Okay, next contraction, you need to help mom ease those shoulders out. I'm not there, so I don't know how big that baby is, but—"

"Doctor thought he or she was about seven or eight pounds." Danni managed before the next contraction completely took over.

"Okay. Okay," Cassandra said. "Dad, you might not have to do too much but let Mother Nature do her thing. Just watch and if it's too much or not much happens on the next push, rotate one shoulder out at a time."

Danni wanted no part of that. She pushed as hard as she could, groaning as loud as she could.

"Oh my God… it's a girl. We have a daughter." Thor placed their child on her chest. A second later, their daughter let out one hell of a cry. More like a bloodcurdling scream.

"She sounds heathy," Cassandra said with a chuckle. "Dad, you need to get a blanket or a fresh towel to keep that precious one warm."

"On it." He wiped a tear that had dribbled from his eye to his cheek with the back of wrist as he jumped to his feet and bolted toward the linen closet in the hallway. When he returned, he wrapped their little bundle of joy in a small towel, placed another one over Danni's legs, and cleaned off his hands. "She's so beautiful." He kissed Danni's temple.

"Did that just happen?" Danni stared at *her* baby. *Her* daughter. "Did I really just give birth in my living room?"

Thor just smiled and nodded like a big goofy kid. "You did."

"Excuse me," Cassanda's voice echoed in the air. "The ambulance is two minutes away. I think that is my fastest birth on record." She chuckled. "Does your little one have a name?"

Thor tossed his head back and laughed. "My wife was so sure we were having a boy she wouldn't even consider picking out girl names much less do that thing where you find out the sex."

"I guess we can't name her Nickalous Mason." Danni pressed her pinky against the baby's lips, and she sucked… and sucked. Her big blue eyes blinked away like she was ready to take on the world. "But I do have an idea."

"Of course you do." Thor smiled. "Lay it on me."

"What about Cassandra Henley Armstrong?" Danni asked.

"I love it." Thor nodded. "It's a perfect name."

"Oh, wow," Cassandra exclaimed. "I've delivered a few babies over the phone, but no one has ever named one after me."

"I'm glad you don't find it weird," Danni said. "It's such a pretty name and your voice was… calming."

"It's not strange at all and I'm so honored," Cassandra said. "But I have to ask, because Henley is so unique, is it a family name?"

"She's one of our dearest friends," Danni said. "She's helped us too, so it seemed fitting."

"The ambulance is rolling down the street." Thor picked up his phone. "I hope we'll get the chance to meet you some day."

"Me too. Take care." Cassandra cut the line.

"I can't believe she's here and it happened so fast," Danni said, glancing between her precious baby girl and Thor.

Baby Cassandra released Danni's finger and let out a wail, as if to let them know two EMTs were standing at the door.

"She's got a heathy set of lungs," Thor mused as he raced toward the door, opening it before returning to Danni's side. He wrapped his arm around her, pressing his lips first to his little girl's forehead, then Danni. "I have to be honest." He let out a sigh. "That was one of the scariest, but most beautiful things I've ever done."

She cocked a brow. "All you did was catch her. I'm the one who had to push her from my body." Danni stared at her husband. The man who was her world. The man who mended her heart and healed her soul. "And you should know, I'm ready for another one."

One of the paramedics burst out laughing. "Dude, my wife said the same thing after we had our first. Now I have five of those things running around. My oldest one—a girl—just turned sixteen and has a boyfriend. My wife caught them playing kissy-face last night in the front seat of that young man's pickup and somehow, it's all my fault we have only one boy and four girls and all the girls are as pretty as my wife and are boy crazy." The paramedic smacked his forehead.

Danni smiled. "I bet it was your wife who made the first move when you got together."

The paramedic chuckled. "Something like that."

"I've got nothing to worry about if my daughter is anything like my Danni," Thor said. "She'll know who the right man is even if he's not smart enough to see what's standing right in front of him."

Danni stared at Thor. He was her heart and soul—her everything. "I love you," she whispered.

*

Thank you for taking the time to read SHELTER FOR DANNI. Please feel free to leave an honest review.

Grab a glass of vino, kick back, relax, and let the romance roll in…

*Sign up for my Newsletter (https://dl.bookfunnel.com/ 82gm8b9k4y) where I often give away free books before publication.*

*Join my private Facebook group (https://www.facebook.com/ groups/191706547909047/) where I post exclusive excerpts and discuss all things murder and love!*

ALSO BY JEN TALTY

*Broken Heroes Mended Souls*

Shelter for Danni

*Brand New Series Co-Written With Elle James!*

**Welcome to…Everglades Overwatch!**

*Secrets in Calusa Cove*

*Pirates in Calusa Cove*

*Safe Harbor Series*

*Mine To Keep*

*Mine To Save*

*Mine To Protect*

*Mine to Hold*

*Mine to Love*

*Check out LOVE IN THE ADIRONDACKS!*

*Shattered Dreams*

*An Inconvenient Flame*

*The Wedding Driver*

*Clear Blue Sky*

*Blue Moon*

*Before the Storm*

**NY STATE TROOPER SERIES (also set in the Adirondacks!)**

*In Two Weeks*

*Dark Water*

*Deadly Secrets*

*Murder in Paradise Bay*

*To Protect His own*

*Deadly Seduction*

*When A Stranger Calls*

*His Deadly Past*

*The Corkscrew Killer*

*First Responders: A spin-off from the NY State Troopers series*

*Playing With Fire*

*Private Conversation*

*The Right Groom*

*After The Fire*

*Caught In The Flames*

*Chasing The Fire*

*Legacy Series*

*Dark Legacy*

*Legacy of Lies*

*Secret Legacy*

*Emerald City*

*It's all in the Whiskey*

*Johnnie Walker*

*Georgia Moon*

*Jack Daniels*

*Jim Beam*

*Whiskey Sour*

*Whiskey Cobbler*

*Whiskey Smash*

*Irish Whiskey*

*The Monroes*

*Color Me Yours*

*Color Me Smart*

*Color Me Free*

*Color Me Lucky*

*Color Me Ice*

*Color Me Home*

*Search and Rescue*

*Protecting Ainsley*

*Protecting Clover*

*Protecting Olympia*

*Protecting Freedom*

*Protecting Princess*

*Protecting Marlowe*

*Fallport Rescue Operations*

*The Matriarch*

*Aegis Network: Jacksonville Division*
*A SEAL's Honor*
*Talon's Honor*
*Arthur's Honor*
*Rex's Honor*
*Kent's Honor*
*Buddy's Honor*

*Aegis Network Short Stories*
*Max & Milian*
*A Christmas Miracle*
*Spinning Wheels*
*Holiday's Vacation*

*The Brotherhood Protectors*
*Out of the Wild*
*Rough Justice*
*Rough Around The Edges*
*Rough Ride*
*Rough Edge*
*Rough Beauty*

*The Brotherhood Protectors*
*The Saving Series*
*Saving Love*
*Saving Magnolia*

*The Lost Sister*

*The Lost Soldier*

*The Lost Soul*

*The Lost Connection*

*The New Order*

# ABOUT THE AUTHOR

Jen Talty is the *USA Today* Bestselling Author of Contemporary Romance, Romantic Suspense, and Paranormal Romance. In the fall of 2020, her short story was selected and featured in a 1001 Dark Nights Anthology.

Regardless of the genre, her goal is to take you on a ride that will leave you floating under the sun with warmth in your heart. She writes stories about broken heroes and heroines who aren't necessarily looking for romance, but in the end, they find the kind of love books are written about :).

She first started writing while carting her kids to one hockey rink after the other, averaging 170 games per year between 3 kids in 2 countries and 5 states. Her first book, IN TWO WEEKS was originally published in 2007. In 2010 she helped form a publishing company (Cool Gus Publishing) with *NY Times* Bestselling Author Bob Mayer where she ran the technical side of the business through 2016.

Jen is currently enjoying the next phase of her life...the

empty nester! She and her husband reside in Jupiter, Florida.

Grab a glass of vino, kick back, relax, and let the romance roll in…

Sign up for my *Newsletter (https://dl.bookfunnel.com/82gm8b9k4y)* where I often give away free books before publication.

Join my private *Facebook group (https://www.facebook.com/groups/191706547909047/)* where I post exclusive excerpts and discuss all things murder and love!

Never miss a new release. Follow me on Amazon:amazon.com/author/jentalty
And on Bookbub: bookbub.com/authors/jen-talty

*There are many more books in this fan fiction world than listed here, for an up-to-date list go to www.AcesPress.com*

*You can also visit our Amazon page at:*
*http://www.amazon.com/author/operationalpha*

JM Madden: Rescuing Olivia
A.M. Mahler: Griffin
Ellie Masters: Sybil's Protector
Trish McCallan: Hero Under Fire
Naomi McKay: Twist
KD Michaels: Saving Laura
Olivia Michaels: Protecting Harper
Annie Miller: Securing Willow
MJ Nightingale: Protecting Beauty
C.K. O'Connor: Delaney's Bodyguard
Danielle Pays: Defending Sarina
Lainey Reese: Protecting New York
Angela Rush: Charlotte
E.M. Shue: Discovering Tyler
Heather Slade: Code Name: Admiral
Dee Stewart: Fighting for Brielle
Lynne St. James: SEAL's Spitfire
Bella Stone: Rexar
Jen Talty: Protecting Ainsley
Reina Torres, Rescuing Hi'ilani
LJ Vickery: Circus Comes to Town
R. C. Wynne: Shadows Renewed
Amanda Zook: Freeing Camila

### *Delta Team Three Series*
Lori Ryan: Nori's Delta
Becca Jameson: Destiny's Delta
Lynne St James, Gwen's Delta
Elle James: Ivy's Delta
Riley Edwards: Hope's Delta

### *Police and Fire: Operation Alpha World*

Freya Barker: Burning for Autumn
B.P. Beth: Scott
Jane Blythe: Salvaging Marigold
Julia Bright: Justice for Amber
Gia Cobie: Saved from Revenge
Leyna Cohan: Embracing Juliette
Nicole Craig: Justice for Francesca
Danielle M. Haas: Crossroads of Betrayal
Deanndra Hall: Shelter for Sharla
Reina Torres: Justice for Sloane

### *Tarpley VFD Series*

Silver James, Fighting for Elena
Deanndra Hall, Fighting for Carly
Haven Rose, Fighting for Calliope
MJ Nightingale, Fighting for Jemma
TL Reeve, Fighting for Brittney
Nicole Flockton, Fighting for Nadia

*As you know, this book included at least one character from Susan Stoker's books. To check out more, see below.*

## SEAL of Protection: Alliance Series
*Protecting Remi*
*Protecting Wren*
*Protecting Josie*
*Protecting Maggie*
*Protecting Addison*
*Protecting Kelli (Sept 2, 2025)*
*Protecting Bree (Jan 6, 2026)*

## Rescue Angels Series
*Keeping Laryn*
*Keeping Amanda (Nov 4, 2025)*
*Keeping Zita (Feb 10, 2026)*
*Keeping Penny (TBA)*
*Keeping Kara (TBA)*
*Keeping Jennifer (TBA)*

## The Refuge Series
*Deserving Alaska*
*Deserving Henley*
*Deserving Reese*
*Deserving Cora*
*Deserving Lara*
*Deserving Maisy*
*Deserving Ryleigh*

## <u>SEAL Team Hawaii Series</u>

*Finding Elodie*

*Finding Lexie*

*Finding Kenna*

*Finding Monica*

*Finding Carly*

*Finding Ashlyn*

*Finding Jodelle*

## <u>Eagle Point Search & Rescue</u>

*Searching for Lilly*

*Searching for Elsie*

*Searching for Bristol*

*Searching for Caryn*

*Searching for Finley*

*Searching for Heather*

*Searching for Khloe*

## <u>Delta Team Two Series</u>

*Shielding Gillian*

*Shielding Kinley*

*Shielding Aspen*

*Shielding Jayme (novella)*

*Shielding Riley*

*Shielding Devyn*

*Shielding Ember*

*Shielding Sierra*

## <u>SEAL of Protection: Legacy Series</u>

*Securing Caite (FREE!)*

*Securing Brenae (novella)*
*Securing Sidney*
*Securing Piper*
*Securing Zoey*
*Securing Avery*
*Securing Kalee*
*Securing Jane*

## Delta Force Heroes Series

*Rescuing Rayne*
*Rescuing Aimee (novella)*
*Rescuing Emily*
*Rescuing Harley*
*Marrying Emily (novella)*
*Rescuing Kassie*
*Rescuing Bryn*
*Rescuing Casey*
*Rescuing Sadie (novella)*
*Rescuing Wendy*
*Rescuing Mary*
*Rescuing Macie (novella)*
*Rescuing Annie*

## Badge of Honor: Texas Heroes Series

*Justice for Mackenzie (FREE!)*
*Justice for Mickie*
*Justice for Corrie*
*Justice for Laine (novella)*
*Shelter for Elizabeth*
*Justice for Boone*

*Shelter for Adeline*
*Shelter for Sophie*
*Justice for Erin*
*Justice for Milena*
*Shelter for Blythe*
*Justice for Hope*
*Shelter for Quinn*
*Shelter for Koren*
*Shelter for Penelope*

## SEAL of Protection Series
*Protecting Caroline (FREE!)*
*Protecting Alabama*
*Protecting Fiona*
*Marrying Caroline (novella)*
*Protecting Summer*
*Protecting Cheyenne*
*Protecting Jessyka*
*Protecting Julie (novella)*
*Protecting Melody*
*Protecting the Future*
*Protecting Kiera (novella)*
*Protecting Alabama's Kids (novella)*
*Protecting Dakota*
*Protecting Tex*

*New York Times, USA Today* and *Wall Street Journal* Bestselling Author Susan Stoker has a heart as big as the state of Tennessee where she lives, but this all American girl has also spent the last fourteen years living in Missouri, California, Colorado, Indiana, and Texas.

She's married to a retired Army man who now gets to follow *her* around the country.

www.stokeraces.com
www.AcesPress.com
susan@stokeraces.com